In the Ghost Detective Universe:

Novels
(Best to be read in order)
Beyond the Grave
Unveiling the Past
Beneath the Surface

Short Stories
(All stand-alone)
Just Desserts
Lost Friends
Family Bonds
Common Ground
Till Death
Family History
Heritage
Eternal Bond
New Beginnings
Severed Ties

R.W. WALLACE

Author of the Tolosa Mystery Series

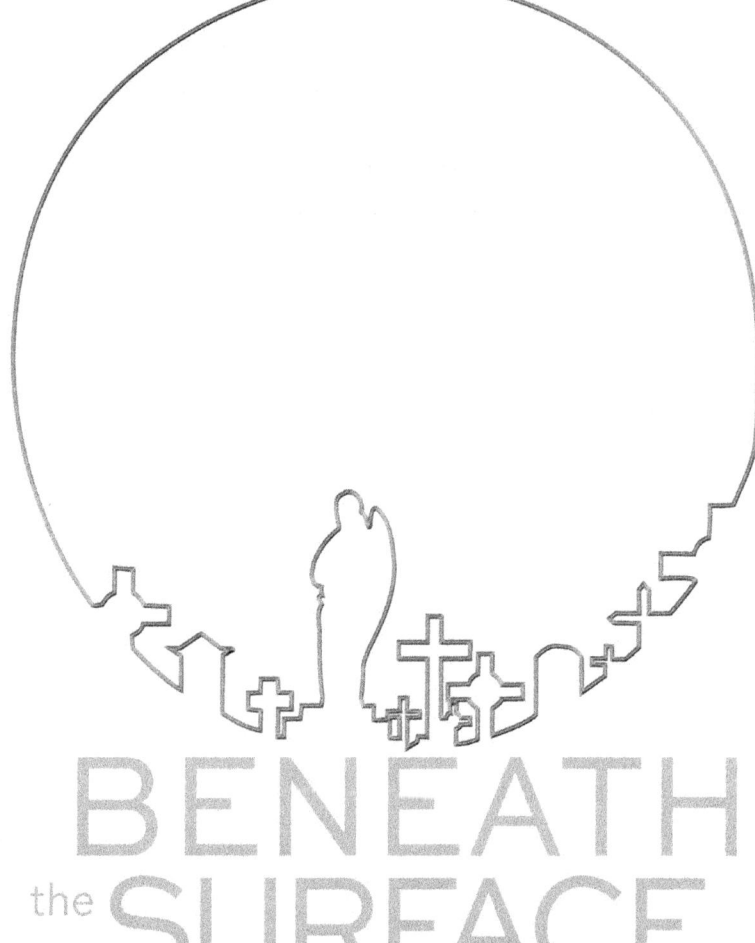

BENEATH the SURFACE

Book 3 of the Ghost Detective Series

Beneath the Surface
by R.W. Wallace

Copyright © 2021 by R.W. Wallace

Copy editing by Alison Scotchford
Cover by the author
Cover Illustration 10926765 © germanjames | 123rf.com
Cover Illustration 51137001 © Tryfonov | Depositphotos
Cover Illustration 263199440 © Nouman | Adobe Stock

All characters and events in this book, other than those clearly in the public domain, are fictitious and any resemblance to real persons, living or dead, is purely coincidental.

All rights reserved. No part of this publication may be reproduced, distributed, or transmitted in any form or by any means, including photocopying, recording, or other electronic or mechanical methods, without the prior written permission of the publisher, except in the case of brief quotations embodied in critical reviews and certain other noncommercial uses permitted by copyright law.

www.rwwallace.com

ISBN: [979-10-95707-74-5]

Main category—Fiction
Other category—Mystery

First Edition

WELCOME TO MY Ghost Detective books. I've been living with these characters in my head for awhile, and a certain number of stories have come out of it. So many, in fact, that there are two parallel timelines.

A quick word to explain.

I started writing short stories about Robert and Clothilde. Had *so* much fun with them. And wondered what had happened to them when they died. They stayed so secretive! Then came the story *Common Ground*, and I got a definite link to Clothilde. And a way to get them out of the cemetery!

"Cool!" I thought, and started writing the next short story. Which wasn't a short at all, but rather the beginning of a series of novels, the third of which you're holding right now.

But I didn't want to stop writing the shorts. So I've done both. In one timeline (this one), the ghosts get out of the cemetery and go looking for their own murderers, and in the other (the shorts), they're still stuck in the cemetery and helping other ghosts find peace.

All of that to say you definitely do not need to read the short stories before starting the novels (though *Common Ground* will give some extra background), and the shorts can be read in any order. The novels, however, are best read in order.

So if you haven't read *Beyond the Grave* yet, you might want to try that one first—although the stories *can* stand alone!

Enjoy!

R.W. Wallace

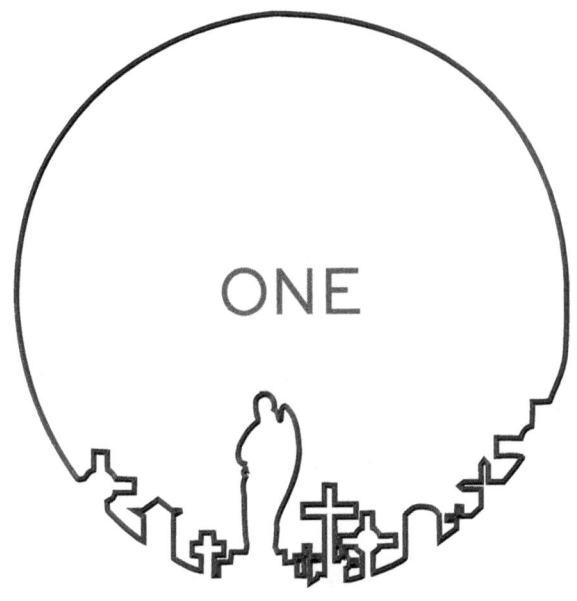

ONE

Is there such a thing as an idyllic setting for speaking with the dead? Emeline Evian doesn't think so but figures it could have been worse.

The last rays of sunlight filter through a small gap in the white curtains and light up the icky brown carpet, the stressfully overcharged old wallpaper, and the pristine baby blue bed covering with its intricate dark blue handmade embroidery. A couple of dust motes swirl through the light, invisible when in the darkness on either side but peacefully and beautifully dancing during their few seconds in the sun.

Emeline Evian is sitting cross-legged on the bed, taking deep breaths, and doing her darnedest to pretend she's not about to do what she's about to do. It's a hot July evening and this apartment is no better than her own across the hall at keeping the temperatures down during a heat wave. She has exchanged her usual jeans and black T-shirt for an old pair of yoga pants and a red tank top. This whole situation is already making her uncomfortable enough; she can at least wear comfortable clothes.

Of course, the way her lovely neighbor Amina lit up at the sight of Emeline wearing something with colors, has made her feel self-conscious. The fact she's now assorted to Amina's living room was *not* part of Emeline's calculations. There *were* no calculations, only icky heat. But she has a feeling Amina doesn't see it that way.

Which makes all sorts of questions arise.

Emeline will have to address those later, though. Right now, she has bigger problems.

Like preparing to talk to a ghost that scares the hell out of her—using a fricking Ouija board.

Yes, yes, the real thing. If such a thing even exists. What makes a charlatan's toy real? Must the board be made of wood instead of cardboard or plastic? Must the letters and numbers be written in that specific font? Why do they all use the same font? Will ghosts not be able to communicate if offered a more lighthearted font? Will that offend them?

It annoys Emeline to no end that she's preparing to use the board—again.

She's a captain of the French Judicial Police, and she's good at her job. She's thorough and logical and bases her conclusions on facts and proofs. Not on whims, not on feelings, not on otherworldly influences. A police captain can't show up in court and ascertain someone is guilty *because a ghost told me*. Ouija boards were made up by charlatans to steal money from gullible people who either wanted an easy scare or had unfinished business with someone no longer of this world. The first part is one thing—there are worse ways to get an easy scare, at least the chance of somebody getting hurt using the board is slim to none—but the second is unacceptable. Taking advantage of other people's pain is not cool.

How she wishes she'd come up with a better way to communicate with the ghosts.

Because, unfortunately for someone as reality-based as Emeline, ghosts *are* real, and she has a particular affinity for them. She can't see them, can't really hear them, but they're able to communicate with her anyway. That sixth sense making the hairs on her neck stand up, the feeling of being watched? For Emeline, it's almost permanent. And from time to time, her mind will be going down one logical route, considering its options, when suddenly a stray thought enters her head, making her veer off in a completely different direction. It *isn't* Emeline's mind coming up with a new idea, but a ghost talking to her, planting the thought in her subconscious.

She had already been like this for a few years before coming to Toulouse, but it only happened occasionally—when she ran into ghosts. Now, it's constant.

Of course, she kind of brought it on herself by stealing the finger bones of each of the two murder victims she was sent to investigate, and keeping them on her, wrapped in two bracelets, at all times. Basically, she made her peace with having Clothilde and Robert around. She has spent enough time looking into their pasts and having their voices talk to her subconscious to have gotten rather attached. She appreciates their help when investigating their murders, and she feels for them. She wants them to get justice, and find peace.

Now this *other* ghost…the one living in Amina's guest bedroom? Her, she's a lot more on the fence about.

Her name is Constantine, and her body is buried in the wall by the window. That's what Emeline's tingly sense is telling her, anyway. The last time they "talked," Constantine told Amina—through Emeline—that she would no longer oppose any workers coming in to fix up the room. And she specified to have a look at the piping in the wall.

Emeline and Amina have been trying to come up with the best way of "discovering" the body without drawing the attention of the police, or too many others. They *could* start the demolition themselves but even then, it's not certain they'll manage to get to the buried body before needing help—or permanently destroying the structure of the building. Neither of them are architects, far from it.

And once they do get the body out, they'll need a place to put it, or hide it, or whatever the hell it is they're supposed to do with it. The plan is for Amina to keep *one* bone, so Constantine can travel with her if she so chooses, but what do they do with the rest? In order to offer the girl a decent burial, they'd have to let the authorities in at some point.

While they debate back and forth on how to proceed, Emeline has—*very* reluctantly—agreed to have another "discussion" with Constantine. And she has been unable to come up with a more efficient way than the Ouija board. Unless she wants to split hairs and show up with a different board, using a different font, only to do the exact same thing.

The board, plus Constantine having had her fun with Emeline by scaring the living daylights out of her the first time she came into this room, and Emeline is understandably on edge.

Taking a deep breath, Emeline reminds herself Clothilde and Robert are also in the room. She was too freaked-out to pick up on the details when Constantine spooked her, but she is fairly certain her two friends called the other girl off. She counts on them to protect her today too.

Amina wiggles on the bed next to Emeline. She hasn't been able to sit still for a second since Emeline agreed to this madness. The lovely woman is wearing a pair of red jeans and a flowing, flowery red and blue blouse. Her hair is the usual dark and curly halo and her green eyes glitter with excitement.

If only the emotion sprang from something other than communicating with a misbehaving ghost. *Anything* else.

"You have the questions ready?" Amina asks for the hundredth time.

"I have the questions." Emeline holds up a sheet of paper with their scribbled notes from the night before. She brought the paper but knows there isn't really a need. Robert and Clothilde were present for the brainstorming session and although Emeline will be asking the questions from the paper, the two ghosts will be doing the actual questioning of Constantine.

Emeline is familiar enough with them by now to know *they* were the ones to give her instructions on where to move the pointer on the Ouija board the last time. Even when she wasn't going completely poltergeist, Constantine felt different from Clothilde and Robert. Emeline took the instructions so well because they came from people she trusted.

Before coming here tonight, Emeline asked the ghosts—so, talking to an empty room—to take charge of the communications with the other ghost. The official story is that she feels the risk of missing something in translation to be less if the instructions come from someone she knows well. The real reason, and she suspects Clothilde and Robert know it, is she wants as little to do with Constantine as she can.

Amina is too caught up in the excitement of communing with "her" ghost again to notice Emeline's reluctance. "Excellent! Let me just get the lights ready." She jumps off the bed, making both Emeline and the stupid board wobble. She whips a lighter out of her pocket and starts lighting the candles she has set up around the room. Three on the dresser, five on the floor along the far wall, four on the windowsill.

When she lights those four, Emeline holds her breath, ready to jump up and run out of the room if Constantine reacts to having her personal space invaded like she did the last time.

All four candles are lit—no otherworldly indignation.

Well. Robert and Clothilde must be doing their part. Emeline will have to thank them later.

"I told you, there's no need to light any candles," Emeline says.

"My teacher says it helps the spirits find us from the other side," Amina says. Because, yes, Amina takes lessons in clairvoyance. Nobody's perfect. Her eyes light up. "Besides, it's pretty!"

Emeline sighs. "Let's get this show on the road, then." She pats the space next to her on the bed. "Come on over here. We're going to start by declaring the bed a ghost-free zone. Anyone breaches that rule and I'm out. Understood?"

Amina stands there gaping for several seconds, until she realizes who Emeline is talking to. Her eyes widen as she scans the room while sidling along the bed to sit where Emeline indicated. "They're here already?" she whispers.

"They're always here," Emeline says. "It's us who aren't always listening." She braces herself, straightens her spine, and places one hand on the Ouija board's pointer.

"Good evening, Constantine. We have a few questions for you."

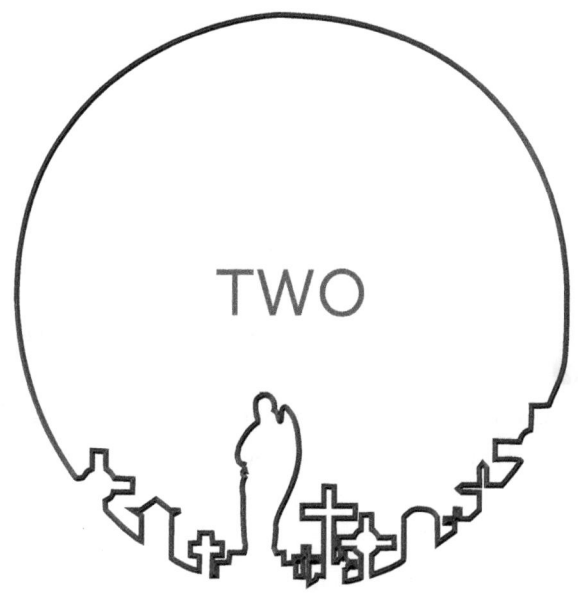

TWO

Clothilde and I have a lot of experience in communicating with ghosts. Not much of a surprise since we're ghosts ourselves, of course, but I'm guessing we have more than your average lingering spirit. Before hitching a ride with Evian, we spent thirty years in a cemetery in the outskirts of Toulouse, helping other ghosts move on.

The thing with ghosts is they only stick around to settle unfinished business. Once it's settled, they move on to someplace we've always assumed to be better. Those who don't have any loose ends to tie up don't go through the wonderful experience of waking up inside a sealed casket, only to be let out when they accept they're ghosts. It was over thirty years ago, but I remember those five days as if they were yesterday. Do not recommend.

Obviously, Clothilde and I are still around because we haven't settled our unfinished business. Thirty years is a long time to carry around a burden like this, but there's a light at the end of the tunnel now—thanks to Evian. She was brought to Toulouse from Paris to investigate Clothilde's murder (her unfinished business) and my inexplicable presence in Clothilde's grave (seems to be linked with my unfinished business). Thanks in large part to Evian's exceptional sensitivity to ghosts, we now get to tag along when she tries to solve our murders.

Constantine…is a bit of a deviation from our path, but I can't turn my back on the poor girl simply because I'm on a mission. My release from this world isn't more important than hers. It may even be less so, honestly.

Constantine has been a ghost for seventy years and has been alone for most of that time. The only human contact she had was from the living people who had the misfortune of attempting to sleep in this guest bedroom. I say misfortune because scaring people half to death seems to have been Constantine's favorite pastime. Which, of course, didn't lend itself to a lot of conversations or human contact. Clothilde and I are the first people she has talked to since she died in the fifties.

Anyone would go a little crazy after spending seventy years with no company.

Once you get her off the idea of scaring anyone who dares enter her domain, Constantine is a sweet girl. She has long blonde hair, wide dark eyes, and wears a worn and dirty wedding dress. It's the dress she got married in, *not* the dress she died in. Somehow, it has gotten worn over the years—a reflection of Constantine's state of mind.

BENEATH THE SURFACE

We don't know who killed Constantine, and it doesn't seem like she cares about finding it out. Her unfinished business isn't with the killer, but with the husband she left behind. If he was in his thirties seventy years ago, the chances of him still being alive aren't great. I can only pray we'll be able to tie up Constantine's loose ends anyway.

The husband—Jacques—is who we're going to talk about today. Maybe Amina and Evian can start looking for him while they figure out a way to bring Constantine's body out of the wall without getting into any kind of trouble.

"How are you feeling?" I ask Constantine. I'm leaning against the wall next to her windowsill, close enough to intervene if she gets any funny ideas of scaring Evian again but not *in* her personal space. "You don't mind the candles?" I'll admit to being surprised she didn't do anything to Amina when the woman lit up two candles currently standing *inside* of Constantine's ghostly form where she sits on the sill, dangling her legs through the wall.

Constantine shrugs and her eyes flicker to the candles on either side of her. I suspect she doesn't like them but likes Amina well enough not to want to scare or offend her.

"We could ask for her not to place any on the sill next time?" I offer.

Another shrug. "That's not what's important."

"First we'll talk about Jacques," I promise her. "But if we have time, I'll also ask about the candles, all right? There's no need for you to feel uncomfortable."

I get a small nod and consider it a great victory. Constantine is going to need some time to get used to interacting with others.

Clothilde, my friend of thirty years, is perching on the dresser. Wearing her favorite jeans, white blouse, and worn Converse, she is seated in much the same way as Constantine, leaning slightly forward with her hands under her thighs and her feet swinging through the wood in total disregard for the rules of the physical world. But while Constantine looks ready to pounce, Clothilde is the careless teenager who has a million better places to be.

Except she doesn't, of course. But that's Clothilde for you and I wouldn't have her any other way.

We've agreed I'll do most of the talking with Evian today and Clothilde will keep her distance. Keep an eye on Constantine in case something sets her off. Clothilde has a bit of a temper and I don't want it interfering when we have a unique chance of communicating with Evian. I know the captain *hates* that Ouija board, so I don't have any illusions of this becoming a regular thing.

When Evian states her ground rule of no ghosts on the bed, I glance at Constantine. She doesn't seem offended. A good start.

Evian places her hand on the pointer and takes a deep breath. Closes her eyes. "All right, Constantine. If we're going to help you, we need to know more about you and the way you died. Can I assume you were murdered?"

Constantine nods and I say, loud and clear, "Yes." Luckily, Constantine wasn't opposed to me being the one to actually answer Evian's questions. The mistrust between those two seems to go both ways.

Evian's eyes open and her hand moves to the "Yes" section.

Amina lights up in a smile that is entirely inappropriate when you learn someone was murdered. I'm glad Evian's eyes are on the board—she wouldn't be thrilled by her neighbor's enthusiasm for talking to ghosts.

"Do you know who killed you?" Evian asks. There's an odd lack of inflection in her voice, probably because she's zoning out as much as possible in order to hear our answers and not attempt to inject her own opinions into the conversation.

Even though I know the answer, I wait for Constantine to shake her head before answering a clear, "No." Before Evian can ask another question, I say, "We have more to add." Then I start spelling.

Evian's mouth opens to ask her next question. Shuts it. Frowns. And moves the pointer. I DO NOT CARE ABOUT KILLER.

When her hand stops moving, Evian shifts her gaze to Amina's notebook. Evian isn't even reading what she's spelling out; she's simply moving on autopilot. Both women wear similar frowns.

"You don't care who killed you?" Amina says. "But they should be brought to justice. Nobody should get away with murder."

"Then again," Evian mumbles, "if the murder happened, what, sixty or seventy years ago, the murderer is most probably already dead. Justice is already served."

"Dying of natural causes isn't justice," Amina says, her voice much harder than her normal tone. "Even if it's postmortem, the world should know who the murderer is."

"And if we happen to figure out who it was, we will do just that," Evian says. She holds up a hand in the direction of the windowsill, as if expecting Constantine to interrupt. "But if this isn't what Constantine needs or wants, we won't waste too much energy on it."

The words are more for Constantine than Amina, to reassure her the message was heard. But it seems Amina also needs to hear them. The usually mellow and smiling woman is straight-backed and tense in her cross-legged position on the bed, and I think she might be in danger of breaking her pen in half. An angry flush is making its way up her neck. She doesn't like the idea of her ghost's death going unavenged one bit.

"It's all right, Amina," Constantine says. I've never heard her voice so soft and kind before. "I've made my peace with it. What I need is for Jacques to find peace. Not some revenge quest."

Amina is in no way as sensitive as Evian, but her anger seems to recede somewhat and the tension in her shoulders lessens.

Evian, who felt Constantine's speech much better than Amina, takes her neighbor's silence for acquiescence. Her gaze turns to the windowsill. "What do you need, Constantine? What can we do to help?"

I again wait for the nod from Constantine before spelling the answer out to Evian.

FIND HUSBAND. LET HIM KNOW. JACQUES LARCHER.

THREE

How many boxes would you need to collect your entire life? What would be in them? Would an outsider see the things as having value or would they throw everything in a dumpster without a second thought?

Clothilde is about to find the answers to all these questions.

Being ghosts, Clothilde and I don't take up much room. We appreciate having some space to ourselves but since we don't have physical bodies, we don't, strictly speaking, need it. We can sit wherever. On Evian's crappy couch without feeling how uncomfortable it is, on the kitchen counter, even while living people are cooking, on the floor, or hanging in thin air if the fancy strikes us. We don't sleep, don't get back pains, and won't knock anything over.

We *will* get bored out of our minds if left to fend for ourselves in a one-bedroom apartment for too long, but that's a whole other story.

We've shared this apartment with Captain Emeline Evian for a little over a month. It was never meant to be anything but temporary, so Evian looked for something small, fully furbished, and close to the police station. This place is all three. What it is *not* is beautiful, comfortable, or thermally insulated. I don't think any of us care about the beauty—except maybe Evian when she invites her neighbor Amina over, it makes her self-conscious—and Evian has figured out where to park herself on the couch to avoid all the broken springs.

But the lack of air conditioning, the single-paned windows, mixed with there being no way of creating a current of air, is slowly getting to Evian. And when she slows down because of the heat, we get restless. When she takes a break to take a cold shower, we pace.

I think our impatience has much to do with not remembering what it's like to live in hot and humid air like this. Not really. Intellectually, I know I complained every time it got hot, especially when I had to wear a uniform for work. I remember sometimes changing my T-shirt three times a day and begging my neighbors if I could come over and use their pool when the afternoon heat was at its worst. But I can't quite remember the *feeling*. Just like I can't remember what it was like to be cold.

Although, to be fair, I don't think Evian remembers that, either.

Right now, I'm trying to decide if I'm comfortable with standing *through* three cardboard boxes filled with bits and pieces of Clothilde's life, with only my head and shoulders poking out over the top one, or if I should move to a place where I can pretend to be corporeal but won't have the same view.

Normally, I wouldn't mind playing ghostly tricks, but we've been doing this for hours already, and there's no end in sight. I feel useless and like I'm a burden, and the constant reminder I'm just a ghost is getting to me. Or maybe it's Evian's crappy attitude rubbing off on me.

The living room wasn't huge to begin with, but the day Clothilde's sister showed up at the door with all of Clothilde's earthly belongings neatly stowed into thirty cardboard boxes, the room went from small to cramped. One entire wall is hidden behind boxes stacked four high and four wide. Some are bothering Evian in front of her bedroom door every time she walks past, and the rest are shoved against the living room side of the freestanding kitchen counter.

They're all labeled. Every single one of them starts with "Clothilde." Then the actual content. *Childhood toys. Books primary school. Clothes 16-18 yrs. Works of art.* You think of a part of a young girl's life, there's a box for it.

Clothilde's mom seems to have kept *everything* her daughter left behind. On first inspection, it's not surprising. Many mothers have trouble getting rid of their children's "works of art" even when the artists are still alive. When the daughter dies a violent death at twenty… I'd expect a shrine and an art museum.

Except this is Clothilde's mom we're talking about. We're still piecing some of the puzzle together, but Madame Humbert seems to have prioritized her husband's job and her own reputation in society over giving her daughter a decent burial and the rest of the family a place to mourn. Clothilde was buried by her uncle, in a grave bearing only her first name and date of death, and nobody but the uncle knew where it was. She didn't have a single visitor during our thirty years in the cemetery.

All the evidence pointed to the mother not caring about her daughter.

Luckily, most of the animosity between the two women was resolved when the mother died and ended up as a ghost in our cemetery. Turned out she *did* love her daughter.

Whatever made Clothilde's mother behave like she did is part of a bigger mystery we're trying to solve. Clothilde's murder was masqueraded as a suicide with the help of corrupt police officers—myself included but that's a whole other ball of ugly—the mother was manipulated by politicians, the uncle was threatened by goons, the priests involved in the funerals harassed.

Something was going on behind the scenes. Something big.

And we're hoping to find answers in Clothilde's old stuff.

I think Evian was overwhelmed by the quantity of evidence. At least, that's *my* explanation for why she started with the box labeled "Works of art." She might not know Clothilde as well as I do, but she knows enough to realize there wouldn't be hints on the back of awkward paintings or inside shapeless pottery projects. Clothilde was—and is—much more direct.

All the same, she took out a framed art piece. The date on the back claimed Clothilde had made it when she was seventeen. "Art project in *première* in high school," Clothilde mumbled. It was a collage of some sort. Lots of aggressive colors, no recognizable shapes. Abstract.

Evian seemed to like it. She walked into her bedroom and held it up against the wall over her bed. "Can I borrow your artwork, Clothilde? This place could use some colors." She stood there, waiting patiently, until Clothilde agreed.

Clothilde would deny it, but I know she was flattered.

Evian "borrowed" two other pieces: one owl-like statue currently taking up shelf space next to an armless Japanese cat some previous tenant left behind, and a painting, another abstract with lots of flashy colors, next to the stove in the kitchen.

Evian closed up the box and shoved it to the side. Since then, we've been going through Clothilde's documents. And for a twenty-year-old, she had a lot of it.

We're focusing on anything pertaining to the non-profit organization Clothilde worked with, one aiming to improve the saturation of traffic in Toulouse. That was back in the late eighties. We don't need to look for the organization today to know it failed. Getting in a car to go anywhere today is synonymous with bracing yourself for a lot of waiting and anger.

We know the mayor at the time actively blocked the organization, but we don't know why. We know he had several helpers, and one of them has talked. Unfortunately, he didn't know much. He was just a lackey.

"There!" Clothilde, who has been sitting cross-legged next to Evian on the floor instead of her usual perch somewhere higher up, points to a page in Evian's right hand. "This mentions Redon." She leans closer. "Huh. I didn't realize I'd already had the misfortune of crossing her path."

Evian's gaze moves to the page Clothilde points to.

She can't actually see us or hear us. She's just really, *really*, sensitive to ghosts. I've been a ghost for over thirty years, and I've done my fair share of communicating with living people. Some are completely closed up and won't be influenced in the slightest, some will hear us on a subconscious level and take our words for their own thoughts and thereby do what we want them to. But Evian…it's like we can have conversations with her. She's *extremely* sensitive and open to listening to the nudges we give her. She knows we're here and has made her peace with it.

She's letting us tag along as she searches for our murderers from thirty years ago. And by "tag along," I mean we're anchored to the small bones Evian has made into bracelets. She has finger bones from each of us, and wherever those bones go, we go.

As she goes through Clothilde's documents, she is clearly counting on Clothilde reading along with her. She skims all the documents but if Clothilde doesn't say anything, she rarely takes notes, or puts the documents in the "to keep" pile.

If Clothilde has spotted the mention of Delphine Redon, I want to get a closer look. Her son threatened Clothilde's sister with a gun a couple of weeks ago, looking for documents left behind by Clothilde's uncle. It seems likely he works with his mother, who has had her hand in dirty business since the eighties. We *know* this to be true but haven't been able to find any proof that might hold up in court.

I lean forward so my torso sticks out of the middle cardboard box, my head over Evian's shoulder. It looks like a form letter of some sort. It has two signatures, one from some guy, one belonging to Madame Redon.

Evian touches the signature and holds it up to study it in the sunlight streaming in her old windows. "It's a stamp, not an actual signature. Still, it's a link."

"It's the refusal for a hearing," Clothilde says. "It's just one of dozens of documents like it. I tried everything to land a meeting with the mayor, but I never could get through. That's why I started showing up at the Capitole—and got kicked out on my ass every time."

"The other name doesn't ring a bell?" I ask.

Clothilde shakes her head. "Probably just a clerk. Which might mean Redon didn't even read my letter. She just told this guy to refuse everything."

Frowning, Evian has pulled out her phone and is tapping

away at the screen. She's typing in the name of the clerk.

"Clerks are usually young, aren't they?" I ask.

Clothilde scoffs. "Way to go on the generalization, Robert. But yeah, I guess it's one of those jobs you have to go through on your way to the top, so they're not often old."

"Hah!" Evian exclaims. "Found him." She holds the phone out—so we can read what it says on the screen without pushing into her personal space—and I see a page from the Regional Council's website, titled "Cyril Legros." It has a picture of a dark-haired man in his fifties, with soft brown eyes and the beginnings of a smile. According to the text, he is the head of a division, and a member of a political party that is *not* the same as Delphine Redon.

Evian jumps up, then immediately groans, one hand going to her back.

One point to being a ghost. Clothilde and I are ready by the door within seconds.

"All right," Evian says as she does some stretches. "I'm getting changed and taking a cold shower, then we're paying a visit to Cyril Legros." She drops the bracelets with our finger bones on the kitchen counter and firmly closes the bedroom door behind her.

Guess there's nothing for us to do but wait.

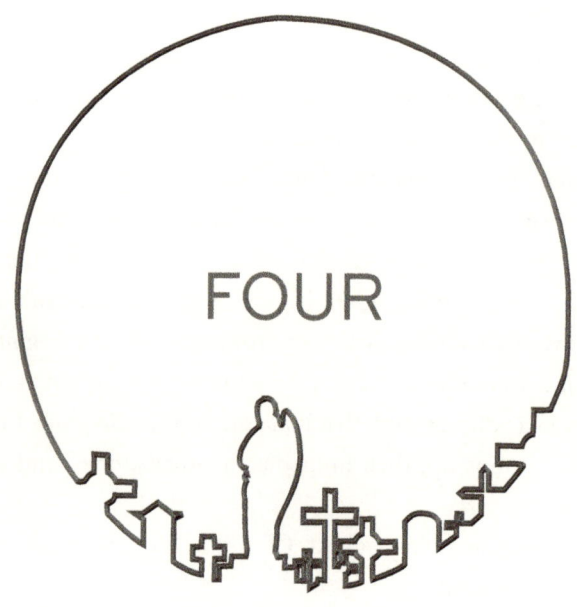

FOUR

Emeline misses having Malik for company when she has to go anywhere in the city of Toulouse. They only worked together for a little over a month, but she got used to him knowing the shortcuts or spots to avoid. Now that her partner is on paid leave awaiting judgment for putting a man's life at risk and not telling his superiors he couldn't stomach pulling his weapon on anyone, Emeline has to figure out how to get from point A to point B by herself.

His capacity as a human GPS isn't the only reason she misses Malik, of course. He is a bright officer with a sense of humor that agrees with Emeline and has a great career in front of him—if he can get his act together. Malik had the misfortune to have fired the shot that ended up killing an old man. It doesn't matter the man was about to shoot *them*, that he was opposing arrest, or that nobody blamed Malik for the man's heart attack. Malik needs more time to digest before he is ready to come back in the field with her.

While Emeline walks the short distance from her building to the metro station, going so far as to cross the street to stay in the shadow and out of the worst of the late morning sun, she ponders contacting Nadine Tulle. The woman is a miracle worker when it comes to searching for information. She has been able to dig up some *very* interesting—and very confidential—information in the past, proving her worth several times over. Emeline wouldn't mind her help in the search for Constantine's husband. Google was no good, nor any other "normal" place a person would go to search. The man must have died before the age of the internet or kept away from it. She *could* search in ancestry records, but that would demand time she didn't have at the moment.

She wanted to help Amina and Constantine, but they couldn't take away from Emeline's search for Clothilde's murderer. One of the men responsible for Clothilde's death is behind bars and awaiting trial, but the others—and Emeline is one hundred percent convinced there were others—are still out there, possibly still killing innocent people. This *has* to be her first priority.

Still, it won't cost her much to ask Nadine to look for Jacques Larcher. The woman *probably* won't turn her down even though Emeline isn't working with her buddy Malik at the moment. But she *will* ask questions.

And Emeline doesn't have any answers that don't include talking to ghosts.

As she validates her ticket and goes through the turnstile on her way down to the metro, she thinks back to the moment

Constantine said she didn't care about going after her murderer. And the sense of peace and acceptance that went with it. The love and longing that went with the husband's name spelled out on the Ouija board.

Without thinking about it too much, she sends off a quick text to Nadine, mentioning it is for a personal project, so the woman won't be using highly confidential police means to do the search.

The ride to the Regional Council doesn't take long. The metro is relatively crowded—for Toulouse. In Paris, this would qualify as almost empty—but Emeline finds a standing place and buries her head in her phone like everybody else until she reaches her destination. The last leg of her journey is on foot, and there's no shade to save her from the heat when she reaches the Garonne River. Malik would have known of a backstreet that could save them from the sun, but Emeline has to follow the directions her phone gives her and walks down the sidewalk with the three-lane road between her and the river, the sun making sweat run into her eyes, causing them to tear up because of her facial cream.

When she stands at the reception desk, waiting for the receptionist to call Monsieur Legros, she wipes her face with the back of her hand while surreptitiously flapping the back of her T-shirt to try to cool down her sweating back in the relatively cool air of the large building. This place is like most French administrative buildings; very clean, lots of windows, some plants here and there to avoid looking *too* stark, the smell of cheap disinfectant, and hordes of lost souls on their way into the rabbit hole of dealing with the French administration. Emeline doesn't envy them.

The receptionist tells Emeline Monsieur Legros will see her immediately and explains the dozens of turns and stairs she will have to take to get to his office. Emeline follows the instructions and five minutes later, finds herself in the office of Cyril Legros.

According to Emeline's information, he is fifty-five, but he looks closer to sixty. What remains of his hair is entirely white and his face is scored with wrinkles, some from smiling, many from frowning. He has a bit of a beer belly straining his white shirt, and spindly legs hiding in too-large jeans. Even though Emeline didn't give him a warning she was coming, he offers her a smile and a firm handshake.

"Thank you for seeing me, Monsieur Legros," Emeline says. She spares a glance at the view, as do probably all visitors. Monsieur Legros must have some power, indeed, to merit not only a large wooden desk and a separate meeting room table touting a live plant, but also an office with a panoramic view of the river. The low hills of Pech David are visible in the south and immediately on the north side, the soccer stadium on the island in the middle of the river. The sun pounding down directly on the windows makes Emeline send up quick thanks for air conditioning.

"How can I be of service, Captain Evian?" Monsieur Legros asks and waves for her to have a seat in one of his visitors' chairs.

Emeline slides gratefully into the seat. She pulls out her phone and opens a photo she took of Clothilde's letter before leaving home. "I'm investigating a cold case from the late eighties," she says, weighing her words, wondering how much she should tell the man. "The murder of a young woman named Clothilde Humbert."

No reaction from Monsieur Legros. The name must not ring any bells.

"I found this letter in her belongings." She hands over her phone so Monsieur Legros can study the document. "I realize it's a form letter of sorts, but it has your signature, so I would very much like to pick your brain on the subject."

Emeline doesn't miss the downward twist of his mouth when he reads the short letter, nor the deepening of the furrow between his bushy eyebrows.

"This *is* a form letter," he says. "So much so, it doesn't even say what subject this person—" He checks the letterhead and realizes it's the name Emeline just said belonged to a murder victim. He clears his throat. "—Mademoiselle Humbert wanted to talk to Madame Redon about."

"She worked with a non-profit organization for the improvement of traffic fluidity in Toulouse," Emeline says. "From what I understand, this is as close as she ever got to Madame Redon, despite multiple attempts to meet with the woman."

Sighing, Monsieur Legros sets Emeline's phone on the desk to return it, and leans back in his chair, making it creak under his weight. His gaze goes out the window but he's not seeing the river, the cars driving past, or the soccer stadium.

"I spent three miserable years working for Madame Redon," he says, his voice low. "Do you know, she's the reason I changed political parties? Simply couldn't stand the idea of being on the same side as her."

His gaze comes back to the office and he looks around as if really seeing it for the first time. "Although, to be fair, I guess she pushed me to discover where my real loyalties and beliefs were earlier than I would have otherwise. Not that I will thank her for it."

Leaning forward in his chair to place his forearms on his desk, he reaches out and taps a finger on Emeline's phone. "She ordered me to send those letters to *anyone* approaching her on three very specific subjects. She didn't care if it was a preschooler or the President himself, she wasn't interested in *any* input or opinions. She had better things to do with her time."

"So I assume traffic management was one of the three subjects?"

"Yes." Emeline doesn't need to formulate the next questions for him to answer it. "The two others were housing management and public transport. The latter is quite close to traffic management, of course, but they are two separate issues to be dealt with. Ideally, you manage the two in concert."

Emeline jots down the two subjects in her trusty notebook. It's slightly damp from the time spent in her back pocket but as long as she can take her notes and read them later, that doesn't matter.

"What happened if someone wouldn't give up?" she asks. "Surely, not everyone was satisfied with this form letter reply?"

Monsieur Legros' snort is flat and devoid of any real mirth. "*Nobody* was satisfied with that letter. It would be followed up by a second letter, a third… Then they'd start calling. Giving that same answer on the phone was *fun*, I can tell you. When *that* didn't work, they showed up in person. Well, the driven ones did, anyway. I suppose I did lose some during the process."

"Clothilde probably showed up in person," Emeline says.

Monsieur Legros throws out his arms, hands up. "I saw a lot of angry people trying to get to Madame Redon or one of the other Council members. And it was over thirty years ago. Maybe I met your Mademoiselle Humbert, maybe I didn't."

"What happened when they showed up at City Hall?"

"They were escorted out by security. Mostly, it happened calmly and without incident. Only once did one young lady make such a scene, only the mayor showing his face and rebuking her in person could get her to *consider* lowering her volume or leaving the building."

Emeline has a feeling, in the pit of her stomach. It isn't even her tingly sense this time, only her own intuition and her knowledge of Clothilde's character. She grabs her phone and quickly searches for another photo she took of something from Clothilde's boxes.

Her school photo from her senior year in high school.

She turns the phone to show it to Monsieur Legros. "You wouldn't happen to recognize this face, Monsieur? Was she the young lady making a scene?"

Monsieur Legros leans so close his nose is almost touching the phone's screen. "I'll be damned. That's her!"

Of course it is.

FIVE

"I wasn't trying to meet with Redon," Clothilde says. She's perched on one of Legros' filing cabinets close to the door. "I wanted Pradel. His form letter responses were a lot more annoying and insulting. Couldn't let it stand."

I smile at my friend. I've opted to take up position in the corner, leaning against the wall behind Evian, with an unimpeded view of the river and cars outside. I keep stealing glances at the soccer stadium behind me—it has been through some major renovations since my time. I'd love to know what the occasion was but unfortunately, I don't think Evian will know—or care.

I miss playing soccer, I realize. Haven't really thought about it before now but I loved being part of a team, pushing myself to my limits, making an ass of myself every time I scored. Even if I found enough ghosts to make up two teams, it wouldn't be the same.

Evian has taken back her phone and is staring at Clothilde's high school picture. It's odd to see her in full color like that. It's definitely my Clothilde, there's no mistaking the mischievous smile or the glint in her eye, but I never pictured her eyes to be that shade of dark green, or her hair to be such a rich chestnut. The flush high on her cheeks is downright surprising.

Yet another reminder of what we've lost. We might still be around and pretending to be equal partners to Evian while solving crime, but we have some pretty severe handicaps. Life isn't quite life without soccer or color.

"Do you know where the order to refute all requests came from?" Evian asks. "Other than Redon, I mean. Do you think she did it on her own initiative, or could the order have come from higher up?"

Legros' frown deepens. "From the mayor, you mean?" He seems to go through memories as he takes a moment before replying. "I suppose it's possible. Might even make sense, to a certain degree. What makes you ask the question this way?"

Evian will have to watch what she's saying so nothing comes to the ears of certain people at the police station. She is still officially working a case but has received increasingly restrictive instructions from several levels of superior officers. She is to work on Clothilde's death and her link to me, and that's it. Throwing around accusations against the long-dead but still-beloved mayor would not go down all too well.

And Legros is a politician. He's cooperating well enough, but the chances of him talking to someone, who talks to someone… and word ending up in Divisional Commander Spangero's ear are unfortunately rather high. It's very frustrating. Both because it hinders us from properly investigating Clothilde's past and because it confirms Clothilde's past is intimately linked to something the big bosses at the police station don't want Evian to look into.

"I talked with Monsieur Pradel not too long ago," Evian says. "He also had some run-ins with Mademoiselle Humbert in the time before she died. In fact, I think she may have been trying to see *him* that time you saw her at the City Hall."

I can't read any emotions on Legros' face but I'm guessing he's heard about Pradel spending some time being "interviewed" by the police recently. "I guess that makes sense," he says slowly. "He *was* working on urban development for a long time. Is this why you suspect Madame Redon wasn't really behind the orders she gave me?"

"Come on, dude!" Clothilde yells from her perch. "You're not the police officer here, she is! *She's* the one asking the questions. *You* should be answering. If you don't, we're going to think you're one of the bad guys."

Evian cocks her head. I think she's confused by what she feels from Clothilde.

She's not yet sufficiently familiar with Clothilde's particular brand of questioning.

It seems to work, though.

"I guess that's not important," Legros says as he suppresses a shiver. "I'll have to redirect you to Madame Redon if you wish to know what made her do what she did. She didn't confide in me, only gave me the most unsatisfying tasks possible. She may have been trying to drive me away from politics."

Evian nods. This is where, logically, we would move on to interviewing Redon. Unfortunately, she's on the no-go list given to Evian by her boss Diome. Too many restrictions.

Evian's phone vibrates. I lean over her shoulder to see it's an incoming call from Nadine Tulle. Could she already have information on Constantine's husband?

Although finding Jacques Larcher isn't as important to Evian as searching for Clothilde's murderer, it seems we won't be getting any useful information out of Legros without letting him know we have our hands tied, so she uses the call as an excuse to put an end to their meeting. They shake hands quickly, Evian leaves him one of her cards, and we're out in the hallway, following Evian toward the staircase as she accepts the call from Tulle.

"You found something already?" Evian asks as she pushes the door to the stairwell open.

I could hear more than tinny noises if I leaned very close to Evian's ear, but I leave her be. I trust she'll share whatever information she gets once the conversation is over. I fall into step with Clothilde a few paces behind Evian as she hurries down the spiral staircase.

"Well, that's quick," Evian replies to whatever Tulle said. "Hang on, let me write that down." She stops just before reaching the exit on the ground floor and pulls out her notebook. She flips to a blank page and jots down "Cimetière de Salonique," followed by a plot number.

Looks like Constantine's husband is dead, and we've found his final resting place.

She also writes down the name Béatrice Larcher and an address that I don't recognize. Next of kin?

Evian thanks Tulle profusely and is about to hang up when she cocks her head. I don't hear anything through the phone.

"Was there something else?" Evian asks. With a quick glance up and down the staircase, she makes sure we're alone, and presses a button to put Tulle on speaker. No sound comes out.

Evian's on-point intuition doesn't come only from her

capacity to communicate with ghosts. Tulle's silence means she has something more than the name of a cemetery. And Evian is giving her the time to decide whether or not to talk.

"It's probably nothing…" Tulle begins, then trails off. There's a faint *click* in the background. I think she might have closed the door to her office.

"I'm guessing it's something," Evian says, her voice encouraging without being condescending. "Does it have to do with Monsieur Larcher?"

"No," Tulle says immediately. "I gave you everything I have on him. It's just… You remember that search you had me do when you first came here? Looking for cold cases with similar profiles to that young woman?"

Here she goes with her secrecy again. Both women know Clothilde's name, and the case Evian has been on since she came here. Tulle is worried about someone listening in and is staying vague.

"Of course," Evian says. She leans sideways to check the staircase again. We're still alone.

"Clothilde will tell you if someone is coming," I tell her. My friend has taken up position half a flight of stairs above us, being the lookout now coming naturally to the both of us.

"Well," Tulle continues, whispering now, "I set up an alert while I did my search. Figured you'd want to know if any hot cases came in that would also fit the profile…"

Evian's breath catches. "You got a hit?"

"Maybe. Yes. I think so."

"Who? Where? When?" Evian sets her phone down on the stairs, so she has both hands free to take notes. She flips her notebook to the next page.

"I can't—" Tulle takes a deep breath. "There's something off with the case, but I can't tell you about it. Boss's orders."

"What!" Two spots of anger appear on Evian's cheeks. "Who—"

"But if you were to go look for the grave of Monsieur Larcher, say this afternoon around four? You might want to take a walk through the neighboring cemetery—Terre Cabade—about half an hour later. It's not often you can see an actual funeral in such an old and overcrowded cemetery. Should be interesting. You know, since you're a tourist in Toulouse, and all."

Tulle trails off while Evian stares at the phone, her mouth hanging open. Her lips form the word "tourist," before she shakes it off and jots down everything Tulle just said.

"Yes, I love taking strolls through cemeteries," Evian says in a completely neutral tone. "I'll jump at any occasion to compare them to Père Lachaise in Paris."

"That's what I thought." Tulle sounds relieved Evian doesn't call her on her weird excuse. If anybody were to listen in on this conversation, a little scrutiny will make it obvious the women aren't actually talking about tourist spots, but it's still better than saying things outright.

Evian thanks Tulle for her help and hangs up. Then she sits down on the stairs and uses her phone to look up the two cemeteries Tulle wants her to visit.

I know them both well, they really *are* Toulouse's answer to Père Lachaise—two very old, very big cemeteries, separated only by a narrow road, and located on one of the city's rare hills, giving the dead a gorgeous view of Toulouse. I used to go there from time to time to take a stroll among the ancient tombs and clear my head.

But that was before I became a ghost.

I wonder if it would still be silent and peaceful now?

SIX

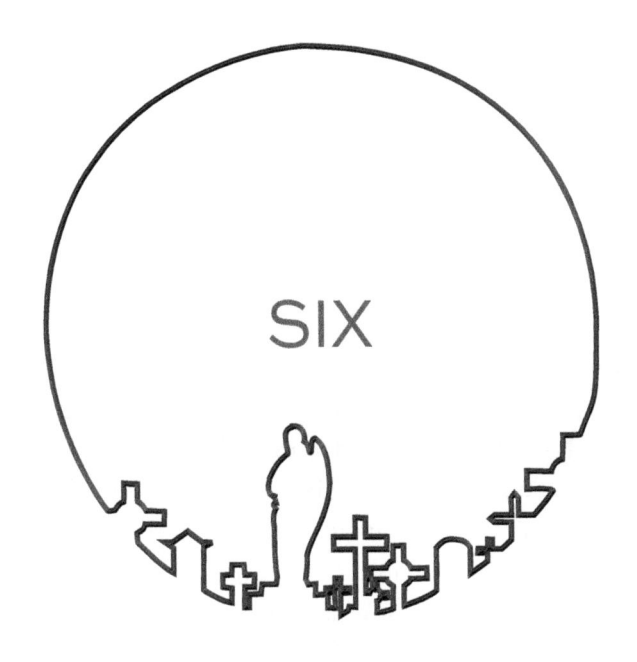

THE ANSWER IS a definite no. Walking through a huge cemetery when you can see the ghosts is *not* as peaceful as when you're blissfully ignorant.

Evian took the metro again, getting off at Jolimont. This way she's already on the hill and we only have to walk a few minutes to get to the Salonique cemetery. With the sun bearing down from a clear, blue sky, and a funeral parlor behind us, we cross the tiny parking lot at the cemetery entrance. Only two cars; one blue sedan and one whitish Peugeot 106 that must have been parked there for several years already.

Evian is sweating profusely. I think she has given up on trying to dry out her T-shirt. When we exited the metro, she bought a large bottle of water and has already drunk half of it. A small part went into her hair two minutes ago. I think she's tempted to pour the rest down her front, but she might need it later. It's not very common to find coffee shops inside cemeteries. Her sunglasses keep slipping down her nose and I have never been happier not to have a physical body.

A cemetery like this one offers very little shade. Some of the tombs and statues are *very* big, and the main avenues are lines with pines and cypress trees, but none seem to throw a shadow a person can hide in. The graves are all gray and stern, most of the statues are missing appendages or faces, and one angel has a clipped wing. The lanes and paths are well-maintained and neat, but the responsibility of upholding a tomb falls entirely to the individual family. Like in our old cemetery, it is clear which families prioritize upholding appearances even in death, and which are keeping the plot because it has already been paid for.

Evian has the location of Larcher's plot on her phone. According to the map, it's on the other side, just past the WWI memorial. With a sigh, Evian chooses the main path toward the center of the cemetery and sets off at a brisk pace.

At first, I don't notice the other ghosts. In my worry for Evian's well-being, I sort of forgot to look for them. But we're not even twenty meters inside the cemetery walls when Clothilde whispers, "There's a girl on the left. And an old man down there by that broken headstone."

I follow her gaze. On our left, sitting on the steps of a narrow mausoleum belonging to the Albouy family, a girl of about ten looks up at us, wispy strands of hair pulled into two messy pigtails and torn trousers under a too-big man's shirt. Her expression is hard to read. The curiosity fits with the ten-year-old body, but the knowledge behind the eyes feels unlimited.

Evian is walking too fast for me to be able to stop for long, but I scan the names listed by the mausoleum door and find one Lisette Albouy, born August 1807, died March 1819.

And she's *still* a ghost.

I stop in front of the girl, opening my mouth to say something, *anything*, but I come up short. What do you say to a girl who's been a ghost for two hundred years? And I'm feeling the pull of Evian moving away from me, like an itch at the center of my ribcage, getting more uncomfortable with each step she takes.

"I'm fine, Monsieur," the girl says, her voice that of a child but her tone that of an adult. "Go with your friends. And stay away from Gérard. He's not right in the head." She nods in the direction of the old man Clothilde mentioned earlier.

I see Clothilde has fallen behind too, and she's approaching the old man by the broken headstone.

"Thank you," I say to Lisette and sketch a bow of all things. "Perhaps we'll meet again someday. Have a good day." I start running after Evian, the itch becoming unbearable. When I pass Clothilde, I slow down. "According to the young girl, there's no point in trying to talk to him. And we need to keep up with Evian."

Clothilde doesn't look happy, but she must be feeling the pull too, and stops trying to talk to the man. I don't spare him more than a glance, but it's enough to see he's missing part of his body—and not because of amputation or anything that might have happened while he was alive, but because he must have forgotten what the lower half of his body looked like.

"This place is like a horror movie." Clothilde shivers and throws her arms around her body, as if she's cold.

I can only agree. As we pass through the enormous cemetery, I spot dozens of ghosts. They're hiding behind graves, dancing on statues, trying to dig through the tiny sliver of dirt between two mausoleums… And they all seem to be by themselves. I can't see a single group.

"Why aren't they at least hanging out together?" I'm keeping my voice down so Evian—now no more than ten steps ahead of us and downing half of her remaining water—won't be freaked-out. As long as the ghosts don't talk to her directly, she doesn't seem to realize they're there, and right now, that's most definitely for the best. This is distracting *me*, who can see the other ghosts, so I can't even begin to imagine what it would be like for someone who can only feel them.

"Maybe you *do* get tired of other people if you hang out together for a hundred years? This could have been us if we'd been forced to do more than thirty years together?" Clothilde is trying for a joke, but it falls completely flat.

This cemetery is *creepy*.

"I'd never grow tired of you to the point of preferring solitude for all eternity, Clothilde."

Clothilde's answer is barely a whisper. "Same, Robert."

I'm suddenly thankful I ended up in *our* cemetery. Clearly, not all cemeteries are born equal.

We've reached the cemetery's center. When Evian reaches the WWI memorial, she slows down so she can look up at the impressive monument. It's about ten meters high and fifty wide, the main wall in the back made of white marble and the decorative front of red bricks and mortar, all set up in an arch with regularly spaced roman columns. On every available marble surface, the names of soldiers from Toulouse who lost their lives in the war. I don't remember how many there are, but it numbers in the thousands.

"Thank God it's just the names and not their bodies," Clothilde says. From her expression, I don't think she intended to say that out loud. She's downright apologetic and hurries to explain. "Can you imagine a cemetery with hundreds of battle-shocked soldier ghosts?"

I smile at Clothilde to show her I understand—and secretly agree. This place is crowded enough as it is.

With a nod to the monument, Evian continues. Here, we find some shade under the pines and Evian's feet throw up dust as she chooses one of the smaller paths into the maze of graves of the "neighborhood" indicated on her phone.

I see several ghosts, but they mostly keep away from Evian when she approaches, preferring to spy on her from afar.

Evian stops at one of the tombstones. It's of a classic sort; a large granite slab made to represent a casket, with a headstone rising at the head and several memorial plaques placed on top. None of them look recent. The family name, Larcher, is spelled out in large letters on the headstone, some moss almost hiding the last letter, and the individual names of everyone buried is engraved on the sides of the "casket."

Jacques Larcher is on the bottom left. Born 1926. Died 1962.

"Only thirty-six years old," Clothilde says, her expression sombre. "Doesn't look like he remarried, does it?"

I scan the other names on the tomb, but none have dates that would fit, nor names to indicate they'd married into the Larcher family. "Having your wife disappear never to be found probably doesn't help with giving it another go. Especially within six years of her disappearance."

Evian has also found the name. She uses her phone to snap several pictures of the grave from all directions. She takes another sip of her water and sighs. "Now what? How is knowing when he died going to give Constantine any closure?" Her eyes scan the cemetery but I'm not sure she's actually seeing anything.

"Knowing he died so shortly after her might have the *opposite* effect of what we want. I don't suppose he's here?"

I start as I realize she's talking to us. "Well, I can't see anybody right now," I tell her, hoping she understands. "But everybody seems to be kind of skittish." I meet Clothilde's gaze. "Maybe we can have a look around?"

"Maybe we don't have to." Clothilde points to a mausoleum two plots down. It's tall and narrow and has a wrought-iron door closing the access to a tiny room with the names of the deceased on the walls.

Just behind the door, a ghost is standing perfectly still, watching us. I can't make out many details, but it's a man and he *might* be in his thirties. The clothing could be from the sixties.

"Hello," I call out to him and wave. "I'm Robert and this is Clothilde. We're visiting." I wish I'd had time to prepare, this is feeling very odd. I'm used to welcoming newcomers to my cemetery, not being the outsider in somebody else's. "You wouldn't happen to be of the Larcher family?"

The man's dark stare moves from Evian, to land on me, but he doesn't reply. Only stares.

Clothilde leans close and whispers, "Do you want me to—"

"What do you want?" the man asks. He steps through the wrought-iron door so we can see him better but stays on the first step of the mausoleum.

"We're looking for a man named Jacques Larcher," I say. I'm about to mention Constantine but decide to hold back that information until I know who I'm talking to.

Evian seems to have realized we've made contact. Her eyes are darting back and forth, and I can tell she's antsy, but she stays quiet and takes up her usual parade rest. She knows we can get this job done without her.

"And what do you want with Jacques Larcher?" the man asks. There's a touch of arrogance to him, but mostly he seems to be holding back a lot of anger. He's practically vibrating with it.

I figure we'll have to give him something. "We have news of his wife."

I don't even see him move. One second he's standing ten meters away, the next he's in my face—quite literally. He's so close I can't see more than his angry eyes and a large nose. "What do you know of Constantine?"

"Hey! Back off, buddy!" Clothilde is trying to pry the other man off me. Unfortunately, it's quite difficult when neither of them is corporeal. "I can go poltergeist too, if needed. Take a step back and we'll tell you all about Constantine."

"Constantine disappeared," he growls, but he does take one step back. I see Evian shaking off a frisson. I'd love to do the same, but keeping a strong facade feels like the way to go with this guy.

"Yes, we know," I say, keeping my voice as level and as neutral as possible. "She's a ghost, just like you."

The man doesn't calm down in the slightest. "How dare you speak of my Constantine in this way! Constantine is not a ghost. She *left* me."

I take half a step back to get some distance between us, hoping he won't see it as a sign of weakness. Clothilde is at my side, ready to fight the other ghost if need be. Yet another thing we never tried: two ghosts going poltergeist at the same time, intending each other harm.

I'd rather not know what it looks like.

"I take it you *are* Jacques Larcher?" I don't wait for his answer. If he's here, right by the Larcher grave, and talks about *his* Constantine, he's our guy. "Constantine is very much a ghost. She never left you, Jacques. She was murdered and the body hidden. She was very sad over how her disappearance hurt you."

Larcher has gone completely still. Ghosts don't need to breathe, or blink their eyes, or even be bothered by gravity—but most of us keep to old habits and imitate life to the best of our abilities. It may be the shock, or the fact he's been a ghost for half a century longer than me so he's had the time to forget, but the man might as well have been a slightly transparent statue for all the life he exhibits.

His eyes dart to Clothilde, who nods confirmation I'm telling the truth.

He whips around to look at Evian, still standing in front of his gravestone.

"You don't touch or bother her," Clothilde says in her midnight voice. "She's an ally and came here to help. You bother her in *any* way and none of us will ever come back and you'll never see your Constantine again."

Evian lets out a long, steadying breath, but doesn't move.

"Constantine would not confide in the likes of you," Larcher practically spits and he's yet again in my face. "If she loved me like you said, she would have come to find me."

"Like you can go find her?" I ask. When he doesn't have an answer, I continue, "We know how this works, Jacques. You can't leave the confines of the cemetery. And the only way to find release is by solving your unfinished business. My guess is yours has to do with your wife."

"You know nothing! Why are you here? You are not one of us."

I've given up on getting some distance between me and the other man. Even if he decides to get physical, what's it going to do? We don't have physical bodies. As long as he stays away from Evian, there's no problem. "And that doesn't even make you a little bit curious?" I ask him. "You don't wonder how we can be here?"

"If we can, so could perhaps Constantine." Clothilde folds her arms, and her right foot is soundlessly tapping on the dirt path.

Larcher bares his teeth at her like he's some wild, rabid wolf. "If Constantine could come here, why didn't she?"

"Perhaps she was afraid you'd have lost your marbles or something," I grumble. "And she'd be right." Making a show of heaving a sigh, I meet Clothilde's gaze. "I think we got what we came for, didn't we? We know he's here, we know he's a ghost. Constantine can decide what to do next."

Evian must sense we're getting ready to leave because she looks around, then down at her phone to find the fastest way toward the exit.

Predictably, Larcher isn't happy with being ignored or made fun of. He stares daggers at both me and Clothilde but can't come up with anything that will hurt a ghost. Or, he knows a way, but doesn't want to try it when he's outnumbered. Not a thought I want to linger on.

When Evian starts to move, though, he figures out how to hurt us.

He leaps toward her with a snarl.

SEVEN

One minute Emeline is calmly starting to walk toward the cemetery's south exit, slightly annoyed she had to stand in the sun for no sane reason, sweating through her clothes and worrying about sun stroke, the next her heart is in her throat, a chill runs down her spine, and she feels such a strong onslaught of *hatred*, her steps falter.

Then she's assaulted by a different feeling. Hurry, goodwill, *run*.

She realizes she knows who's talking to her. It's Clothilde. How attuned *is* she to ghosts if she can tell them apart?

Another bloodcurdling *scream* she can't actually hear, and Emeline drops all pretense of logical thought. And she runs.

She tries to keep the fear and horror off her face so the few people she encounters won't think she's pursued by an attacker—even though she is—and when someone looks at her askance, she raises her hand to look at her watch. Like she just remembered she is late for a meeting.

The horrible feeling of being attacked and *hated* comes back at regular intervals but she feels her friends fighting the other ghost off, looking out for her.

Down the last gravel path, and the exit is in sight. There's no one around, so Emeline pushes a last sprint. In the last few meters, her head feels like it'll explode—is the ghost *inside* her?—but she doesn't need to see to make the last, faltering steps.

The horror stops.

Hands on her knees as she's heaving for breath, Emeline squeezes her eyes shut, forcing the memory of that awful feeling away. If felt almost like she was back… No, no thinking about it. Focus on the present.

Scorching hot sun. High, stone cemetery walls reflecting even more heat. The dark asphalt under her feet and two cars slowing down to go over a speed bump behind her.

And silence in her head.

Robert and Clothilde are still there—they don't really have a choice in the matter as long as she's carrying the bracelets—but must be keeping quiet.

What the hell just happened in there?

Slowly, she straightens, brushing off her pants even though there's no need. She's alone, with the Salonique cemetery behind her, a narrow road running left to right, lined on both sides by the walls of the two cemeteries. Why even bother claiming it's two different cemeteries if they're separated by nothing but a five-meter-wide street?

Emeline checks her watch—and actually looks at what it says this time. Twenty minutes past four. She needs to get into the Terre Cabade cemetery immediately. When Nadine Tulle gave her vague hint, Emeline didn't think to ask for directions or details. There's a funeral in a cemetery, how hard can it be to find?

When the cemetery's the size of a small village and on uneven ground, quite hard.

Downing the rest of her water and throwing the empty bottle in a trash can by the exit, Emeline crosses the street and walks up to the entrance of the Terre Cabade cemetery. It's just a nondescript door in the tall stone wall. The main entrance is on the other side, the part facing the city center. That one has two obelisks, wrought-iron gates, and guards.

When she steps through the door, she's met with more of the same: mausoleums, statues, memorials, crumbling gravestones. Where the first cemetery was on flat terrain, this one is on a gentle slope down toward the city. Visible above the graves, the entirety of Toulouse is gleaming in the sun, from the hill of Pech David in the south, past the many church towers and numerous red brick buildings in the city center, and to the Blagnac Airport in the north. The Garonne River meanders through the landscape, and the green lines of plane tree canopies mark the locations of canals and large avenues. It's a beautiful sight, but right now Emeline doesn't have the time to admire it.

"I'll take all the help I can get, guys," she says. "There's a funeral starting in ten minutes—I need to find it."

She gets no reply, of course, but she's confident the ghosts are helping. After all, it's *their* murderers she's after.

Emeline takes off at a quick pace, aiming for the central paths. It should allow the two ghosts to spread out.

No more than five minutes later, while Emeline is eying the statue of a man who was apparently a famous writer in the nineteenth century, she feels a tug to the left.

Ah, they found the funeral.

Switching off her own brain as best she can, Emeline wanders in whichever direction her feet will take her. A left turn here, a right one there, across a tombstone here.

She ends up on a small butte underneath an enormous cypress tree with roots digging into the nearest graves, in a spot with a view of a gathering group a few plots down. One of the graves is open—a large, black hole in the ground looking like it leads right down to hell, waiting for its next victim.

Suppressing a shiver, Emeline forces her gaze away and instead focuses on the gathering mourners.

The group is relatively small, maybe twenty-five people. If Emeline were to venture a guess, she'd say the deceased was fairly young, based on the average age of the mourners. A large majority look to be in their thirties, and another group fifties or sixties. So the group of friends, and the parents' friends. The rest must be extended family.

Could this be the funeral of their serial killer's latest victim? If it showed up in Nadine's search, it must have ticked a certain number of boxes.

She's very tempted to go down there and talk to the people. There's only so much she can do from up here. But if Nadine was so careful in her wording, and someone gave her the express order *not* to say anything to Emeline...she should stay out of sight. For both her own and Nadine's sake.

However... "You guys can go down there and listen in, right?" She sighs as she realizes what she'll have to do to get her report. "I'll ask Amina if I can borrow her Ouija board when we get home so you can give me all the details."

Now that it's decided there's nothing more to do, Emeline slides down to sit with her back to the cypress's trunk, thrilled to finally be in the shade. She's not really hiding but as long as she doesn't make any big or sudden movements, nobody from the funeral should notice her. She takes out her phone and starts snapping pictures of the mourners—you never know, she might need to identify someone later.

Or maybe Nadine has the tools to run facial recognition software?

That probably won't be necessary, but it keeps Emeline's mind away from other things while she waits.

Less than five minutes later, a hearse pulls up. Looks like the Mass was someplace else, and the mourners got here before the casket. Now they all line up to form a passage from the hearse to the open grave, faces morose. Even though she's too far away to see many details, Emeline sees the tears on almost all their faces.

The doors to the hearse open, revealing the end of a white casket covered in wreaths. Emeline snaps one picture—

Her hand shoots to her head, covering her ear. When that doesn't help, she drops her phone and covers the other one.

What is going on?

It's like someone's *screaming* in her head. It could be one of the mourners below, except the sound isn't coming through her ears—it's *in. Her. Head.*

Panic. Pain. Desperation.

So. Loud.

Her hands still over her ears, Emeline stares down at the group. Nobody seems to be reacting, no more than the usual crying and hugging at a funeral, anyway. Can nobody else hear the screams?

Unable to block out the sound, or diminish the volume, or even identify where it's coming from, Emeline starts to slip.

Instead of hearing the screams of whoever that is, she's hearing her own. In place of her cozy spot in the shade, she's in the dark…the walls closing in…her screams going unheard…

A soothing presence and a gentle hum ease their way into her consciousness.

It's still dark, but the screaming subsides. *Her* screaming subsides. The other person's screams, the ones from below, are still there, but they're slightly muffled. Something else is inserting itself over them—a song?

Emeline's wits come back enough for her to recognize the presence. It's Clothilde again.

She's being rocked, enfolded by, and sung to, by Clothilde.

Not even caring how odd it is, Emeline focuses on the song just out of reach, and on the sensation of arms around her. Of not being alone in the dark.

And she waits for the horror to pass.

EIGHT

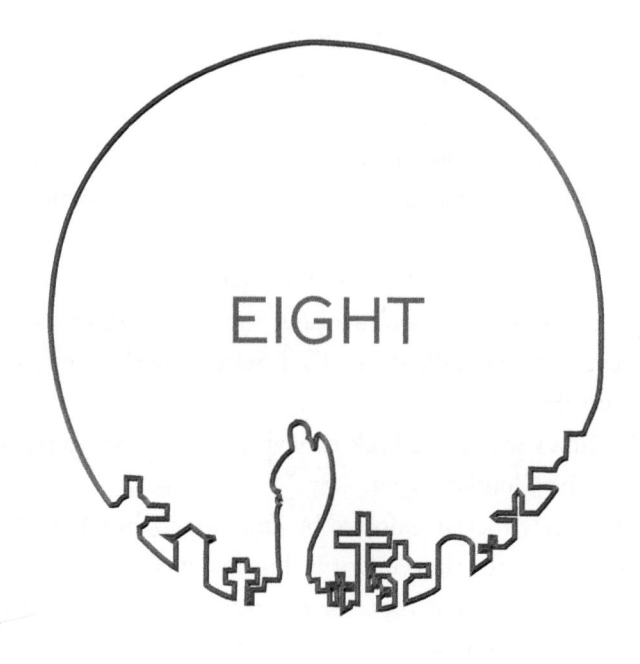

EVIAN SEEMS TO think it was her idea to send us down to eavesdrop on the mourners. We don't feel the need to correct her. While she settles in underneath the huge cypress tree to get some well-deserved rest, we run down the short slope to the group of mourners.

It feels odd to be doing this again. It's familiar—because we've been to hundreds of funerals like this in our old cemetery, where we'd listen in on what the mourners had to say about the deceased in case they woke up as a ghost and might need the information—and yet completely new, because the cemetery is unknown to us and we've been getting used to moving around in the world of the living.

We split up immediately. Clothilde goes to the family and I take the friends.

Most of them are standing around waiting, not talking. A funeral isn't the ideal spot for small talk. But two guys standing on the outskirts of the group, wearing matching ill-fitting suits I'm willing to bet they only bring out for weddings and funerals, have their heads together, talking. Both blond and in their thirties, one is rather burly and looks like he was once of the athletic sort while the other is almost worryingly thin.

I rush over to eavesdrop.

"I'm telling you," the skinny one whispers, "the case was closed before it was even opened. How can you conclude someone committed suicide and not check with any family members or friends if the person showed signs of depression?"

The burly guy sighs as he stretches his neck from side to side. Sweat is running down his face and I think his tie is too tight. "He jumped off a building, JP. It does kind of scream suicide."

"You find it believable that Hélori would do that? And why wasn't there an autopsy?"

"You often don't suspect who wants to take their own life," the burly guy counters weakly. "If it was obvious, people would watch over their friends closer."

The skinny one rolls his eyes as the hearse pulls up. "Did you Google that?"

I think he did but can hardly judge him for it. It is, unfortunately, the kind of information one looks up when it's too late. In this case, however, if Nadine Tulle sent us here because she thinks there's a link with Clothilde's murder, it probably *wasn't* suicide.

What surprises me is the name. It's not one I'm familiar with, but I'm pretty sure it's a man's name. All the victims we've found so far were women. Young, pretty women.

Does this mean the murderer is branching out? That the victim profiles have changed now that the usual executioner is in jail? Or that we were missing a large number of the victims in our first search?

I don't get the time to take the thought further because the hearse's doors are opened—and we have a screamer.

I really haven't missed this.

When someone has unfinished business, they become ghosts. This transformation happens in the casket during Mass. And I cannot begin to describe the pure terror of waking up inside a sealed casket while being carried to your grave.

The casket only lets the ghost out once they've accepted what they've become. This can take anything from hours to weeks. Personally, I screamed for five days before emerging.

Hélori has become a ghost—and he's good at making his displeasure known.

The living, of course, can't hear him. So I ignore the screams as best I can to lean in and continue listening in on the two men's conversation. But they've fallen silent to watch the casket be pulled out of the hearse.

Suddenly, Clothilde rushes past. "You have to manage all of them, Robert," she yells. "Emeline can hear the screams." She sprints up to Evian's hiding spot.

I can't make out many details since she's in the shade, but it looks like she's on her knees, both hands to her head as she's rocking back and forth.

That can't be good.

Clothilde reaches her and drops to her knees. Enfolds her in a hug. She meets my gaze over Evian's head and signs for me to get on with my job. She's got Evian covered.

Right then. While the casket is set up on the lift that will be lowered into the grave after the priest has said a few words, I stroll through the group, trying to catch the rare conversations or observe the expressions and attitudes of the mourners.

The family is the closest to the casket, of course. The parents, and a young woman with a toddler on her hip. Looks like Hélori was a father. The toddler is fussy because Maman is crying, and the grandmother looks like she wants to take the little girl, but probably more for her own sake than for her daughter-in-law's.

Just awesome. As if we didn't have incentive enough to catch these guys—now they're killing young parents too. I'm fairly certain none of the victims that Tulle identified for us in the past were mothers.

As I amble through the small crowd, I realize a large number of the friends are side-eyeing two persons in the back. None of the glances are friendly. When I'm close to the two blond guys, the skinny one grumbles, "They're spending more time making sure he's below ground than they did on investigating his death."

They're police officers? I rush over to study the pair more closely.

I've never seen either of them before but that's not surprising. We've only met a handful of officers since we started hanging out with Evian. Neither of them is in uniform but now I'm looking I see they're both armed. One woman, in her late fifties, with short salt-and-pepper hair and moderate but visible eye makeup, lets her eyes roam over the mourners, studying everyone, not even pretending to be there for the actual funeral. The man, much younger and probably fresh out of officers' school, is trying to do the same but seems too nervous about the angry stares he's getting in return to actually notice anything important.

Police officers showing up to a funeral isn't surprising in and of itself. But coming out of uniform, not caring about the deceased, and several mourners murmuring about a badly done job?

This is why Tulle stayed cryptic. She was expressly forbidden from telling Evian about this death and the funeral, and these officers are here to make sure she didn't show.

I glance up toward Evian's hiding spot. The shadow was enough to hide her from mourners focused on the casket, but will the officers—who are looking for her—notice?

I realize I can't even see Evian anymore, only Clothilde. She is kneeling under the cypress tree, her focus on the ground before her. Evian must be lying down. Not a good sign for her mental state, but at least she's out of sight.

The new ghost in his casket is still screaming and I can hear him pounding against the wood. We're going to have to come back once he's calmed down and hope he remembers who killed him.

In the meantime, I'd very much like to get the names of the two officers before me. Neither is wearing a name tag, of course, and since they're not talking, they won't drop names in conversation. I doubt asking them, no matter how sensitive they might be, is going to be enough for them to just say their own names out loud.

So I settle for committing their faces to memory.

Once the priest has finished his speech, there isn't a dry eye in sight. Hélori seems to have been a loved man. And I catch more than one comment questioning if he could really have killed himself. Not a single one of them speaks up to say *but you remember that time…*

Once the casket is at the bottom of the grave and the family has thrown in their spadefuls of dirt—and *boy*, did the screams increase when he heard and felt that—people start to leave in small groups.

Now, we *could* find this family and groups of friends later, but it would require a lot of work and time. It feels like a waste when we have all of them right now. I would especially like to interview those two blond guys.

The two police officers don't leave straight away, unfortunately. The young man makes movements to start walking away, but the woman grabs his forearm and holds him in place. "We're the last to leave," she tells him.

Waiting them out at the grave isn't going to work.

Besides, if Evian is that affected by the screams while over fifteen meters away, she isn't going to want to come down here.

I somehow have to get the witnesses to her.

NINE

I GO WITH the old and tried method of being annoying and insistent. Very few people are as sensitive to ghosts as Evian, but none are completely immune. If we talk to them long enough, our words will end up making their way into their subconscious and their thoughts. Then, of course, comes the question of whether or not they'll listen to the odd thoughts that pop up, but that part is out of my hands.

Right now, I think the fact there are two guys to influence is playing to my advantage. I'm saying the same thing over and over to the both of them—"Go for a walk through the cemetery before going home. There are cold drinks at the other end"—with the only goal to get them away from the police officers and to a place Evian will be able to function. I hope they won't hate me for the lie about the cold drinks, but it's the most tempting thing I can think of on the spur of the moment.

"I've never been to this cemetery before," the skinny one says as he glances around. They've just said goodbye to the wife and the parents by the graveside and told everyone they will be heading home.

The chubby one looks around, stretching to see over some of the larger tombs. "I have a friend who likes to come here to stroll through from time to time, to look at the tombs and odd names and stuff. Kinda weird, but I guess it's peaceful enough."

I'm repeating my instructions over and over, speaking straight into their ears, first one, then the other. They're not very sensitive at all, but I'm not giving up until they're out of reach.

"I'd kill for a cold drink right about now," the chubby one says as he loosens his tie and removes his suit jacket. His shirt is soaked in sweat.

"Maybe there's a place in here that sells drinks," the skinny one says doubtfully. He looks confused. He doesn't understand why he suddenly thinks that statement makes sense.

"Excellent idea!" the chubby one says and almost sends his friend flying with a slap on the shoulder. "Let's go for a walk and see what we find, shall we? Nothing fun waiting for me at home anyway." He throws a glance over his shoulder at Hélori's grave. An afternoon of staring at the wall and missing his friend probably doesn't sound very appealing.

Having mutually convinced each other there is sure to be a stand selling cold drinks in an old cemetery, the pair takes off toward the north, and not south like everybody else who parked at the main entrance.

I'm *very* happy to see the police officers haven't noticed anything amiss.

Now I need to get Evian in the same direction.

I run up to the small butte where I saw her last. By the trunk of the cypress, Clothilde is on her knees, bent over a prone Evian. Clothilde is running a hand from Evian's head to the middle of her back, petting her like she's a cat and she's humming a lullaby I vaguely remember from my own youth.

"Two of the friends are going for a walk in the cemetery," I say, speaking loud enough to be heard over the screaming from below. "I'd *really* love for Evian to talk to them before they disappear."

"Okay. You hear that, Emeline?" Clothilde's voice is smooth and calming like a mother talking to a sobbing child. I'm taken aback by how strange it is to hear it from my friend. She's usually scathing, or witty, or disdainful. Never soothing. "We're going to get away from the screams now. You're going to have to get up on your own, but then I promise we'll move away from the noise."

A whimper escapes from Evian and her hands tighten over her ears. I notice her T-shirt is completely glued to her body with sweat. It seems unlikely to be from the heat. She also has dirt and needles from the cypress sticking to her front. Even with a black T-shirt, she's going to be quite a sight once she recovers.

"He's going to keep screaming for several days, maybe weeks," I say, doing my best to match Clothilde's tone. "We have some experience with these things. And lying here isn't going to be a viable solution for you because *he* certainly isn't going anywhere."

As if to prove my point, Hélori gives out a *roar* that should have been heard on the other side of the city. It's absolutely not helping with Evian, but it makes me very curious about what happened to him. We *have to* come back here.

And that's a conversation which is *not* going to go over well with Evian.

One thing at a time.

After a long, shaking inhale, Evian struggles up onto her knees, her hands still over her ears and her back bent so she's barely off the ground. "Get me away from here," she forces out. "Get me the hell away."

She stumbles to her feet, almost going face-first into the tree trunk, and I worry she's going to tumble down the small slope and be spotted by the police officers despite our best efforts.

She must feel where the noise is coming from, though, because she quickly sets off on a course directly away from the screaming Hélori and the remaining mourners—and yes, the two officers are still there—stalking across graves, not caring who or what she steps on, as long as it takes her *away*.

Clothilde keeps up the supportive comments. She even looks like she wants to put a reassuring hand on Evian's shoulder, but pulls away. Even though the intention is good, touching Evian right now is not the best idea.

I stay behind long enough to confirm the police officers didn't see her, then run ahead to find out where the two blond guys have gone off to.

Five minutes later, we've crossed two of the cemetery's larger paths running from the top of the hill to the main entrance at the bottom, and even I can barely hear the screams anymore. Evian has removed her hands from her ears and is taking deep breaths to regain her composure. She hasn't noticed the state of her clothes yet and I can't decide if it would be better to point it out and have her realize there's nothing much she can do about it, or wait for her to discover how she looks when she gets home.

The two men have reached the cemetery's northern wall when Evian catches up to them. They're arguing over whose idea it was to search for cold drinks inside a cemetery—surely neither of them is that stupid.

Sorry, not sorry. We got them where we wanted.

"Good afternoon, Messieurs," Evian says as she approaches. "I'd like to have a minute of your time, if you don't mind?"

The chubby one stops talking mid-sentence, his mouth hanging open as he takes in Evian's appearance. He seems fascinated with her hair, which is sticking out in all directions and—oh—there's a whole patch of needles stuck just above her right ear. The skinny one is more focused on the dirty T-shirt, though he seems to be trying to look without looking.

Frowning, Evian runs a hand through her hair—only to get her fingers stuck in the gooey sap, making the pines stick to her hair. She looks down at herself. Winces. Makes a half-hearted attempt to brush the dirt off.

She's sort of successful. No more needles or patches of dirt. Just dirty.

"I've had a rough afternoon," she says, her scowl making it clear the men would do well to keep from commenting. "I have some questions about the man whose funeral you attended. He was a friend?"

The skinny man takes a step backward, then eyes his friend. Studies Evian in a way suggesting he's judging their chances against her in a fight.

She's fiercer than she looks, dude. You wouldn't stand a chance.

"What's it to you?" he spits out. "You the one who pushed him off that building?"

Breath whooshes out of Evian. Her shoulders slump a little. "He was pushed off a building?"

I lean in and speak in her ear. "They have suspicions it wasn't a suicide."

Her back practically shoots up straight. "It *was* ruled a suicide?"

The men don't answer but their expressions are all the confirmation Evian needs.

"He fell off a building, the cops came in and ruled it a suicide in no time, and there was no autopsy?" She perks up like she was just offered a cold beer. "Was he involved in any political non-profits?"

The chubby guy's mouth is still hanging open and his eyes keep widening. I'm scared he might topple and hurt his head.

The skinny one, however, frowns and takes a step toward Evian. He's angry enough to try his chances in a fight, even without the support of his buddy. "All right, lady. That's enough. Who the hell are you?"

Evian draws up short. "Oh. I'm terribly sorry. I think I might have suffered heatstroke earlier. My brain isn't at its best. I'm Captain Evian, of the Judicial Police."

The chubby guy's mouth snaps shut, and he comes back to the present. Takes a step to stand shoulder-to-shoulder with his friend, arms crossed. The skinny one is so angry his whole neck turns a blotchy red.

"You're a *cop*?"

TEN

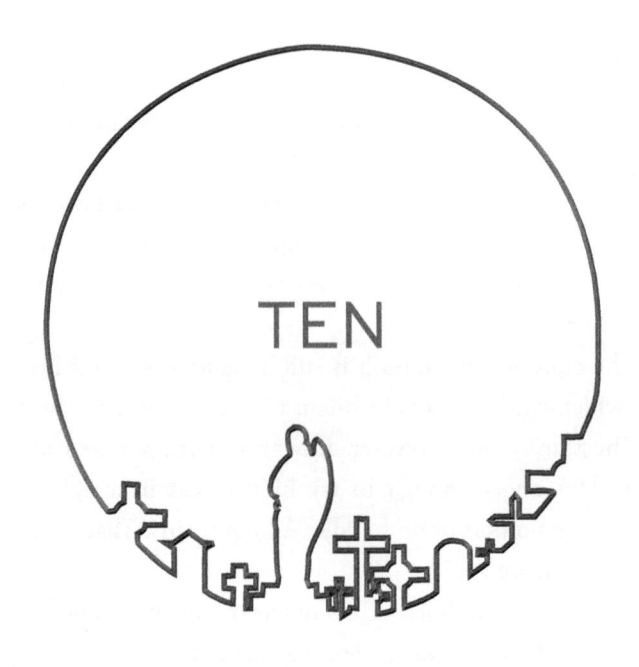

Emeline wonders if perhaps she *did* have a heatstroke. Her brain is sluggish, skipping from one thought to the next, never staying long enough to make any sense. And she's fairly certain it isn't even because of the ghosts. She simply isn't making much sense. For some reason, she was hoping this cemetery would sell cold drinks, but that doesn't sound very logical, does it?

She runs a hand down her face, somehow finding her palm to have a cooling effect on her forehead. If only she'd kept some of her water from earlier. Or thought to have this conversation in the shade instead of in this horrible heat, standing in front of a tombstone with a gargoyle sticking out its tongue at visitors. Who'd think that fitting for a grave?

Focus, Emeline.

"I'm not one of the officers who worked on your friend's crime scene," she blurts out. "I was not supposed to be here at all, so I had to hide during the ceremony." God, this was coming out all wrong. What she wouldn't give for a glass of water.

"That why you're so dirty?" The solid one cocks his head, already more curious than angry.

His skeletal friend, not so much, unfortunately. "Were you spying on us? Waiting for a chance to get us alone?"

"Yes, actually." With such a miserable excuse for a brain, Emeline might as well be honest. "Well, I was spying on the funeral because I was told it was somehow connected to the case I'm working on, and I was hoping I could talk to someone afterward, away from the officers."

"How'd you know they were officers? Friends of yours?"

Emeline scoffs. "Never seen them before in my life. I'm from out of town. But those two screamed police officers, even in civilian clothing."

Sniffing, the skeletal man seems to take her analysis as proof she's telling the truth. He takes a step back and scans the graves surrounding them. "Why don't they sell cold drinks in this place?"

Oh, for… The bloody ghosts again. That's how they got the two to split from the rest of the group? And Emeline fell for it as well, parched and questioning her sanity in accepting a job south of the Loire. It never gets *this* hot in Paris.

"Look," she says, doing her best to appear in control and capable. "I believe your friend was murdered, no suicide. I think his death is linked to the case I'm working on right now. But I can't think in this heat. Would you be amenable to finding a bar or a café nearby and having a chat over a cold drink?"

She should have started with the cold drink. Five minutes

later, they are strolling out past the large, red obelisks guarding the cemetery's main gates, aiming for the closest open bar by the Canal du Midi.

Emeline draws a few glances when they enter the small bar and aim for a booth in the back, but she ignores them. If she has sap in her hair, there isn't much she can do about it until she gets home, and her clothes aren't in worse shape than the workers sulking at the bar.

Their seats are next to a closed dartboard and under the signed photographs of the owner posing with various rugby players from the Stade Toulousain, the oldest at least a couple of decades old and the newest no more than a few months if Emeline has her roster information right.

The freshness of the air-conditioned room allows her to draw the first real breath since the screaming started in her head up at the funeral. The smooth, cool leather of the seat under her thighs makes her exhale with gratitude.

And the glass of chilled water down her throat? Pure heaven.

The two men get beers and clink their glasses solemnly together before their first sip. In remembrance of their friend.

Emeline waits until they're all halfway through their drinks before she starts her questioning. Now that's she finally firing on all cylinders, she has to take advantage of the situation as best she can.

"I have reason to believe your friend's death wasn't accidental or suicide." She holds up a hand to stall their questions. "I can't tell you the reason I believe this at the moment. And I'm going to ask you not to repeat it too loudly. There are too many elements I don't understand yet. All I know is people with enough power to get police officers to do their jobs badly are involved, which means it's dangerous." She pauses a moment to make sure they understand. The skeletal one—who introduced himself as Jean-Philippe, or JP for short—seems to follow and will probably keep his mouth shut. The big one—Walter, apparently—is back to catching flies in his open mouth. Emeline's best hope is for his friend to keep him from blabbing or posting on social media.

"You said Hélori's death was linked to a case you're working?" JP asks. "Couldn't you just work with your colleagues, like normal people?"

He's likely worried Emeline is going rouge, or downright lying. She's going to have to give them something, to earn their trust.

"I'm working on a cold case," she says. She keeps her voice low, even though there aren't many people in the bar, and the front door is firmly in her line of sight. For some reason, she keeps expecting the two officers from earlier to barge in and ruin everything. "Thirty years ago, a young woman named Clothilde was found dead in a hotel room. Her wrists were slit, and it was declared suicide. Within a half hour of the first police officer's arrival at the scene."

Walter has managed to shut his mouth but has completely forgotten about his beer. He is one hundred percent focused on Emeline, and she has to reluctantly revise her opinion of him. He might not be as stupid as she first thought.

"I ended up with Clothilde's case when I was investigating several similar cases that have taken place over the last thirty years—all the way up until three months ago. The same person or persons have been killing people and sweeping them under the rug as suicides for three decades. I'm wondering if perhaps your friend is the latest victim."

"What makes you think so?" JP asks. He's sipping on the last of his beer and is leaning back in his seat with an elbow on the backrest. He looks relaxed and barely interested. Except for his eyes. They're intensely focused on Emeline, making her feel increasingly self-conscious about the messy hair and dirty clothes.

Emeline gives a mirthless smile, knowing how this sounds. "An anonymous tip." Might as well have been. She isn't going to tell these men she got information from someone inside the station. Nadine Tulle is going to get as much protection from Emeline as she can.

JP's right eyebrow shoots up. "An anonymous tip. How convenient."

Sighing, Emeline places both hands palm-down on the worn table and meets the gaze of each man in turn. "Look, I'm here to help. The only thing you'll obtain by keeping information from me is, well, nothing. If you *do* help me, we may get some justice for your friend. Closure for his family.

"His death was ruled a suicide, yes? No autopsy to test for drugs in his system? *Was* he involved in any kind of political activity, or a member of a non-profit organization?"

Eyes never leaving Emeline, JP gives a tiny nod. "Non-profit to find housing and jobs for homeless youth."

Excitement bubbles in Emeline's chest. She's on the right track. This death is linked to all the others and someone is trying to keep her from learning about it. It's a damned shame Malik isn't here to work with her. His fresh take on things was always helpful.

"He fits the profile almost perfectly," she says, forcing her voice to stay even.

"Almost?" Walter speaks up for the first time since they entered the bar. His dazed look is long gone, replaced with almost the same level of intensity as his friend. Seems like Emeline wasn't the only one affected by the heat and sun.

"All the others were young women. The others that we know of. The fact we now have a man could mean we've overlooked other victims in the past, or one of the members of the team of murderers has changed, and that changes the MO."

"*Team* of murderers?" JP removes his arm from the backrest and leans forward to rest his elbows on the table to get closer to Emeline. "How many are we talking about here?"

"I *really* can't give you any details," Emeline says, genuinely sorry she can't share more with them. "It's an ongoing investigation. But I can tell you we caught the man who did the actual killings, so it would make sense for the MO to change if they've found someone else to do the deed, and he was *definitely* not the brains behind the operation."

Walter scratches his ear and runs the back of his hand down the beginnings of a beard on his chin. "If these people can buy off cops and have been doing this to people who work with non-profits for three decades, we're looking at some seriously powerful bad guys."

Emeline doesn't say anything because she can't openly confirm, but she lets them understand the silence means yes.

"You working all on your own?" Walter asks.

Moving her now-empty glass on the table to watch the condensation make a wet track on the dark wood, Emeline shrugs. "Not quite. But close enough." Malik is supposed to come back, after all, and Nadine will definitely help as much as she can.

"So..." She lets go of the glass and clasps her hands together on the table. "Will you help me find out who killed your friend?"

ELEVEN

OF COURSE THEY'LL help. Presented like that, who wouldn't?

Evian pulls out her trusted notebook and starts asking questions. The most important one for us right now: what do the two men know about Hélori's work for the non-profit.

Quite a bit, as it turns out, since they also work there as volunteers. Hélori was the boss, got a paycheck and everything, but JP and Walter helped out when they could. Nobody knows who will take over for Hélori, but Walter admits he's playing with the idea, both to try something new and to make sure his friend's legacy lives on.

"If you're telling me Hélori was murdered because of the work he did," Walter says, a strong undercurrent of anger in his voice, "I'm definitely not going to let it run aground. Never negotiate with terrorists."

Clothilde, who has slipped onto the neighboring table, gives Walter a once-over. "He's not so bad once he gets out of the sun. Wouldn't want him to fall off a building."

I'm sitting next to Evian in the booth, like I'm part of the group. While Clothilde rarely bothers with pretending to be corporeal, I like to pretend. Focusing too long on the fact I'm a ghost makes me grumpy.

I *really* wish I could have a taste of JP's beer. I may not have felt the heat, or remember what thirst feels like, but I do remember how good a cold one tastes after a long day. Evian has allowed us to relive and review many things from our old lives, but cold beers will stay forever out of reach.

"You do realize," Evian says, "that taking over your friend's job will most likely make you the new target?"

Walter's brows draw together, and his hand tightens around his empty glass. "Let them try. I will *not* be scared into backing down."

Evian smiles tightly. "While I appreciate the sentiment, I would much rather you stayed alive. We *will* catch these guys, but they've caught bigger guys than you in the past."

"I thought you said it was only young women?" JP says.

My finger tingles as Evian touches the bracelets on her wrist. "We know of at least one male police officer. He was killed around the same time as Clothilde, the murder I'm investigating."

"Is this your way of telling us not all cops are bad?" JP says in a flat voice I realize is him making a joke.

"Actually," Evian says, "that particular one *was* 'bad.' He was the one to rule Clothilde's death as a suicide. But it seems he changed sides and thereby signed his own death warrant."

Will hearing people talking about me like this ever stop hurting?

Maybe the day I've done enough to atone for my sins.

While the two men exclaim over this revelation and ask for more gory details, Clothilde swings her legs and meets my gaze. "I wonder what happened to *my* organization when I died. You think it survived?"

Happy to disengage from the conversation between Evian and the men, I focus on my friend. "That's an excellent question. Were *you* the problem or was it the entire organization? If it was the whole thing, the reason for the murders is definitely politics. But if it was you personally, it may have been simply one particular point that you kept nagging them on, but your successor left alone."

"Hey! I never *nag*."

I grin at my friend, only now realizing to what point the reminder of my past sins was pulling me down. "A specific point you found particularly important and wouldn't let go of. Is that better?"

Clothilde nods. "Yes." A frown. "I think. I wasn't even the boss, though, like Hélori. I was still a student, barely out of high school, and focused on one or two details. There's no way my death stopped the whole thing from running."

I reach out to squeeze her knee—as close to squeezing as we can get without actual hands or knees, anyway—and turn to face Evian. She needs to know about this.

Evian, of course, has already caught on to our conversation. "What are the risks of the organization disappearing now that Hélori is gone?" she asks JP and Walter. "Could his death mean the death of the non-profit?"

"No way," Walter replies without hesitation. "I haven't

decided if I want to take over, but if I don't do it, somebody else will. It's far from being a one-man operation."

"You're thinking this means the reason he was killed has to do with something specific." JP leans forward, interest piqued.

"It's one theory," Evian says, somehow managing to make it sound like she didn't just come up with it. "Do you have access to his files, his workstation, his office? Could you give me a list of the subjects he saw to personally?"

"Consider it done." Walter raises his glass to drink, only to discover it's been empty for a while. He sets is down, aiming to align exactly with the circle of condensation on the table, before leaning back in his seat and glancing around the bar as if seeing it for the first time.

He sends a quick glance at his buddy. "Feels good to have something to do. Won't bring Hélori back, but…"

JP nods. "We can at least find him justice."

Evian questions them some more on the non-profit, getting the scope of the operation, their goals, major hurdles… Anything that might help to link it to the other victims' work.

Well, I know what we're doing tonight: we're checking if Clothilde's organization survived her death.

TWELVE

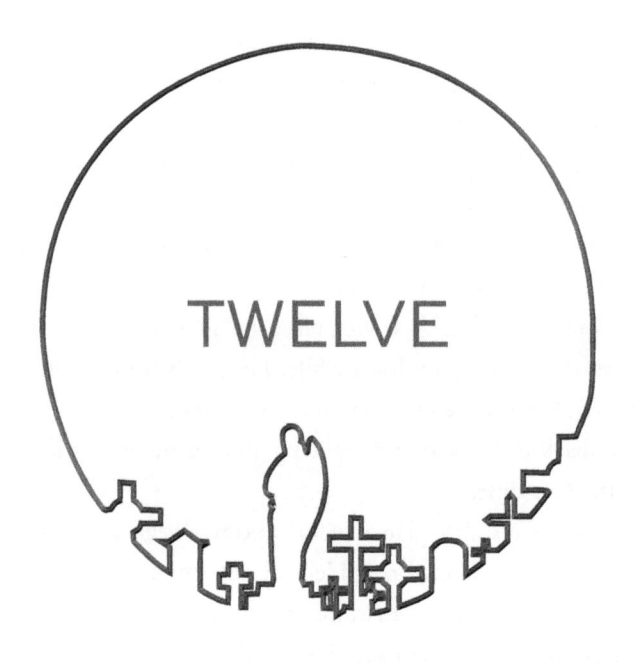

Evian's living room floor is completely covered in papers when Amina knocks on the door just before nine. Evian is sitting in the middle of it all, four different notebooks open and full of indecipherable notes, her hair a complete mess. She never got around to washing it when she got home—she just needed to check this one thing first, and that lead her to follow up on that other thing, oh, and that made her think of something she saw in one of the boxes…— and I think she has forgotten about the sap in her hair and the dirt on her clothes. There's nobody here to give her the side-eye or remind her she looks like she's been sleeping outside for a week, so she is entirely focused on her research.

She has also completely forgotten about eating, which is where Amina will get her.

"I heard you come home a couple of hours ago," Amina says with her usual brilliant smile when Evian opens the door, and not a glance at the messy hair or dirty clothes. "I just wanted to come by to say hi and check if you'd be interested in some food? I cooked way too much."

A hand going to her hair—interesting how she suddenly worries how she looks—Evian blushes and stutters. "I don't— There's no need— I haven't even showered…"

It's adorable, and even Clothilde, who has been reading the documents Evian has kindly spread out for us non-stop for as long as Evian has, with a focus I've rarely seen from her, comes over to grin at the two women. "That's so nice of her to invite you for dinner, *again*. You should totally go. Tell her you'll take a quick shower and be right over."

Evian opens her mouth to say something, then unfortunately catches it before it escapes. She throws an annoyed look over her shoulder, at the empty room. She knows where the thought came from.

Amina, bless her, isn't about to take hesitation for an answer. "You have to eat, Emeline. There's no point in you ordering takeout and me throwing food away. Won't you please keep me company for an hour or two?" She glances past Evian at the mess on the living room floor. "It's not good for you to be working twenty-four seven. You must also have some fun. Make friends." The warmth behind her smile makes *me* melt, and I'm not even in the direct line of fire.

Evian doesn't stand a chance.

"Fine." She sighs. "Let me take a quick shower and I'll be right over. You, uh…" She grits her teeth so hard I can hear it from where I'm standing. "You might want to bring out your Ouija board. For *after* dinner. I think we may have some information for Constantine."

"Excellent thinking," I say loudly. "We do need to talk to Constantine. And Amina." I had almost forgotten about the crazy husband. We desperately want to figure out who's murdering so many people, but we can't abandon the poor couple completely.

Bouncing and clapping with joy, Amina returns to her apartment. Dinner will be ready and on the table in thirty minutes.

Once the door swings slowly closed, Evian looks down at herself. Vaguely tries to brush off some dirt from the front of her pants.

"Next time I forget I'm not a ghost, will you tell me, please?" She gently removes the bracelets and leaves them on the kitchen counter, before slipping into the bathroom, firmly closing the door.

Twenty-seven minutes later, we're standing in front of Amina's door. Not knocking. Just staring at the door.

"What's going on?" Clothilde asks. She's a bit distracted tonight, from all the reading. I'm not sure if she found a lead or if it's simply all the reminders of her life before dying. She'll tell us when she's ready.

"Amina said thirty minutes," I answer, not even attempting to hold back my amusement. "It's only been twenty-seven."

Hands on hips, Clothilde frowns at Evian. "You're weird, you know that? Just knock on the door. The food was ready when she came by earlier. She only gave you half an hour so *you* could get decent."

Evian closes her eyes and sighs. "If you're not going to be helpful, just shut up, will you?" It's barely more than a whisper but it's clear she's not actually rebuking us. It's the type of response you make to a friend.

It makes me feel all warm and grateful.

Evian raises her hands and knocks. Not even ten seconds later, Amina greets us with another of her smiles. I think she has done something to her hair, and she has definitely changed her dress. Earlier it was short and yellow, now she has chosen long and white.

She'd match Constantine perfectly. It's a good thing Evian hasn't seen what Constantine wears, or this dress would probably have put her off completely.

Evian, of course, is wearing her usual jeans and T-shirt. But everything is clean, as is she. The entire building must have heard her swearing when she cleaned out the sap. I think she even put on some perfume—then grumbled to herself for being stupid.

She smiles back at Amina and I'm honestly gobsmacked. I didn't know she could smile like that, with her whole face, eyes crinkling and one dimple forming on her right cheek. "Thank you for forcing me to eat," she says.

Clothilde and I mostly leave them be while they eat. It feels like we're intruding. I settle in on the couch and Clothilde perches on a cluttered desk in the corner and we chat in low tones, so we won't hear the details of what the two women are saying. Amina is recounting some anecdote from her day as a masseuse and Evian is drinking it up with more enjoyment than the cold drink she got in the bar this afternoon.

"So what do we tell Constantine?" Clothilde asks. "That her husband is dead, has become a ghost, and has gone completely crazy? That should go over well, don't you think?"

"There's a good chance they'll both find peace if we can just get them back together," I say. "I don't think Constantine is much more stable than Jacques, so I prefer to avoid giving too many details about what we saw. It certainly didn't do Jacques any good.

We'll tell her we found her husband and that our goal is to get her to him. If she asks for details, we'll say we were short on time and barely had time to ascertain it was him."

Clothilde nods and shoves her hands under her thighs. "So what do we say through the Ouija board? That we need to get Constantine out of here so she can talk to her husband?"

"Yes. We have to figure out a way to get her out of that wall. It's not going to be easy, but getting Jacques exhumed would be much harder." I don't mention it, but I know Clothilde agrees that we'd rather have Constantine around until we get her to her husband than the other way around. We'd all go crazy within hours if that man gets to scream at us around the clock.

We sit there in silence for awhile. I let myself drift while listening to the voices of Amina and Evian without really hearing the words and let my gaze roam over the numerous and colorful souvenirs and decorations Amina favors.

"Did you find anything in your old papers?" I ask Clothilde gently. "Any clues to what set off the killing machine?"

Clothilde shrugs. "I worked on a lot of issues, but most of them were basically finalized when I died. From what I can glean, I think it might have been one of two issues that set them off. One I was just starting off on, and the other was kind of stalling because I could never get feedback from the mayor's office."

I'm about to ask her what the issues were when I realize Evian and Amina are heading for the guest bedroom, Ouija board in hand.

We'll have to continue our discussion later. Right now, it's time for some clairvoyance.

THIRTEEN

During dinner, Emeline mostly manages to forget about the ghost, the guest bedroom, and what she will have to do in there later. She focuses on the lovely Amina and on the delicious food. Amina pretends it's a "simple" meal because there's no starter and no wine, but Emeline isn't fooled. The woman has cooked up a *frog leg pie*. The recipe in itself isn't too complicated but putting your hands on that many frog legs is. They don't sell them in the store like chicken.

The pie is fabulous. The frog legs are drowning in some brown sauce where Emeline picks out at least thyme and basil. And the crust is just decadent.

Emeline compliments Amina profusely and Amina blushes prettily.

Halfway through the meal, Emeline suddenly wonders if this is a date. She took a shower before coming over, picked out clean if not nice clothes, and she's *wearing perfume*.

To her, it *is* a date.

But for her lovely neighbor? Who is Emeline kidding? She has never known when someone is interested. Sure, Amina changed her dress, but that doesn't mean anything.

Does it?

By the time they finish dessert, Emeline is dizzy from all the mental gymnastics. Which has one positive silver lining: she's eager to go talk to the ghosts. That feels like safer ground than trying to figure out if the pretty lady likes her.

Amina enters the bedroom first, Ouija board in hand. Emeline follows—carefully—on full alert. She won't be taken by surprise again. If Constantine shows any signs of aggression, Emeline will hightail it out of here in the blink of an eye. The ghost can figure her business out on her own.

The Ouija board is dropped on the bed, then Amina proceeds to light all the candles. Emeline could tell her, again, there's no need, but it seems to please her to light them and follow the instructions she learned in her clairvoyance class, so she stays silent.

Until Amina reaches the one on the windowsill. "Maybe don't light that one," Emeline says kindly. "It's Constantine's spot. She might not like being invaded by a lit candle."

Amina freezes, comically stopped with her lit match only centimeters from the candle and her eyes widening. "She's there right now?" she whispers.

Emeline shrugs and starts opening the box with the Ouija board to have an excuse not to meet her neighbor's eyes. "I can't actually *see* them. But that's definitely her spot."

The sigh escaping Amina is reverent. "Right. I'll just put it with the others on the dresser." She pats the spot on the sill. "So sorry, Constantine. I didn't know."

Emeline feels a wave of gratitude. "She says thank you," she grumbles.

"Really?" It's no more than a squeak.

Emeline sighs. "Or something along those lines." She gets comfortable on the blue bedspread, Indian style, with her back against the wall. The stupid letters grin up at her, gloating to have her back so soon. "This really isn't going to be a regular thing," she mumbles.

A faint smell of incense fills the room and Amina comes to sit next to Emeline, adding in her own scent of lavender. "I'll write down what you spell out, like last time?" When she adjusts her position, her knee touches Emeline's.

As if this wasn't hard enough as it is.

Emeline grunts something that is supposed to be a "sure," then addresses the empty room. "All right, guys. Give us the rundown of our visit to Constantine's husband. And be brief, please." She is going to have to spell out what they say letter by letter on the stupid board.

She places her hand on the pointer, places it in the middle of the board, and waits.

And waits.

"Are they not there?" Amina whispers. "Maybe I should put the candle back in the window, so it's exactly like last time."

Emeline, who has put herself in what she's coming to consider a type of trance to be as receptive to the ghosts' messages as possible, has an odd feeling of being ignored. Like she's four again and trying to catch her parents' attention during dinner, only to be told to stay quiet until the adults have finished their conversation.

"I think they're telling Constantine about our day," Emeline whispers to Amina—which makes her lean even closer to Emeline and her delicious smell becomes all-encompassing—"We'll give them a minute to chat and figure out what they need from us."

Amina licks her lips as she glances toward the empty windowsill. She doesn't say anything, but Emeline can tell she wants to have a lengthy conversation with "her" ghost. She wants to know everything, learn everything.

Emeline is ready to do quite a bit for her beautiful neighbor but becoming a permanent translator through the Ouija board is a no-go.

Suddenly, she feels an urge to move the pointer.

"Ah, here we go," she says as she lets her hand move wherever it feels like. "You ready with the notebook?"

Blushing with eagerness, Amina leans forward to note where the pointer lands. Emeline doesn't look at the letters. She discovered quickly it was easier to land on the right letter if she didn't think about it or look where she was moving at all.

Which means this looks one hundred percent like a ridiculous clairvoyance seance.

Bloody hell.

She lets her hands move as they want while she zones out completely. She gets lost in the sweetness of the night pouring in through a crack in the window, the scratching of Amina's pen on her notebook, and the smell of lavender shampoo.

When her hand stops moving, she has to blink several times to come back to the present. She shakes her hand, as if this will banish the ghosts from having power over her body, and turns to Amina.

"What did we get?"

"Must get Constantine out of wall," Amina reads, her voice shaking. "Husband needs her."

"All right, fair enough," Emeline says. "Guess we'll prioritize finding a way to open up that wall."

Amina isn't done, though. "Must talk to Hélori. Should be done screaming in a week or so. Sorry." She looks up at Emeline, her eyes so wide the whites are showing all the way around the iris. "What does that mean?"

Emeline can't stop the whole-body shiver running through her body. She can hear the inaudible screams again. The panic. The anger.

She remembers the *other* screams from her past. The darkness. The pounding.

She jumps off the bed and starts brushing non-existent dirt off her pants. Runs a hand through her hair, expecting to find needles and sap. Moves around the room to prove to herself she's not stuck.

Singing.

Except there's no singing. It's in her head again, like the screaming.

Clothilde is singing to her, like she did in the cemetery earlier, trying to soothe her.

And damn if it isn't working. Emeline stops pacing and takes a deep breath.

Amina drops her notebook on the Ouija board and approaches Emeline with wide eyes. "Are the ghosts bothering you? What are they doing?" She shoots a glance at the windowsill, then the rest of the room, searching for signs of her invisible guests.

"The ghosts aren't doing anything." Emeline runs a hand down her face. Whispers, so low she hopes Amina can't hear, "Thanks, Clothilde. I'm all right."

Amina is right in front of Emeline. Grabs her hand in her own and gives it a squeeze. "Is there anything I can do to help?"

Well, if the goal was to slow down Emeline's heartbeat, this isn't helping. But while the stress of being scared to death is something Emeline would like never to feel again, the stress of having the most beautiful woman she has ever met standing too close and with so much emotion in her gorgeous eyes is a complete thrill. It doesn't even matter if Amina has that kind of feeling for her in return. Just standing here, so close together, makes her happy.

"I'm all right," Emeline says with a smile that isn't even forced, and squeezes Amina's hand in return. "I just had a stressful afternoon and that message brought it all back. Why don't we start to make some plans for opening up that wall? We have a couple of lovers to reunite."

Amina squeals with happiness and jumps forward to give Emeline a strong hug, putting her voluminous and lavender-smelling hair right into Emeline's nose.

Yep, total thrill.

FOURTEEN

When we enter the guest bedroom, Constantine is in her spot on the windowsill, legs dangling and cutting through the wall on every back swing. Her wedding dress is back to looking dirty and tattered but the woman herself seems sane and reasonable.

"Good afternoon, Constantine," I greet her affably as we enter behind Evian and Amina. "How are you doing?"

Constantine's eyes had been on the Ouija board in Amina's hands when they entered, but they shoot to me with an almost scary intensity when I ask my question. I don't think she's angry, even though that's what her face is saying at first glance. She's touched someone would ask how she's doing. Being alone for seventy years and nobody even bothering to ask for your name can do a real trick on you.

"I'm well, thank you," she finally says, as if trying on the words for the first time in, well, decades. "How was your day?"

"We met your husband." Clothilde jumps up to perch on the dresser, trying but failing to find a spot where she won't touch any of the candles, and sends a kind smile in Constantine's direction. "He's a ghost too."

Constantine seems to solidify. "You met Jacques? He is dead?"

"He would have been over one hundred years old today," Clothilde says calmly. "Chances were very good he'd be dead. But there was no guarantee he'd also be a ghost."

Amina is lighting the candles, her arm and match passing through Clothilde. Clothilde ignores it completely, focused on Constantine.

"You said only people with unfinished business become ghosts," Constantine says. "Does this mean he is not happy?"

That stops me short where I'm leaning against the wall next to Clothilde's dresser. I've always been focused on the unfinished business, not the emotions this would entail.

If someone lingers after death because they have unfinished business, *can* they be happy? Everybody will have left *something* dangling when they leave this world, but it's rarely important enough to stay behind to fix it, or we'd have met a lot more ghosts.

And the logical next step: am *I* happy? Clothilde?

I glance over at my friend. She looks content enough. We've shared countless laughs over the years. We're friends.

But are we really happy?

Probably not. We have to find the people who killed us and countless others before considering moving on to the afterlife. And without that closure we can't be happy. Not *only* happy, anyway. I'm also not *unhappy*, so there's that. Good enough for now.

I come back to the present, where Clothilde still hasn't answered Constantine's question. She was saved, somewhat, by Evian asking Amina not to light the candle on the windowsill and Constantine very seriously thanking them.

"I believe Jacques's unfinished business has to do with your disappearance," I say. "We need to get you out of here and over there to meet him as soon as possible."

"What did he say when you told him I am here? Did you tell him I never left him?" Constantine is so solid I can't see through her at all. It's like her density is directly proportionate to her level of interest in a subject. I bet she could move tiny objects when she's like this.

"I'm afraid we didn't have much time to talk," I say. "We only had a short time while Evian was in the vicinity and she had to attend another funeral shorty after."

"Did this funeral involve another ghost?"

I'm surprised this is what she focuses on. I don't know if she's worried we're spending time on a different case, if she's jealous, curious about other ghosts...

I realize Amina and Evian are waiting for us, Evian's hand hovering over the Ouija board's pointer. "We'll be right with you, Mesdames. We simply need to debrief with Constantine first."

Evian gets the message, and I can return to Constantine. "Yes, there was another ghost. This has to do with *our* murders. For Jacques, we only had time to locate his grave and identify him as the ghost. He talked about you straight away, so I'm certain reuniting you will help. Both of you."

"You did not tell him I never left?" Her voice is faint and her body back to slightly transparent like the rest of us. She's not angry we didn't deliver her message, she's sad.

"You can tell him yourself very soon," Clothilde says. "How

about we ask the ladies to get on with the whole breaking-up-the-wall thing so they can get you out of there? Then we'll figure out how to get you to your husband's cemetery."

Constantine agrees, and we start the tedious process of instructing Evian to spell out what we want. She's opting not to look at what she's doing, so when I tell her a letter, she moves to the right area, then waits for me to say a little to the right, forward five centimeters, that's it, stop.

We make no mistakes and I'll admit to being quite proud. Teamwork at its best.

The line about freeing Constantine goes over well. I'm sure they'll decide which route they want to take within a week. The line about going back to talk to Hélori… Evian reacts much like when Constantine rushed her that first time.

She's freaking out. The mere idea of going back there, hearing those screams again, and she's out of her seat, eyes wild, hands all over the place, and her breath erratic.

I understand that hearing and feeling ghosts can be scary, but this is Evian. She's been hanging out with us for months already. She hardly batted an eye when we influenced her to steal parts of our skeletons. Why does *this* put her in such a state?

It's a good thing Clothilde is here. While I'm pondering the mysteries of Evian's mind, Clothilde realizes she needs help—and moves to give it. She jumps down from her perch and places herself in front of Evian. Puts a ghostly hand on Evian's cheek.

And starts to sing.

It's the lullaby again. About a dragonfly landing on the moon and birds sleeping in the forest. Do not worry about the growling wind or the stray dogs, the brilliant stars are watching over you.

Constantine's hand goes to her heart. Looks like she knows the song, too. I worry she'll be unhappy with a lullaby being sung in the room she planned for her own children, but she seems to approve. In fact, she seems touched.

Clothilde's voice is clear and pure, and a smile plays on her lips as she finishes the first verse. She's looking at Evian but I'm willing to bet she's seeing whoever used to sing that song to her when she was a child. My money is on her mother.

There's no need for a second verse. Evian calms down enough to reassure a rather freaked-out Amina. She even thanks Clothilde and if my friend had had any actual blood running through her body, she would have been blushing.

As is Evian, by the way, when Amina gives her a hug. Even though she can't see me, I grin at Evian. I wonder if anything will ever happen between the two, or if Evian is of the sort to pine in silence. Amina certainly *isn't*, but I haven't been able to tell if she likes Evian that way or if she's just very friendly.

The two settle back on the bed—after Evian packs the Ouija board away and hides it under the bed—and they start their planning. Clothilde returns to perching on the dresser, I lean on the wall next to her, and Constantine stays in her windowsill.

"We have to hire professionals to do the work," Amina says. "I have no idea how to go about destroying a wall and even if I did, I honestly doubt I have the strength for it."

"You're stronger than you give yourself credit for." Evian is blushing again, poor thing. "But I agree we should get a professional. Because even if we do manage to destroy the wall, I don't want us to destroy the building—or your pipes. The pipes go through in there, right?"

Frowning at the wall in question, Amina chews on her lip. "Probably. The bathroom is just behind there, so it would make sense... How did you know that? Is it the same way in your apartment?"

Evian sighs. "Probably. But the information must come from the ghosts. I couldn't care less about where the pipes are in my temporary rental apartment and I know next to nothing about architecture."

Again, Amina seems awestruck. She's *really* into communicating with our side. I hope it won't become a problem with Evian, who is reluctantly doing it because she doesn't have much of a choice. "Are they still here?" Amina whispers.

"They're *always* here." Evian glances around the room, taking in the old dresser, the ancient and stressful wallpaper, the icky wall-to-wall carpet. "But how do we get the professionals to open up the wall? That's hardly needed to redo the wallpaper."

"Good point." Amina pulls a lock of hair into her mouth to chew on it and Evian blushes furiously. "I could ask them to install a larger window?"

"Won't you need the validation of the rest of the residents for that?"

"Ah, shoot." Amina blows out the lock of hair. "I'll even need the validation of the *city* for that. This building is too old. And they'd never agree to something that modifies the exterior of the building."

Evian cocks her head as she focuses on Constantine's windowsill. Constantine is still sitting there, legs dangling, silently following the conversation.

"What if we ask them to carve into it just a little bit? We'll claim to want a bookcase inside the wall, or something of a bench under the window, to sit and gaze out the window?"

Amina laughs. "Gaze out at the neighbor's wall? Sure, why not?" Her eyes linger on the exact spot where Constantine is sitting, then her smile falls. "And what do we do when they find the remains?"

"We act surprised," Evian says. "Or rather, *you* act surprised. I'd rather not be officially involved in this business in case they call in the cops."

FIFTEEN

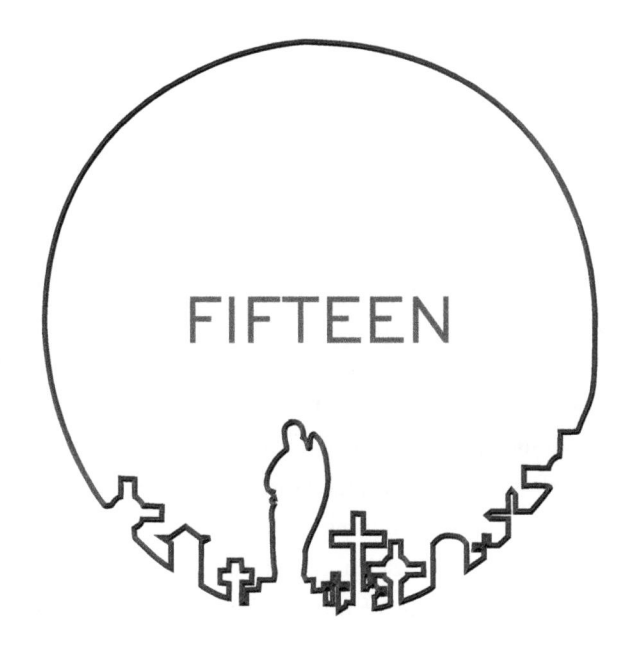

The café was chosen for its air conditioning and its location. Evian has picked a spot toward the back, right below one of the fans in the ceiling spewing out fresh air. She has her back to the wall with an unimpeded view of the front door and the swinging door leading to the kitchen. If her wince is anything to go by, the coffee isn't very good, but she moaned through every bite of the lemon meringue pie.

I have vague memories of lemon pies. Both sweet and tart, right? But "tart" is nothing but a word to me now; my memory won't tell me how it would feel in my mouth, what messages my taste buds would send to my brain. I'm more upset at having forgotten the taste than at not being able to eat it.

If we never find the people who killed us, will I someday forget the taste of coffee? Or freshly baked croissants?

While I'm pondering these existential questions, Clothilde is snooping into everybody's business. She got bored of waiting for Walter after about thirty seconds—how she survived thirty years in a cemetery without going crazy is a bit of a mystery—and now seems to be experimenting with how to get people to do what she wants. She read an article on a young lady's phone over her shoulder earlier and spooked the poor girl every time she scrolled down the page too rapidly. The guy with the long, thin hair in the corner turned the volume up on his music when Clothilde asked him to, ruining his own ears so Clothilde can figure out what today's youth is listening to. Her words, not mine.

We have spent the last week going through so much paperwork I'm starting to wonder if ghosts can need glasses. My eyes cross at the mere thought of the hundreds of piles of papers in Evian's living room.

It's not just Clothilde's stuff anymore. Evian contacted the mothers of Manon and Lise, the two last known victims of Gérard de Villenouvelle, the guy who did the dirty work of killing all the young women for whatever group we're after. Their murders were what brought Evian to Toulouse in the first place. The two young women, who we met as ghosts in our old cemetery, were active in their own non-profit organizations. Their mothers have been more than willing to give Evian all the information they can find on their daughters' activities.

Today, we're going to compare notes with Walter. He has decided to take over Hélori's job and has spent the last week learning the ropes, focusing especially on the subjects Hélori supervised personally. He told Evian in a text he has started carrying pepper spray with him everywhere. On my prompting,

Evian told him to not accept food or drinks from people he doesn't know.

Poison seems to be the weapon of choice for this group.

Twenty-five minutes after their agreed rendezvous, Walter stumbles through the door. He's wearing a crumpled white business shirt folded up to his elbows, a pair of blue Bermuda shorts, and flip-flops. His face is red from the heat and he orders a large red slushie from the counter before making his way to Evian's table. His messenger bag is slung across his torso and the minute he sits down across from Evian, he pulls out a sleek travel-sized laptop.

"Sorry I'm late." He lets out a great sigh of relief when his ass hits the rickety wooden chair and a happy shiver when he slurps down a mouthful of his slushie. "I was stuck in the metro because of some technical incident for fifteen minutes, then had to walk here from Esquirol when they finally let us out. I *hate* summer in Toulouse."

Evian doesn't appear to be bothered by the man's tardiness. Her smile is sincere when she shakes his hand. "I'm told fall is agreeable in these parts, but I'll stay skeptical until I see proof."

Walter barks a laugh, drawing the attention of several patrons. The guy with the long hair appears to realize his music is too loud and turns it down with a frown.

Clothilde comes back to our table and jumps up on the for-now empty neighboring table to perch there.

"Did you find anything interesting in Hélori's affairs?" Evian asks once they've gotten the pleasantries out of the way and Walter has downed two-thirds of his slushie.

"I've certainly got my work cut out for me." Walter opens his laptop and logs in. His background is a picture of him, JP, and a third man I'll assume to be Hélori. Three tall, blond men, as different as night and day—JP skinny, Walter chubby, and Hélori clearly a gym rat.

"Hélori had his hands in almost everything," Walter explains. "Makes sense, of course, him being the boss and all. I've compiled a list of the various actions that were still open when he died, and I'll send it to you once I'm connected to the internet."

"Excellent," Evian says.

"Now, I figured if he was killed because of something at work, there wouldn't be much point in it if the project would just continue on once he was gone. Nobody else is dead, after all. So I've tagged the stuff where he was acting only as a consultant, or the guy to sign the letters or checks. A couple of things he was definitely active on, but not alone, so although they've been delayed by his disappearance, it hasn't stopped."

We're all hanging on his every word. Clothilde is leaning forward, her eyes alight and intense, while Evian is jotting down notes in her trusted notebook. I'm sitting on a pretend chair, my hands clasped on the table, leaning forward to try to read what's on Walter's screen.

"What remains," Walter continues, "are two projects where Hélori worked alone, and they have completely stopped now that he's gone. He wanted to start a new homeless shelter in the outskirts of Toulouse, out here to the west." He turns his screen so Evian can see the map displayed there. It has a red pin in an industrial area filled with what looks to be businesses or warehouses. Hardly prime real estate.

"Hélori liked to work in places like these. It's not the most sought-after locations, which makes it affordable, but it's also not a dangerous place to live. It has schools nearby, so it wouldn't have been too difficult to convince some of his guests to go back to class if they're up for it. What this place *doesn't* have is efficient collective transportation to get into the city. Which is what the *second* project was all about. Prolonging the planned route of the *site propre*."

"Clean site?" Evian asks.

Clothilde is still leaning forward, her nose so close to Walter's screen I'm afraid she might pass through it. She's no longer actually *on* the table; she's perching mid-air as she frowns at the map.

Walter grabs a napkin to wipe some sweat from his brow. "They're building new roads going in as many straight lines as possible—not a mean feat in a city like Toulouse—to be used only by public transport and bikes. The point is to diminish the number of cars on the roads, thereby lessening pollution and traffic jams. One of these is planned to reach this area here." He points to a spot some kilometers east of the red pin. "Hélori wanted them to prolong it by five kilometers. He was in the process of looking into the availability of the real estate on his proposed trajectory."

"Robert," Clothilde says, her voice shaking. "That's the exact area I was starting to work on when I died." She points to a large intersection no more than three hundred meters from the red pin. "This thing created so much trouble. At any hour of the day, hundreds of cars would be blocked in all directions. Everybody got annoyed and pushed their way in even when there was no space, blocking passage completely for the cars coming from the other directions and then it just kept piling up. We wanted them to change it into a roundabout. It wouldn't solve everything, but it would have helped."

And thirty years later, it's still an intersection.

"I don't remember seeing anything about this in your stuff," I say.

Clothilde's eyes dart from one side to the other as if she's sifting through memories like they're pages in a book. "I never got as far as making it official." Her voice trails off. "I was trying to gather information before preparing my dossier. Checking out who owned the land like Hélori was doing, because a roundabout takes up more space than an intersection and trying to get ahold of the politicians who might help move things along."

I haven't needed to breathe in over thirty years, but I'm holding my breath anyway as my gaze goes from the laptop, to Walter, to Evian.

Who catches on beautifully. "Do you know if Hélori was in touch with any political figures for this project? He'd need their support to push something like this through, right?"

The intensity in Walter's blue eyes increases as he studies Evian a long moment before replying. "Interesting you should ask, Captain. He *would* need it, and it should have been his logical next step. But I couldn't find any trace of it in his emails, snail mail, or various calendars."

Evian nods and jots down the information in her notebook. This means we'll have to focus on the real estate angle.

"But then I talked to his wife." Walter's pulse is beating rapidly on the side of his neck as he turns to check if anyone is nearby and might be listening in. Wiping his brow again, he leans forward, his usually loud voice down to a whisper. "He had a meeting with someone the day he died. He shared his online calendar with his wife, and she remembered it was there, because she had to pick up their daughter at day care on a day when it was usually Hélori's turn.

"When she checked her calendar yesterday, the meeting had been deleted."

SIXTEEN

Once she knows what to look for, Emeline finds an abundance of leads. Manon wanted to transform an old but solid factory building into a student housing complex. The factory is less than five hundred meters from the building Hélori was aiming for and one of the buildings that would have had to be destroyed if they'd been able to push through on the green road. Lise had her eyes on a different building, one that had been constructed as a retirement home, then abandoned because of technical issues that were troublesome for housing elderly but the homeless wouldn't care so much about.

Both young women had contacted the City Hall several times by email in the weeks before their deaths. They had also made several inquiries about the real estate, going through the official channels.

Neither had meetings in their calendars on the day they died.

Emeline obtains access to the women's emails and social media accounts from their mothers. It seems their lawyer already made the same request, and they don't need much convincing. Emeline would have *loved* to contact Maître Clément to discuss the case but can't find a way to bypass her direct orders from Commander Diome to "stay the hell away from the trial against de Villenouvelle and anyone involved in his case."

While Emeline sits ensconced between the two broken springs of her ancient couch, scouring through the calendars with various notebooks spread out around her, she feels the ghosts trying to communicate with her. They have something to say about this, but she can't figure out what, exactly.

She'd been so sure she was done with the stupid Ouija board.

As she stares angrily at her screen and Manon's empty calendar, her gaze falls to the keyboard.

Lots of letters! And no stupid font.

She opens an empty text file. Closes her eyes. And poses one finger above the keyboard. "All right, guys. If you have something to say, spell it out for me." She feels oddly peaceful, considering, sitting there all alone except for two ghosts, the noise from the bus station outside reminding her of the busy city she's starting to think of as home, and the mouthwatering smell of fresh baguettes wafting up from the downstairs boulangerie. The temperature has dropped below thirty degrees for the first time in two weeks, allowing her to properly breathe without feeling like she's in a sauna.

She's happy to have the company of Clothilde and Robert, happy to try to help them. And *thrilled* she might have found a way to avoid that bloody board.

Dictating the message on a computer takes a little longer than on the Ouija board, possibly because Emeline doesn't instinctively know where all the letters are on the keyboard. But they get there, with a nudge left or right here and a shift up or down there.

LISE REMEMBERS KILLER USING HER THUMB TO ACCESS PHONE, WIPE CALENDAR.

Well then.

Emeline jerks up straight. "Are Lise and Manon still around? Did we leave them back in your cemetery?"

The feeling of reassurance comes immediately. To make things clear, she gets a message dictated: THEY MOVED ON THANKS TO YOUR WORK. Emeline breathes out a sigh of relief and sinks back into her uncomfortable couch.

"Clothilde, do you remember anything useful from the day you died?"

Emeline is ready with her finger over the keyboard, but she doesn't need it to understand the reply. Clothilde doesn't remember.

"It's that bloody poison they're using on everybody, isn't it? It makes you forget."

Probably, yes.

She needs to figure out a way to order a proper autopsy on Hélori. He hasn't been dead long, so they may still find traces of the poison in his body. Which would change his official cause of death from suicide to murder and merit—demand—an investigation. But how does she do that when she's not even supposed to know about the man?

"Once he gets out of the sun, Walter seems like the kind of guy who can get people moving, right?" Emeline isn't even sure if she's talking to herself or the ghosts anymore. "It feels counterintuitive to ask a civilian to make noise with my own colleagues, but I think it might be the right way to go here."

She makes a quick call to Walter, staying very vague on her reasons for believing his friend was poisoned but very clear on the fact he has to keep her name out of it. "My name is only going to do you disservice in this case." When he asks her why, she replies honestly, "I wish I knew. Except I'm pretty sure knowing would mean having solved the case—both mine and yours. Just make as much noise as you can; it worked for the last two victims' mothers."

With Hélori out of the way for the time being, Emeline focuses on how she can figure out who Lise, Manon, and Clothilde were meeting with on the day they died. She already knows Gérard de Villenouvelle was there, was the one to do the deed, but he wasn't the man in charge. He was the willing henchman. Someone else was pulling the strings.

The lawyer Laurent Lambert certainly had his finger in things too. It's the name that pops up everywhere. But from everything Emeline has read about the man, she doesn't think he's in charge either. He's simply a valuable player in the group, the one who makes sure nobody else gets caught. Emeline would love to get him behind bars, but again, not the top priority, the top guy. Or gal. That Redon woman seems to be pretty high in the food chain.

What she needs is access to the backup data of those calendars. Clothilde's is out of reach, but Lise's and Manon's should be on the cloud somewhere. Emeline can't access such files without jumping through a million hoops—and nobody at the station is going to even let her try.

Nadine Tulle could do the work in her sleep, though.

With her near-magic abilities on mining data and accessing servers even high-raking officers aren't supposed to have the clearance for, this would be child's play.

But she sounded rather scared the last time Emeline talked to her. Her hunch on Hélori being part of Emeline's cold case was spot on the money and she *knew* somebody higher up didn't want Emeline to get that information.

Yet she gave it anyway.

Emeline is getting more paranoid by the minute. She only has Nadine's professional phone number, one bound to leave a trace, at least to the people who count. The last time they talked, Emeline asked about Jacques Larcher, who, okay, wasn't in any way linked to the case she is working on, but also wasn't linked to Hélori, Lise, or Manon. If anyone asks, Emeline can be perfectly honest and say she was helping out her friend and neighbor in… searching through the history of the past residents of her apartment. Or something.

Could she come up with a valid excuse to call her now? Nothing to do with the case?

She thumbs through her contacts and calls Nadine. Only when the other woman replies, does Emeline realize it's almost nine at night and Nadine is most definitely not at the station working office hours.

"I'm so sorry to call this late," Emeline exclaims. "I didn't realize what time it was. This is Emeline Evian, by the way," she adds belatedly with a face-palm. Sighs. "I'll call again tomorrow."

"No, don't hang up!" Nadine sounds like she's laughing. "If I answer the phone, it means I'm available. And I'm tech savvy enough to have your name in my phone already, Captain."

"Right. Sorry again. Actually…" Emeline can't quite decide if this is going to make her sound more or less suspicious, but she really doesn't like her chances of surveillance on the work phone. "Could I call you on your private number? I promise I'll delete it straight away after we're done. I'd rather not use taxpayers' money when I'm inquiring after a mutual friend." That sounds credible, right?

Nadine doesn't miss a beat. "Sure, no problem. I also prefer keeping the two worlds as separate as possible. I'll text you my number." And she hangs up.

A text comes through less than thirty seconds later and Emeline enters it into her personal cell phone. When she places the call, Nadine picks up halfway through the first ring.

"Looking for news of Malik? Or is that just a ruse?"

Emeline chuckles and she leans her head on the backrest as two men are yelling at each other for something or other out on the street. She smiles to herself. It's like being back in Paris. There's even someone leaning on their horn.

"I'd definitely like some news of Malik, if you have it. But I'll admit to an ulterior motive for switching phones."

"Figured. Well, you're in luck. I talked to Malik this morning." There's some clanking in the background, like she's doing the dishes or clearing the table. "He's being allowed back into active service as of tomorrow, but they're putting him on cases where there's basically zero risk of him needing to pull his weapon."

"That's good," Emeline says. "I take it it's not a desk job, though?"

"Oh, no. He was really happy to know he was going into the field, even if it was to look for missing cats."

"Do police look into missing cats in Toulouse?" If the police of this city had enough time on their hands to take on that type of case, she really would need to consider the possibility of moving here permanently.

Nadine's peal of laughter is so free, it removes all doubts about calling her. This was a *good* idea. "God, I wish. I'd sign up for that in a heartbeat. No, from what I understood, they're putting him on some cold cases. Ones where the perpetrator should be long-dead and they're just looking for official closure."

"That sounds all right, I guess." Though the cases she was brought down here from Paris to look into were also cold cases and look where that got them.

"Malik's happy about it." Nadine's voice is soft. There's no doubt these two are real friends outside of work and Emeline is happy to hear it. "It'll do him good to feel useful again while he's working through his fear of that stupid weapon."

There's some more noise on Nadine's end—sounds like more dishes and closing cupboards—and Emeline tries to figure out how to approach her second reason for calling Nadine. Or first, if she's being honest.

Nadine beats her to it. "So, what's the other business you wanted to talk to me about? You need me to dig up some more information for you?"

"I do." Emeline sighs as her finger traces the edges of her laptop's keyboard. "I swear I'm working on my Clothilde Humbert case. But I keep finding links to the two young women who started the whole de Villenouvelle case."

"And those are out of reach for you."

"Yes. So I don't dare going through official channels for the stuff I need right now."

"What do you need, exactly?" Nadine's tone is all business and Emeline gets the feeling she's ready to take notes and launch right into the research. Bless her.

"I have reason to believe both Lise and Manon had meetings with their killers on the day they died. Then all trace of the meetings were deleted from their online calendars, probably using their own phones once they were dead. How are my chances of getting information on those meetings? When, where, with who.

When it was deleted?"

Nadine whistles softly. "Without using the station's tools and without the proper paperwork in order? This is a high order, Emeline." A short pause. "I should be able to do it, though."

"I don't want you to get into trouble for this," Emeline says. "I don't want you to lose your job and end up in jail because of this."

"All right." Nadine hums and Emeline can practically see her throwing that long braid of hers over her shoulder. "Let me think about it, see what legal solutions I can find. Can I get access to the calendar as it is today? Even though it's deleted?"

"Yes! The mothers gave me their daughters' passwords and everything. Let me just check with them they're okay with me passing it on to you."

"Brilliant! That I can work with." The woman is like a teenager being told she's allowed to stay up all night playing video games.

"There's one more thing." Emeline runs a hand through her short hair, fretting about setting the woman on *another* potentially dangerous search. Still, what other choice does she have?

"Hit me," Nadine says.

Praying she won't regret this later, Emeline says, "I need information on some real estate."

SEVENTEEN

THE FIRST DAY the workers show up to fix up Amina's guest room, both Evian and Amina are on edge. Amina got their contact info from one of her regular massage clients, who vouched for them being prompt, efficient, and honest—and available because someone had canceled on them last minute. But some woman claiming they're honest doesn't necessarily mean they won't get rid of Constantine's body in secret and pretend nothing happened in order to avoid delays on their job.

Amina and Emeline both make sure they can work from home that first day and keep coming up with excuses to see how the workers are progressing, checking if anyone has started in on the windowsill yet. They're so obsessive about it that the boss ends up asking them nicely—but quite firmly—to stay out of their way and let them do the job they were hired to do.

So Amina goes back to work and Emeline continues her research in her apartment.

But she leaves the bracelets behind in a decorative cup on Amina's bookshelf. Clothilde and I are standing watch.

I feel almost bereft not to be there when Emeline sifts through yet more information, but I guess some separation won't do us much harm. Also, it gives us the opportunity to chat with Constantine without a timer hanging over us like every other time we've been in here.

The door between the living room and the guest room is open, so we can go in freely. In theory, Constantine could also come to us, but she refuses. I think it scares her. And since this whole thing is about moving her out of her room, I don't push her to move until she has no choice.

One of the workers is quite sensitive to ghosts. The two Portuguese guys who have been removing the wall-to-wall horror carpet give no sign whatsoever of being aware we're there, but the blond guy in his fifties who's removing the wallpaper… He keeps whipping his head around as if he saw something in his peripheral vision only to find it gone when he looks straight at it. This something is usually Constantine, who can't stop flitting back and forth, wanting to see what the men are doing up close but also not wanting to leave her spot at the window. She was seconds away from giving him the scare of a lifetime while he was up on a stool to reach the ceiling, but Clothilde convinced her to leave him be at the last moment.

They don't get around to opening up the wall until the third day. It's the day we meet with Walter—Evian drops by Amina's apartment "to check if they need anything" and takes the opportunity to pick us up before leaving, then drops us off again after, pretending to have forgotten something in the kitchen—and we weren't really expecting them to start today. When Evian goes back to her place, the workers are discussing what to do with some rotten planks in the floor, so she doesn't notice the beginnings of a hole under the window.

The minute Evian is out the door, though, the blond guy picks up a large sledgehammer and pounds it into the wall. Two hits later, he yells for his buddies to come see.

"That's my leg," Constantine says, her intensity level dialed up to a maximum and her dress going back and forth between a pristine white and the dirty frayed piece we first saw her in. "I can feel his dirty hands on my thigh. I don't like it!"

"It's okay." Clothilde is by Constantine's side, an arm over the other woman's shoulders. "I know it feels awful. We suffered the same thing when they did our autopsy after our exhumation. Like a tingle, right?"

Constantine nods. She's still not happy, but knowing we've shared this experience helps.

"Guys," the blond worker growls. "There are bones in the wall here. I don't think this belongs to a dog." He holds up the femur.

"Oh shit," the youngest of the dark-haired ones says. "You think the boss lady killed somebody and hid him in the wall? Or maybe her crazy neighbor?"

"Don't be daft," the blond one says. "You saw the state of this room. Nothin's been done here since the last big renovation. And I'm betting that was before either lady was even born."

"Oh. Right. So what do we do then? Just throw them out with the rest of the rubble?"

The flat stare the blond guy gives his younger co-worker makes me think this isn't the first time they're having this kind of discussion. "No, Pedro, we do not throw them out with the rubble." He turns to poke a finger into the crumbling mortar. Several more bones are already sticking out.

"You should tell the lady next door!" Clothilde yells. "She'll know what to do!" And to steal one of the smaller bones for Constantine to latch onto.

The man shivers and frowns but oddly enough doesn't do what Clothilde tells him to. Someone that sensitive would normally go with what we tell them, thinking it's their own mind coming up with the ideas.

"We have to call the police," he says. Growling, he points a finger at the third worker. "You two continue digging out that wall. Snap pictures every couple of minutes. And sort the bones into a pile."

"Actually," I can't help but inject, "the police won't want you to touch anything. The position the bones are in could give clues as to what happened."

Clothilde gives me an incredulous look. "*What* are you doing? We *want* those bones all over the place. Emeline can't come in and steal the bloody femur!"

I'm about to argue that it could still be possible to find Constantine's murderer and the position of the body in that wall could very well be the *only* clue the police will find, but then I remember Constantine doesn't care about justice. She only wants her husband. So I shut up.

Unfortunately, the guy listens to *this* instruction. "Actually, no, we shouldn't touch it. You continue working on the floorboards and I'll call the police. There's a good chance we'll have to take a break on this job for a few days while the police do their thing." Shaking his head, he walks into the living room, his phone already in his hand.

"I don't know who made *him* boss," the young

one—Pedro—grumbles as he shuffles over to the other side of the room and the wonky floorboards.

"He's *not* the boss," the older guy replies calmly. "But I don't need to be the one to make all the decisions and give all the orders to know that. What he said is sound and that's what we'll do. Now get to work." He gestures vaguely at the floor.

Constantine still won't leave the room—in fact, now that her femur is lying discarded on the floor, she seems unable to unglue her eyes from it, or move more than a couple of steps away—so I leave Clothilde the task of looking after her while I go after the guy on the phone.

He's so calm and professional about it, you'd think finding dead bodies in old walls was an everyday occurrence. Maybe it is, what do I know? He gives them the address, Amina's name, a description of what he's found this far.

"You should tell the neighbor," I tell him when he hangs up. "Or at least call the owner. She deserves to know a dead body has been found in her apartment."

The man is sweating profusely—more than he did while wielding the sledgehammer—and his breath is short. His hand keeps going to the back of his neck, much like Evian did before getting used to having us around.

"I'm not calling any of the ladies until the cops get here," he grumbles. "There's something weird going on with those two and I'm not messing up another crime scene. This one is *not* on me."

Great. Finding bodies *is* common. And this guy has been burned before.

I make another attempt at convincing him, without luck. He sits down in one of Amina's chairs and stays there, frowning fiercely while clutching his phone, until the police show up.

And things only get worse from there.

EIGHTEEN

Doubira is back.

At first, I'm thrilled to see him. We get a guy we know on the scene. A guy who looks up to Evian and should want to please her any way he can. He's the first one through the door, followed by two crime scene investigators in white overalls. It's the first time I've seen Doubira in uniform. Investigators like Evian aren't required to wear one—in fact, it's better if they don't so they won't be so visible—but whatever role Doubira currently occupies clearly does. It seems he has muscled up since the uniform was made for him; the fabric is bursting at the seams in the shoulders.

His face is one giant frown when he walks through the door. "Is the lady who lives here still not home?" he asks the sweating blond guy in a curt tone.

"I didn't want to do anything stupid," the man says defensively. "Didn't want no hysterical woman on my arms. *You* call her."

Doubira checks the time on his phone. "She should be home soon anyway. We'll get started without her."

I'm not sure he's allowed to snoop around in Amina's affairs without her at least being informed but there's enough tension in the air without me adding more doubts. I wish I understood why Doubira is so morose.

Doubira steps toward the open bedroom door and glances in at the mess under the window. He stops short. "That's where you found the body?" He's remembering it's the exact spot where Evian freaked out the first time they were in the room. Where she was spooked by a ghost.

"I've pulled out a femur at the moment," the worker says. "Plenty of others already sticking out but I didn't want to mess with your crime scene." He's wringing his hands and I hope he's not planning on sitting in Amina's couch—it would get soaked in sweat in seconds.

Doubira stares at the bone on the ground for several seconds before replying. "You did the right thing." He gives the all-clear to his colleagues for them to start working and asks the two darkhaired workers to come out to the living room.

"The lady who lives here," Doubira says to them, apparently wanting to pretend he doesn't know Amina, "does she live alone? She the only person you've been in contact with for this job?"

He's fishing for information about Evian. He *knows* she lives next door. And yet, he hasn't told her he's here, working Constantine's case.

"There's also this other lady who drops by from time to time. A neighbor. They must be close. She's been by twice already today."

Doubira pauses from taking notes on his phone and frowns. "Why is she dropping by? Is she checking on the work you're doing?"

"Not officially. Looked like she borrowed something from the kitchen. She fiddled with the pots in the corner there both times." The young guy points at the container where Evian dropped off our bracelets.

Doubira walks over to look into the pots. My little finger tingles when he pokes at the bracelets. "Left you here to keep watch, did she?" With his back to the room, nobody else will have heard his mumble, but I've moved closer to make sure I don't miss anything.

"Please call Evian," I tell him. "She needs to be here. We're trying to help Constantine, the ghost who has haunted that room for decades. There's nothing illegal going on, I swear."

Clothilde pokes her head out of the bedroom with a frown. "Who's touching the bracelets? Oh... Why isn't Emeline here yet?"

"He hasn't called her."

"You have to call your partner, Malik!" Clothilde yells, making the blond guy jump. "She needs to be here." Then she returns to Constantine.

Doubira grinds his teeth together and the hand hovering above the pots curls into a fist. "Stop telling me what to do," he growls.

I step away and hold my hands up as if he could see me. "All right, Doubira. We'll shut up." And I clamp my mouth shut, swearing I'll try to do just that. Doubira is not as sensitive as Evian, but clearly, when he knows about us, he does feel the pull, if not the exact message.

And I have to respect his wish not to have us pushing at him when he's doing his job.

He makes quick work of interviewing the workers. They tell him how long they've been there, what Amina is paying them to do, and the fact they only landed the contract a few days ago through a common contact. Then he sends them on their way, saying it's unlikely they'll be able to come back tomorrow and asking them to wait a few hours before contacting "the lady who lives here."

They've already told him Amina's name several times. He *knows* her name. Yet he chooses to make it as impersonal as possible.

I'm getting nervous.

Doubira joins the investigators in the bedroom. One seems to be finishing up taking pictures of the room from all angles as well as the halfway open wall, while the other is gently placing the femur in a plastic box he brought with him, complete with label.

"Looks like it's a woman's body," he says without looking up at Doubira. "There's no way she was just forgotten in there or something. I guess she *could* have died in an accident but placing her body in there like that most definitely wasn't."

"So it's likely she was murdered."

"I'd say so, yeah." The man scratches his forehead with the back of a gloved hand. "But this place hasn't been touched since at least the sixties, possibly earlier. I mean, look at that wallpaper. Your chances of figuring out who did it are non-existent. You'll have to be *very* lucky to identify the victim."

Doubira's jaw flexes. "Let me worry about identifying the victim." He knows exactly who to go to, after all. "Make sure you get every bone. Count them out. I don't care if it takes all night. We're not going to miss a single piece. And let me know about your findings, no matter how insignificant."

"Well, I can already tell you one thing." The investigator pokes at what looks like metal between two bones. "She was wearing a bra, and not much else. If she'd been wearing clothing, I would have already found traces. All I've seen so far is this underwire of a bra. The tissue is crumbling but it's there."

"But I was wearing a dress!" Constantine is standing over the investigator, glaring at her own remains. "Why would they remove my beautiful dress? What use would it be to them? I've been *naked* for decades?"

Clothilde moves to stay close to Constantine. Her left leg is cutting through the investigator's head, but he doesn't seem to notice. "It doesn't matter what clothes your dead body was wearing. You decide what you wear as a ghost, and your wedding dress was a beautiful choice. Hey, if it's any consolation, my mom buried me in a horrible yellow dress that I hate."

"But yellow's a lovely color."

Good job on distracting her, Clothilde. Constantine is understandably on edge today, but I'd like to avoid her scaring Doubira or his colleagues.

Clothilde pulls Constantine a couple of paces away so they won't be in the way and I zone them out the minute I realize they're discussing fashion. I'm going to have to thank Clothilde profusely for her sacrifice later.

I watch as the investigator removes Constantine's bones one by one. He catalogs each of them, naming the bone and describing where it was found and indexing pictures. He's definitely doing what Doubira asked and is keeping a count.

If we want to keep one of them, we're going to have to distract them somehow.

He's up to fifty when Amina comes home. Doubira is sitting at the dinner table, on the phone with Nadine Tulle, asking her to get a list of all missing persons from Toulouse from the approximate time period of the death. When Amina's surprised face appears in the doorway, he hangs up on his friend and shoots to his feet.

"Malik," Amina says. "What a pleasant surprise. Did Emeline let you in—" She steps into the living room and spots the investigators through the open bedroom door. "Oh."

Doubira stays quiet.

"Don't give anything away," I plead with Amina. "Don't make it official you know there was a dead body in the wall. And get Evian over here."

Amina stops in the middle of her living room, her gaze jumping from the bones in the plastic box, to the two investigators, to Doubira, to the empty kitchen.

"Emeline isn't here?"

Doubira shakes his head, his eyes narrowing.

"Then how come you're here? What's going on?" She leans through the bedroom door to check the one corner hidden from view. "Did those guys just let you in and then *leave*?"

"They found a dead body in your wall," Doubira says.

"Oh my God!" A hand over her mouth, Amina is quite convincing. Or would have been to someone who didn't know she had a ghost in her apartment.

"I guess it might be true you have a ghost in there after all." He throws a glance at the pot in the kitchen. "An extra ghost."

Some of Amina's usual animation falls away. Her smile fades into a serious frown and her eyes become hard instead of sparkling. "Why haven't you called Emeline, Malik?"

"I don't need Captain Evian to do my job." Doubira pulls his shoulders back, making him tower over the short Amina. "I was assigned the task of looking into a cold case, only to discover it was at your address. If anything, I should *avoid* talking to the women who claimed to see a ghost in the exact spot we found the body in. At least until I can secure the scene."

I can tell Amina is dying to ask questions, but she holds out admirably. Head high and hands clasped in front of her, she waits patiently without rising to the bait.

"Do you have anywhere else you can stay tonight?" Doubira asks, making both me and Amina frown. "It's going to take a few hours for us to finish extracting the body and I'm afraid you won't be able to sleep here. This is an active crime scene."

"An *active* crime scene?" Amina scoffs. "Nobody has touched that wall in well over fifty years, if not more. The murderer is long gone. Can I—" She glances over her shoulder toward Constantine's bones piling up in a plastic container. "Can I at least have a look?"

Doubira shakes his head. "I can't have you messing with the evidence. Wouldn't want any bones to go missing."

I step so close to Doubira I can see the fine hairs in his ear as I speak right into it. "Don't do this, Doubira. You have to let her keep one of the bones. Otherwise, you're going to have a half-crazy ghost on your hands! Let Constantine stay with us so she can finish up her business with her husband."

Clothilde and Constantine join us in the living room. Constantine keeps shivering whenever the investigator touches one of her bones, but she's following Clothilde like she's a lifeline.

"You have to let Amina keep one of the bones, Malik," Clothilde says loudly. "One finger bone more or less isn't going to make a difference to your investigation."

Doubira clamps his jaw shut so hard I can hear his molars cracking. He's not very sensitive to ghosts, but he's not completely immune either.

"I'm in enough trouble for not doing my job correctly as it is," he growls. "Nobody goes into that room until we've removed everything. And the box will be sealed shut when it's carried out of here. Mademoiselle Kettani, could I ask you to come by the station tomorrow so I can ask you some questions?"

Constantine has finally caught on to what's going on and starts yelling at Doubira that she doesn't want to leave and that she needs to stay here with the nice lady. Clothilde seems to hesitate between getting the other ghost to step down and jumping into the fray and going poltergeist herself.

I stay quiet, wondering how we're going to get Constantine out of the mess we've created for her. Because there's no way we can abandon her now.

NINETEEN

When there's a frantic knock on her door, Emeline has been feeling off for about five minutes. It's not quite the feeling of a ghost trying to communicate with her—they're all over at Amina's place anyway, and there better not be any more lurking around—but she's still fairly certain this feeling of worry isn't coming from herself. It's a bit like hearing Hélori in the cemetery, but from several hundred meters away.

The moment she opens the door, the feeling intensifies. Definitely like Hélori.

A panicking ghost.

Barely even noticing Amina standing before her, wringing her hands, Emeline rushes out the door without bothering to lock it behind her, taking long, quick strides toward Amina's apartment. "What's wrong? Who's screaming?"

"Oh, God. She's panicking, isn't she?" Amina scuttles after her. She's still wearing her coat and it's just after five, so she must have just gotten home from work.

"I assume they found the body? What did they do?" If those workers did anything to the body, Emeline is going to make it her mission to make them pay—and then move on to Amina's friend who recommended them.

Emeline enters Amina's apartment, wincing at the increasing volume of the screams she can't actually hear. And finds herself face to face with Malik.

"They called the police." Amina sounds resigned as she stops right behind Emeline. "My apartment is now an active crime scene."

Emeline scrambles to make all the connections. Why is Malik here? And in uniform? Nadine said he would be back on the job today, not behind a desk, but out in the field, on a case where he wouldn't need to use his gun.

Investigating a crime that's obviously decades old definitely fits the bill.

But why is his expression so hard? What did he say to make Amina so panicked, and Constantine freak out?

And how is Emeline supposed to focus with all this noise in her head?

"I'm happy to see you back on the job, Malik," she says tentatively and reaches out a hand for him to shake. They aren't close enough to do *la bise* yet. She steps farther into the room to get a view of the bedroom. "They couldn't have found a better fit for—"

"Do not step into the bedroom, Captain." Malik's voice is void of inflection and matches his expression. "Like Mademoiselle

Kettani said, it's an active crime scene. Nobody goes in there until we're finished."

Emeline stops short. There are two investigators in white overalls in there, digging Constantine's body out of the wall.

"Did you know there was a dead body in the wall?" Malik asks.

Closing her eyes, Emeline takes a deep breath. How could this go so wrong so fast? And will she be able to avoid having a nervous breakdown from listening to Constantine's wails? She assumes Robert and Clothilde are also here, possibly talking to her, but they're completely drowned out by the screams.

She replies in a whisper. "You know we knew about the body, Malik. You know there was a ghost in that room. If there's a ghost, there's at least part of a body." She holds his gaze for a moment. "Is the entire body there?"

"I'll be asking the questions," Malik says. "And I'm afraid I won't be able to share that information with you at this time."

"Why?" Emeline is getting annoyed, and it's proving an efficient method for ignoring the background panic. "Because we're your prime suspects? You know as well as I do nobody has been in that wall since before any of us were born. Amina hadn't been able to change even the wallpaper since she moved in here, and I'll bet you everything I own you'll get the same story from all previous owners and tenants. We *can't* be the murderers."

"How do you explain knowing about the body?"

"You know how I explain it, Malik. I've *already* explained it to you. And if you put it in your report, sure, you'll expose me to ridicule. Except I don't really care. I'll only be here for a few more months, tops, then I'll go back to Paris. *You* will stay here for years and believe me when I say you do *not* want to be the guy who talked about ghosts in his report on a cold case."

Malik is grinding his teeth together so hard, Emeline can hear it over the screaming. He's not happy but he knows she's right.

"I guess I'll just have to say the owner didn't know anything," he finally says. "I *could* omit the fact I ran into you here, but only if you're actually *not here*." Before Emeline is able to reply to that, he talks right over her. "In any case, you're not getting into that room to steal any bones, Captain. I'm not messing up this case, no matter what you say."

As her own anger wanes, Emeline is once again submerged in Constantine's anger and panic. What will happen to the poor girl if she's dragged out of here against her will and with nobody to accompany her?

"Malik," she whispers. "Please leave just one bone behind. It'll be enough for her to hang onto. We need to reunite her with her husband so she can find peace."

Malik's laughter is flat. "Oh, sure, let me get right on that. So the autopsy can say there's a bone missing, and the investigator can confirm I told him *not* to get that last bit. And then we'll both have fun explaining ourselves to the commander. Tell you what. Why don't you give me the name of the victim, and her husband, and I'll see what I can do?"

Emeline hesitates. She's not going to convince him to leave a bone, which means Constantine will be shipped out of here. Will it do more harm than good to give Malik the information they've managed to gather? Will he be able to help her? Or will it simply mean he can make their job even more difficult?

Is there any way to ask for Constantine's opinion?

She tries to listen to the other side of the veil. Can she make out anything apart from the screaming? Are there two calmer voices there too?

She can't be sure, but in the end decides to trust her partner. "Her name is Constantine Larcher. She disappeared in 1954. Her husband's name in Jacques Larcher and he's buried in the Salonique cemetery. Nadine can give you the exact location of his grave."

Malik's lip lifts in scorn. "Nadine is in on this too?"

"Nadine isn't *in* on anything. I asked her for a piece of information, and she found it for me. Without the need for any special police accesses, I might add."

Malik grumbles something inaudible but notes the names on his phone. "You think the husband killed her?"

"I wouldn't know." Emeline sighs. "It's your job to find out now, isn't it? I hope you'll keep us updated on what you find and do. We were only trying to help Constantine."

Squeezing Amina's shoulder on her way out, Emeline turns to leave. She decides to leave the bracelets for now, so Robert and Clothilde can stay with Constantine as long as possible. She'll come back for them once the police have left.

Running a hand over her face as she crosses the hallway to return to her home, the screams already waning, her shoulders slump. "I'm so sorry, Constantine."

TWENTY

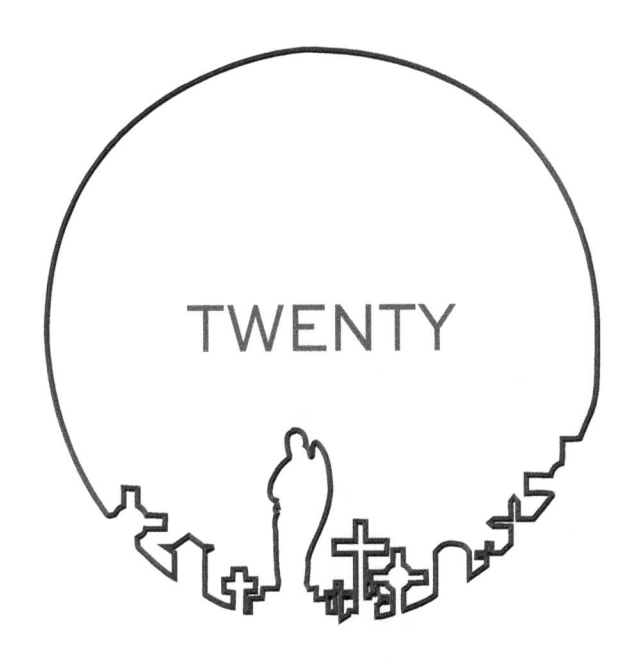

Constantine's departure is horrific.

We're used to screaming ghosts. We spent thirty years in a cemetery and welcomed hundreds of new arrivals over the years, every single one of them screaming their heads off when they woke in the casket. But they were always *arriving*, and we knew that once they'd calmed down, we might be able to help them. With Constantine, we've *been* trying to help her, and in doing that, have condemned her to be sent away to God knows where, all alone.

When Doubira carries the box of bones out the door, Constantine is flitting between him and Clothilde, moving so fast she's nothing but a blur, her dress a sparkling white and not a loose thread in sight, and her blonde hair floating around her head like she's under water.

"Don't let him take me! I don't want to leave. This is my home! Why is he allowed to steal my body? I can't—"

The door slams shut behind Doubira and Constantine is pulled out with him.

Silence.

Amina, who has stayed in her bedroom for the three hours it took Doubira and his men to finish up, emerges wearing a pink tank top and shorts pajamas and red eyes. She carries an empty container of Cookie Dough ice cream that she listlessly lets drop into her trash.

She shuffles into the guest room and stares forlornly at the hole in her wall for a good minute.

"Maybe you should call Emeline?" Clothilde suggests gently. "She'll want to get an update."

And pick us up. Hopefully.

Sniffling, Amina returns to her bedroom and sends off a text to Evian. Not even two minutes later, a knock sounds at the door.

"They're done?" Evian asks briskly when Amina opens the door. Then trails off on a gulp when she sees what Amina is wearing.

Amina doesn't notice. "I heard them counting out the bones, one by one. Malik made sure they had everything and then told me I'd hear from him, *within a week or two*! The nerve of the man."

If Doubira had any aspirations of winning Amina's favor, he has certainly not made his job easy. But he's understandably more focused on saving his career than on pursuing a pretty woman he met a couple of times.

Evian steps inside the apartment and closes the door behind

her. Her eyes scan the living room, looking at anything but her pretty neighbor. "She's gone, then? Couldn't find anything here to hold onto?"

That question is for us. "Yes, she's gone. Kicking and screaming."

"All right." Evian takes a deep breath. "Guess we'll just have to figure out where he's taking her. If he's treating it like a cold case, he'll request an autopsy, right?"

"He did say something about an autopsy." Amina perks up a little. Enough to take in Evian's attire: her usual jeans and dark T-shirt. "Were you waiting up for news?"

Evian meets Amina's gaze for the first time since she saw the pajamas. "Of course I waited up. I'm not going to be happy Constantine is gone and just move on with my life. We're going to help that girl. I promise."

Clothilde, who was as morose as Amina up until this point, smirks and leans in to whisper in Amina's ear, "You should give her a hug."

Matchmaking Clothilde. Finesse isn't really her thing, but that wouldn't work for a ghost anyway. And in this particular case, I have a feeling the manipulated party would have done what Clothilde suggests unprompted.

Amina throws her arms around Evian. "Thank you! I'm so worried about her. She hasn't left the apartment in over seventy years!"

"She'll be all right." Evian is frozen with her hands held out from her sides, as if she's terrified to accidentally touch her neighbor. Then she gets a whiff of Amina's hair and visibly mellows. She returns the hug, taking care to place her hands well above Amina's waistline.

"There isn't much that can happen to a ghost, you know,"

Evian says with the beginnings of a smile. "I know she'll be scared, but nobody can hurt her. Actually, I'm more worried about the people performing the autopsy. That woman can be *loud*."

Amina lets out a strangled laugh and a hand flies to cover her mouth. She leans back slightly so she can look Evian in the eye.

And Evian didn't let go, so now they're in each other's arms, staring into each other's eyes.

Clothilde lets out a gleeful *whoop* and claps her hands.

Which Evian must hear, because she lets go of Amina as if she got burned and clears her throat while shoving her hands into her pockets.

Amina doesn't move and remains frozen as if she's hugging an imaginary friend—I'm tempted to step into the space just for the hell of it but decide she's had enough ghostly experiences for one day—blinking several times as she's trying to process what just happened.

And I do believe she understands.

Slowly, she lowers her arms and a soft smiles spreads across her features, making her eyes sparkle. "Would you like a cup of herbal tea, perhaps? We could plan out what to do next. For Constantine."

Evian's eyes widen. She draws a quick breath. Opens her mouth…

And her phone chimes with a message.

"Oh, come on!" Clothilde groans. She has jumped up on the kitchen counter and was ready to watch the play-by-play between Evian and Amina as if it was prime TV.

Evian whips her phone out of her back pocket. I walk over to read over her shoulder. "It's from Nadine Tulle," I say for Clothilde's benefit. "She found something in the calendars."

"Well," Clothilde says with a huff. "I guess that puts an end to the romantic evening before it could even get started." She points at Amina, then Evian, staring at them as if they'd meet her gaze if her focus is strong enough. "But this isn't over."

Evian, for once, doesn't seem to notice Clothilde's shenanigans. "I'm really sorry, but I have to go home and call this person back. It's for the case I'm working on."

"To find the murderers of your two ghosts?" Amina is more subdued than usual, but anything concerning ghosts is still of interest to her. She doesn't *only* care about Constantine.

Evian sighs in resignation. "Yes. It's for my cold case." As if suddenly reminded we're here, she walks over to pick up the bracelets. My finger tingles as she ties them to her wrist.

"Is there anything I can do to help?" Amina asks.

"Thank you, but no." Evian approaches the door but stops in front of Amina. "I appreciate the offer but we're most likely on the traces of a serial killer who is still at large. It can be dangerous." Knowing what Amina is about to say, she speaks over her. "It's part of my job and I'm trained for it. You're not. And I wouldn't be able to live with myself if something happened to you because of me."

She lifts her hand and traces the back of one finger along Amina's jaw. Amina's eyes widen, Clothilde's jaw drops, and my eyebrows shoot toward my receding hairline. When Evian realizes what she's done, she whips her hand away as if she was burned.

"Anyway," she says, stepping away and clearing her throat twice. "I have to get going. I'll let you know if I hear anything about Constantine. I'll even ask my contact at the station if she can get me any information. I hope you'll do the same. Tell me if you hear anything, that is. Good night and sleep tight."

She jumps out the door so quickly, Clothilde and I don't have the time to follow. I catch the smile playing on Amina's lips before I'm sucked out into the hallway when the door closes.

Evian is stomping toward her apartment door, hands clenched and cheeks flaming. "Not a word," she growls. "Or you're sleeping in a kitchen cupboard tonight."

We make sure our snickers are silent.

TWENTY-ONE

BLUSH UNDER CONTROL, Evian settles onto her lone kitchen chair, her laptop open on the counter, and her trusted notebook ready with a pen lying across a blank page. The windows are closed despite the heat, to avoid the noise of the bus station, and the drapes are closed, giving the room almost a cozy feel. I say almost because all the cardboard boxes and files filling up every available space makes it look like someone is either on the verge of moving in or out.

I opt for leaning against the refrigerator, while Clothilde perches on a pile of boxes. She tends to prefer that pile to the others; I'm not sure if it has to do with the height or the content of the boxes. It contains a couple of old teddy bears and posters from her room. I suspect it's nostalgia talking but wouldn't dream of mentioning such a theory to her face.

When Evian calls Tulle, the other woman picks up after the first ring.

"You found something in the calendars?" Evian asks. "That was quick." She puts the phone on speaker—for us—and places the phone next to her laptop.

"Well, it's easy when I can do it all as a civvy," Tulle replies, a smile in her voice. "That other task is going to take a lot more time and effort. But I'm making headway on that one, too."

"Great. Just make sure you don't get caught, all right?" Evian stares intently at the phone, as if it can transmit the power of a look through sound only. "I do not want you to get in trouble over this."

"Don't worry. I know how this works. It's usually my job to *catch* the people snooping, remember? Anyway, the calendars were a piece of cake. I just used the credentials you gave me and asked to retrieve a six-month-old backup. It's not *easily* done, but possible. Now, you might not want to talk about this too loudly, because it's officially identity theft, but we did have the approval of the parents, so…"

Evian shifts in her chair and clicks open her pen, ready to take notes. "So you found the meetings? How many details?"

"The one for Lise had basically nothing. The location, which was the hotel her body was found in, the time, and the title 'Meeting Cèdres.' That's the name of the senior center she wanted to transform into a homeless shelter, by the way."

Evian nods and jots everything down in her notebook.

"Now Manon," Tulle continues. "She put *everything* in her calendar. Location was the hotel she was found in, with the detail 'meet at hotel bar, will hold meeting in hotel room.' The time was eight thirty at night, which is about one hour before the estimated time of death according to the autopsy report. There are two names. Laurent Lambert."

Evian grumbles under her breath and Clothilde swears loudly. That lawyer *again*.

"And Delphine Redon," Tulle finishes. "I checked, and there's only one Delphine Redon in the entire south of France. It's the woman on the Regional Council."

Evian underlines the name three times on her notebook. "Redon again."

"So it *is* her. You weren't kidding about this being big."

"And it confirms the link with my case. Clothilde Humbert also had some run-ins with the woman before her death. *And* with the lawyer."

I start pacing on top of all our research. Leaning is too static for what I'm feeling. Are we really catching up with the bastards? Will this be enough to bring in Lambert?

Tulle whistles softly. "Are you telling me she brings a lawyer when she plans to kill someone?"

"A lawyer and a henchman." Evian runs a hand through her hair and glances toward the window, only to wince at the drawn drapes. "But the henchman she used in the past is in jail awaiting trial, so she must have found someone new for her latest victim. Someone who prefers pushing people off buildings rather than slitting their wrists."

Tulle remains silent for several moments. "So there was a link with the man who was buried the other day?"

"Yes. But the less you know, the better. I don't want to get you into trouble."

Tulle doesn't say anything. She's probably dying of curiosity, but common sense wins out.

"How much of this could I use in court?" Evian asks.

I stop pacing and Clothilde leans forward as we wait for the answer.

Tulle's sigh comes through as static on the phone. "If you can get the mothers to claim to be the ones to request the backups, the information should be sound. But it's just an annotation that some young woman made in her own calendar. You'd need the corresponding one in Redon's to make anything stick."

"I think it's pretty safe to assume we won't find anything. Assuming we could get a warrant to get into her system."

"Yeah, good luck with that one."

The two women chat for a few minutes, but Tulle has given us all the information she could find. Manon was meeting with Redon to discuss her student housing project but it's just confirmation of something we already knew.

When Evian disconnects the call, she gets up to stretch and to open both drapes and windows. She seems to enjoy the noise of the busy street and bus station outside and draws a deep breath of what I can only assume is not-so-clean city air. Big city girl, through and through.

"Redon and Lambert keep showing up everywhere," Clothilde says, her legs dangling, passing through the cardboard boxes on each backswing. "Redon is probably the brains behind the operation, right? The lawyer is there to make sure the others don't get caught?"

I shrug as I pace back and forth in the little free space in Evian's living room. I don't have any blood flooding through my veins anymore, so I reap no physical benefit from moving around, but old habits die hard. Especially if you never try to lose them.

"There's no way to tell with the information we have so far," I say. "So we must be careful with drawing any conclusions. But I am tempted to agree with you. It doesn't feel like Lambert is the boss with the politicians following him. It's most likely the other way around and it's just a lucrative job for him. But I'm willing to bet he still has quite a bit of power. If he's there to give counsel, it means the others are primed to listen to him."

Evian speaks up. She is still at the window but is leaning against the metal balustrade with her back to the city. "I need to focus on Redon's link to Clothilde and forget about her involvement with Lise and Manon. Whoever is working their case will have to take that angle. I know Clothilde tried to contact Redon before she died. I know she tried hard enough to make a scene at the City Hall."

She crosses her arms and lets her gaze roam over the boxes with all of Clothilde's things. She ends up on the form letter of rejection, which has occupied a spot of honor on her coffee table since the day we found it.

"I think it's time I pay Madame Redon a visit," Evian says. "But I need more than a thirty-year-old form letter to put some pressure on her."

She returns to her phone and after a wince when she sees the time, she starts a call to Walter. Who picks up on the second ring. "Talk to me, Captain Evian." His voice sounds tinny through the loudspeaker on Evian's phone, but I much prefer this to squeezing close to Evian's ear to eavesdrop on the conversation.

"Have you figured out how to restore your friend's calendar yet?"

"No. But it's on my to-do list. I've been spending the last days making a lot of noise with the police to get them to reopen Hélori's case. Contacting that woman lawyer you told me about seems to have done the trick. It's no longer officially a suicide, but an open investigation."

"That's excellent news," Evian says and taps the kitchen counter twice in satisfaction. "Do you know who will be working on his case?"

"Not yet, but I have a meeting at the station tomorrow. I'll let you know."

"I appreciate it. Make sure you don't mention my name to anyone, though. That'll just bring trouble for the both of us."

"Do you think they will be able to help with the calendar issue?"

Evian chews on her lip as she considers the question. "They might. But if you have the login credentials for your friend's account, you might not even need them." She explains how to proceed to request a backup of old data for the calendar, repeating back what Tulle told her earlier almost word for word, sounding like a real geek. "Ask them to give you official proof that this was the actual retrieved data, that you haven't had the opportunity to modify anything. Then, if you do find something interesting—and I'm sure you will, otherwise they wouldn't have deleted it in the first place—get the police to look into it straight away. We want that as official proof."

Walter promises to look into it immediately. He's all business and entirely focused on finding his friend's killer and keeping his organization afloat. It seems like he'll be an excellent successor for Hélori, which is great news all around.

When the call ends, Evian leans back in her chair and stretches like a cat.

"We're going to get that woman." She turns to scan the room, eyes narrowed as she plots out her next steps. "How can ghosts help intimidate someone during an interrogation?"

Clothilde lifts her arms in victory and cackles. "Yes! This is going to be so much fun!"

TWENTY-TWO

Emeline was surprised to discover Madame Redon lives less than three hundred meters from the police station. Somehow, she expected a woman suspected of being the brains behind multiple murders to stay as far away from the police as possible. Although hiding right under their noses seems to be working too.

It's been three days since Constantine was forcibly removed from Amina's apartment. Emeline has sent texts to Malik every day, asking for updates and telling him his victim cares more about reuniting with her husband than about catching whoever killed her, but she's trying not to push him too hard. She can't abandon Constantine, but she also won't push Malik so hard he cuts her off completely.

Emeline has searched the police's database for any information on Redon. Or her son. For some of it she had help from Tulle, for some she worked alone, mostly from her laptop at home.

She didn't feel like going to the police station if everyone was going to look at her sideways. Maybe she imagined the looks, maybe she didn't.

In any case, her notebook was filled with information she could use against Madame Redon, and her phone had an impressive number of screenshots she could show as proof, if needed.

She's keeping to the shade as she walks down a narrow street running from the Canal du Midi, past the police station, and through the Minimes neighborhood. From what Emeline has gathered, the neighborhood grew from marshes to city in the first half of the twentieth century. It's a fairly popular place to live, due to its proximity to the city center, well-served public transport, and easy access to the airport and Airbus.

Most of the buildings are houses, tightly packed but with cozy gardens in the back where passersby can't see, but there's also a fair share of apartment buildings. Some rather recent and pricey because of the location, some from the not-so-charming sixties, often city-owned, and housing less fortunate families. It makes for a varied mix.

And then there's the one percent. Every so often, when walking down one of the narrow, winding streets, there will be an opening in the red brick wall of houses. A tall fence. A fancy wrought-iron gate. A large garden, often with a fountain. And a mansion. Made from the same red bricks as the neighboring houses, but with taller windows, prettier shutters, higher ceilings, and grander entrances.

Guess which type of house Madame Redon lives in.

Emeline is standing across the street, wondering how much a house like this might cost, when her phone rings.

"Malik," she answers with a smile. "To what do I owe the pleasure?"

"The coroner won't finish his autopsy of the dead body." Emeline can hear his annoyance, loud and clear. He's grinding his teeth again.

Emeline straightens, ready to fight. "Why? Is someone putting pressure on him not to find anything?"

"Nobody *real*, if that's what you mean. He tells me he keeps getting freaked-out about nothing. Seeing movement when there's nobody there. Being scared to touch the bones for no good reason." He growls into the phone. "The ghost is *haunting* him, Captain."

"Oh, dear." Emeline spent less than thirty seconds being haunted by Constantine and it scared the living daylights out of her. Suffering that for days? She wouldn't wish it on anyone.

Except maybe Madame Redon. Emeline *is* about to bring a couple of ghosts to her home for an interview, after all.

"Oh, dear? That's all you have to say?" Malik must be in a place where he's afraid of being overheard because he's yelling, but in a whisper.

"What do you want me to say, Malik? It's not my fault Constantine is haunting the poor coroner. I didn't want her to go with you. I tried my best to keep a small bone so she could stay with us, remember?"

"I wasn't going to let you *steal* part of a murder victim. Not when I'm in charge."

"It's a good thing you weren't in charge when we exhumed Clothilde and Robert, then." The words slip out before Emeline can think better of it.

Malik is silent. But he's probably fuming so hard smoke is coming out of his ears. "You *stole* their bones?"

"I'm pretty sure I acted on their behest." Emeline sighs. "I wasn't really aware they were talking to me at the time. Once I started to second-guess taking the bones, it was too late to take them back. The ghosts didn't want to go back to the cemetery, Malik."

"The—" A growl. "You can't know that."

"Yes, I can. But I can't prove it. Not that I feel the need to. Who's hurt by a couple of missing bones, Malik? Do you think Clothilde's family cares? Robert's? Would your coroner have missed a vital clue if a bone from her little finger was missing? Actually," she can't help but add, "he'd probably be able to do his job better without it, because it would also mean *no ghost*."

"I just need her to calm down so the man can do his job."

"I'm pretty sure the only way to do that is to get her out of there. You *could* try to take a bone and tell her you're bringing it to Amina. If she believes you, she should be able to attach to the bone and follow you out. But that's a big if considering what you've done to her. Which leaves taking Amina down there to get the bone, I guess. I'd recommend inviting the coroner to do something else. You know, so he won't see you stealing the bone."

"I'm not going to steal a bone!"

"Then I'm afraid you're stuck with being haunted by an angry ghost, Malik." Emeline knows she sounds cold, but she doesn't believe in coddling in *any* situation. Malik is a big boy; he can figure out how to solve his case. Especially when she has given him all the elements needed to get rid of Constantine.

"Maybe I'll just conclude we didn't find anything and have her tossed in a pauper's grave."

"You want your first case to stay unsolved? Autopsy interrupted halfway through? Suit yourself. But if you do, let me know which grave she's being sent to, all right? That poor woman doesn't deserve to pay for your insecurities. Now, if you didn't need anything else, I have to get back to my own case. Goodbye, Malik."

Emeline ends the call and slips her phone into her back pocket. Malik isn't going to be happy, but this case is going to be good for him. Yes, as police officers, it's their job to make sure laws and rules are followed. But there is also a time for stretching the rules a little. Even the best of laws will have an exception where following it isn't the right thing to do. There's always room for interpretation and a good officer has to be able to think for herself and not simply follow the rules blindly.

Malik knows this, deep down. Emeline has no doubt he's a very good man. He just needs to remember that for himself and he'll find his way back.

The woman who lives in the mansion across the street, though... That's a whole other story. Emeline is increasingly convinced she has done more than bend and stretch the rules. She has obliterated them completely.

Emeline has made sure Madame Redon is home. Her secretary wouldn't say where her boss was, other than not in the office, but a call to her home—thank you, Nadine, for finding the non-listed number—confirmed her presence. The trick was to not ask the person who answered the phone whether or not Madame Redon was home, but to ask a question they would invariably relay immediately. When the reply came within thirty seconds, Emeline took off from her apartment straightaway.

Now she only has to make it inside and not get kicked out without talking to the woman.

Waiting for an unmarked police car to drive past way over the speed limit, Emeline crosses the road and presses the buzzer. The house is too far away for her to hear ringing.

It doesn't take long for a man's voice—sounds like the same one who answered the phone earlier—to ask her to state her business over the speakerphone.

"I need to see Madame Redon," Emeline says, looking into the small camera.

"Madame Redon isn't home. She doesn't receive visitors in her home. Contact her secretary at the Regional Council."

Emeline nods. "I don't believe she will want to have this conversation in her office, Monsieur."

Silence. No way to tell whether it's a refusal to rise to her bait or if there's a discussion going on with the microphone off.

"I'm a captain with the Judicial Police," Emeline says. "I'm looking into a thirty-year-old murder case. Madame Redon's name keeps popping up and I thought she might wish to clear up some issues *before* I bring them to the attention of the commander."

Still no reply, but this time Emeline leaves them more time. She waits patiently, her hands clasped behind her back, and watches as a couple of magpies splash around in a small artificial pond in a corner of the garden visible through the latticework of the gate. The place looks immaculate but not very lived-in. No children's toys, no lawn chairs, no lazy hammock.

Five minutes after the last sign of life, the gate buzzes unlocked. It squeals on its hinges when Emeline pushes it open. No instructions from the intercom, so Emeline makes her way toward the house and its grandiose double staircase leading up to a set of beautiful hardwood doors that are slowly sliding open.

Let the ghostly interrogation begin.

TWENTY-THREE

I HAVE TO admit I'm kind of excited. Until now, when Emeline has questioned people, be they victims or suspects, we've kept out of it. Us trying to influence or scare the interviewee would only hinder Evian from doing her job, and there was always the risk of disturbing the interview.

Today, we *want* Madame Redon perturbed. Evian has collected evidence and interesting tidbits Redon shouldn't want leaked to the press or the opposition, but there's nothing that would hold up in court, or even be enough to bring her in for questioning. Redon is experienced enough to know this, so the only way to get anything out of her will be by throwing her off her game.

Clothilde's moment of glory has arrived.

We flank Evian as she enters Redon's house. Nobody's there to greet her, only a wide, well-lit hallway with potted plants on the floor, colorful paintings on the walls, and black-and-white checkered tiles, running straight across the house to an open door leading to the garden in the back. Two doors on each side of the hallway; two closed ones on the left, one closed and one open on the right.

I rush ahead of Evian to have a peek inside. No need for her to get ambushed if I can do some scouting first.

It's an office. Or maybe it could qualify as library. A cozy room with lots of dark wood, the far wall covered with bookshelves from floor to ceiling. The books range from beautiful old ones that are more decoration than reading material, to well-worn thriller paperbacks. The floor is covered in worn woven rugs, and the window on the left opens on the garden in the back, with a palm tree front and center.

Occupying a large part of the floor space in front of the window: a large wooden desk, with a laptop, a computer monitor, and a variety of scattered papers. And a furious Madame Redon in the large leather office chair.

I see no guns, no goons, and no other immediate threats to Evian. "Coast is clear," I tell her when she reaches the doorway.

Evian stops just inside the door. She doesn't so much as glance around the room; her eyes are on Redon and stay there. "*Bonjour*, Madame Redon. I'm Captain Evian."

Redon's lip lifts in a sneer. "I'm aware who you are, Captain. What I do not know is why you've forced your way into my home when I'd be perfectly willing to meet with you in my office during business hours."

We expected this type of welcome, of course. While Clothilde and I *could* attempt to influence Redon to accept to talk to Evian, there's a good chance it would have the opposite effect of what we want. So we stay silent, and instead, start snooping through the papers on Redon's desk while Evian talks her way into the room.

On one end of the desk lie two opened letters. I recognize the insignia of the Judicial Police and aim straight for them.

"You probably won't believe me," Evian says calmly, "but meeting here is actually in your best interest because it stays private. Secret, even. If I show up at the Regional Council, people will see me and ask why I've come to see you. I'm fairly certain you wouldn't like them to hear my answer to the question."

While Clothilde is trying to read the documents in a pile on Redon's right, I'm reading the first letter from the police. The second one is unfortunately hidden beneath the first and there's nothing I can do to move either. The top one is addressed to Madame Redon and informs her Monsieur Mathieu Redon, her son, will have to remain in jail until the time of his trial. He is considered too high of a flight risk to be let out until a judge has ruled on his case. This also means they're basically one hundred percent certain of his guilt—not too hard to understand when he kidnapped Clothilde's sister in her own home, threatened her at gunpoint, and then proceeded to do the same to two police officers.

Redon's brown eyes are dark with anger as she stares at Evian across the room. "Why, what would be your answer?"

Evian lets her gaze roam the room, ending up on her feet on the doorstep. Still on the outside of Redon's study. "Are you inviting me in for a chat?"

I'm close enough to see the twitch in Redon's left eye and the clenching of a muscle in her jaw. Neither would be visible to Evian from the door. "I don't react well to threats, Captain Evian. Is this how the Judicial Police does their work nowadays?"

She's trying to threaten Evian right back. She knows Evian isn't doing things by the book and could get in trouble if word got back to the wrong people.

Clothilde seems to have found something of interest. She is leaning over a messy pile of documents at the end of the desk, her brows drawn together in concentration. She's trying to push the top sheet of paper to the side with her hand, but I don't think she's having much luck at the moment. We *can* exert *some* influence over physical objects in the realm of the living, but it takes a lot of effort, and the results are minuscule. Paper is very light, though, so it shouldn't be impossible.

Evian, her face set to an agreeable neutral I'd expect of someone waiting on a pleasant customer, shrugs. "I have no issue with coming to your office tomorrow morning, Madame. But you will not come crying to me afterward when your colleagues start asking questions."

"*What* questions?"

I grin from ear to ear. Evian definitely doesn't need our help in getting a reaction out of Redon. She's warming up our subject beautifully.

Clothilde signs for me to come join her. "Help me with this," she whispers when I'm close, remembering the instruction to not influence Redon in any way until Evian gives the signal. "I need to see the rest of this address."

I glance at the papers she's working on. The top sheet is separate; a letter from a notary's office. *Please find enclosed the deed for the acquisition signed two months ago.* The pile underneath it is a thick stack of stapled-together papers—the deed.

Which would list the address of the purchase on the first page. In fact, we can see the first part already, but it's just "34, rue." Which could be anywhere.

"You think it's important to the case?" I whisper back to Clothilde as I try to do what she has been doing, using my hand to push the first sheet of paper away.

"They have interests in that particular part of the city," Clothilde says. "It would make sense they're buying stuff up, don't you think? I need to see this address."

In the meantime, Evian hasn't replied to Redon's question. She simply stands there, on the threshold, hands casually clasped behind her back, as she waits for Redon to invite her in.

Redon's attention is on Evian. She shouldn't notice if one of her documents moves a couple of centimeters.

"All right, Clothilde, let's do this," I whisper. "Friction isn't our friend, though, so I don't think pushing it off is the way to go. How about we both blow on it from the side? Aerodynamics would be on our side." And we can move small particles if we concentrate very hard. Moving air should be feasible.

Clothilde grumbles something that I think is "aerodynamics" and a swear word, but she lines up next to me, so we'll be blowing the paper in the right direction.

Redon is still having a staring match with Evian, under the illusion the captain could back down first.

"On three," I whisper. "Aim for the top of the sheet of paper, not under it. It's air moving across the top that's going to make it lift." I make the count, and start blowing.

This part of being a ghost is so frustrating. If a living human made this kind of effort, the entire pile of papers should be flying off the desk. All we manage to produce is barely a flutter.

But it's there.

We blow and we blow and we blow, so hard we would have been going red in the face if we'd had any blood in our veins, and when the sheet looks like it's on the verge of lifting up, we both shove our hands at it, adding in what we have of physical influence to get it to move in the right direction.

The sheet of paper shifts. No more than four or five centimeters, but it's enough to display the address.

And draw the attention of Redon.

The Regional Council member suddenly jumps into action. She grabs the entire pile of papers, reaching through me to get there—ever wonder what it feels like to have an arm sprout out of your chest? Not as fun as it sounds—and dumps them unceremoniously into one of her desk's drawers.

"Don't just stand there in the doorway, Captain," she snaps. "You're creating a draft. Get in here and close the door behind you." She grabs more documents, shoving them all into the same drawer, then slamming it shut. With a frustrated grunt, she remembers the letters from the police at the other end of the desk, and they also end up in the drawer.

Evian steps slowly into the room, and gently closes the door. While she approaches the visitors' chair, I move to stand next to Clothilde, who got out of the way when Redon started her cleaning frenzy.

"Did you see the address before she snatched it away?" I ask.

Only now do I notice her hair is lifting, as if dancing to an eerie tune nobody can hear. Her voice is already approaching the midnight voice that only comes out when she's very, very angry. "I got the address."

Clothilde's gaze is locked on Redon and I'm surprised the woman doesn't notice. Clothilde might be invisible, but she's so *intense*. "She bought Lise's retirement home."

TWENTY-FOUR

"Now I've invited you in, tell me what these incriminating questions are, Captain Evian." Her desk clear of clutter, Delphine Redon fixes Evian with a hard stare, her hands clasped on her desk, her legs elegantly crossed with the toes of one foot hooked behind the heel of the other. Immaculate and discreet makeup and an elegant blue pantsuit; it all adds up to the perfect image of a woman in charge, who knows what she's doing.

Evian, dressed in her usual black T-shirt, jeans, and black sneakers, isn't intimidated in the least by the older woman. In fact, I'm beginning to think she enjoys these situations, where others look down on her and underestimate her. It means the only direction she can move in is up.

"I'd like to talk to you about Clothilde Humbert." Her tone is light, as if she's discussing the weather.

"Who?" Redon looks genuinely confused.

And Clothilde genuinely insulted. With a huff, she stalks off toward the bookshelf, where she jumps up to perch on a shelf about halfway up the wall. I'm used to her feet swinging through whatever she's sitting on, but her upper body melding with three shelves of books is disturbing, even for me. I guess the only natural place to perch—Redon's desk—was suddenly removed from the list of viable options.

"Clothilde Humbert," Evian patiently repeats. "Here, I have a picture." She holds up her phone to show the screen to Redon. It's Clothilde's high school picture. "She was three years older when you interacted with her, but I don't think she changed much."

Although I'm still fascinated by Clothilde's picture—seeing her younger, carefree, and in color is a shock every single time—I keep my eyes on Redon. I don't want to miss any microexpressions that might give her away.

She actually leans forward to see the picture better and squints at it. "I'm quite happy to say the face doesn't ring any bells. If this is your shocking revelation, I'm afraid you'll be leaving quite disappointed, Captain. And I'll be sure to have a word with Commander Diome next time I see him."

"Feel free to do that," Evian says with a smile. "He is the one who requested I investigate Clothilde's murder."

"Well, if I never met her, I couldn't have killed her, could I?"

Clothilde jumps down from her perch and saunters over to lean over Redon's desk so she's in the other woman's face. "I don't think you did kill me. But I think you're responsible anyway. You're the one who lured me to that hotel thirty years ago."

We're extrapolating slightly on this point. Not that it should be much of a problem, since Redon can't actually hear us and won't be able to prove we threw suppositions at her. Clothilde didn't go to that meeting to meet Redon. It was for a different subject. But we've come to the conclusion she was lured there under false pretenses because she was about to poke the sleeping dragon on the issue of the intersection.

Redon made a preemptive strike.

"How many people have you sent to their deaths," Clothilde says, "if their names don't even ring a bell? Where's your humanity? Seriously, you've been at this for *decades*?"

The flinch on Redon's face is faint, but it's there. I don't think she's anywhere near as sensitive as Evian, but enough for us to be able to mess with her a little.

Evian, who can feel we're participating, pretends not to notice. "It's possible to be responsible for somebody's death without being the one to wield the knife. You're certain the name doesn't ring any bells? She made several attempts to contact you and your team."

Clothilde is sitting cross-legged on Redon's desk, her elbows on her knees and her chin on her folded hands as she leans toward Redon. "Come on, lady, admit it. I made enough noise for you to feel threatened and you had your goons come after me. I was going to mess with your plan in that stupid neighborhood, wasn't I? Since I was one of the first, you were probably just starting out? Didn't want someone to mess with it right out of the chute?"

We're no closer to finding out what they're trying to do. They've been at this since the late eighties and don't mind taking their time. But it should mean their goal is something big, something with a huge impact on the city, or their bank accounts. Probably both. Evian hasn't heard back from Tulle on her research on the subject. I don't know if it means she's having trouble getting to the information or if there's too much to sort through.

"I meet a lot of people in my line of work," Redon says in a cold voice. "And I've been at this for most of my adult life. You cannot expect me to remember someone who tried to contact me thirty years ago, someone I never met."

I feel a grin spreading across my face and Clothilde straightens, gleefully leering at Redon. "Oops," I whisper.

Evian simply frowns and lets the silence settle.

Redon, like most people, tries to fill the silence. "Surely, you're faced with similar issues, Captain. You must meet a lot of people in your line of work. Do you remember every single one of them since your first day on the job?"

Evian pretends to ponder the question for a moment, making Redon increasingly nervous. She has unhooked her foot and it's currently jumping up and down under her desk, a dead giveaway.

"I do remember the names and faces of everyone who died, actually," Evian finally says, her voice low. "Be they murder victims or someone killed during our search for the culprit."

She cocks her head. "What I'm infinitely curious about, Madame, is how you managed to place the time of Clothilde's death if you have no idea who she is."

A sharp intake of breath, and Redon's foot increases its cadence. "You told me when she died."

Clothilde and I exchange gleeful grins. We were hoping repeating the information several times would make her pick up on it.

"I did not." Evian's frown is deepening. "I told you she tried to contact you several times and I showed you a picture. All remaining information you have, comes from you."

Redon is straightening, her hands squeezing together so hard it looks painful. She's preparing to counter-attack and I don't think she'll play nice. "The picture is obviously quite old and—"

Evian cuts her off. "I can actually prove you knew the young woman. Well, I can't prove you knew her while she lived, but we have the very believable testimony from a witness who claims to have heard you bragging about putting a stop to her funeral. When you threatened the poor priest who was in charge of laying Mademoiselle Humbert to rest?" She adds in the hint of a smile, as if politely inviting Redon to review her memories.

Clothilde is enjoying herself immensely. She reaches out to bop Redon on the nose.

Redon scoots back in her seat. Did she feel Clothilde invading her personal space?

She's definitely angry, though. "And who is this person whose testimony you put so much trust in? I'd very much like to know who is attempting to blacken my name without proof."

"Maybe it's your son." Clothilde shifts closer so she can poke a finger into Redon's cheek. "He's in jail for kidnapping and threatening my sister, and a whole bunch of other stuff, remember? Are you really so sure he wouldn't turn you in to save his own ass?"

Redon runs a hand down her cheek as if swatting away a fly. Her breaths are shorter, and her hands are clenched into fists below her desk.

"I'm afraid I can't divulge that information," Evian says smoothly. "But the report states you bragged to have put pressure on the priest and the mother to make certain Clothilde wouldn't have a funeral where her family and friends could be present."

"You know," Clothilde says conversationally as she pulls on Redon's hair. "I find it kind of odd you've set your own son to do the grunt work in this operation of yours. He's doing the same job as the people who threatened my mom, and they were just goons.

Is he really not smart enough to get a little more responsibility? Although I guess we saw how incompetent he is firsthand when he threatened my sister." She has another go at Redon's nose.

Redon's nose twitches and she runs a hand through her hair. "Mathieu would never tell such lies. If he did, it only means you've been threatening him during interrogations. He would *never* sell me out."

Evian purses her lips. "I assume you're talking about your son? Mathieu is quite a common name. Why would you assume he is the source? Was he in on your schemes already as a ten-year-old? I certainly hope he wasn't the one to murder Mademoiselle Humbert."

Clothilde cackles and claps her hands. "This is so much fun! She's quite receptive, don't you think?"

"Seems like just the right amount," I agree. I decide to join the fray and add another layer. "Your son must be desperate to get out of jail right now. He didn't seem like the kind of guy who would keep calm under pressure. Am I right? And what better way to get his get-out-of-jail card than to snitch on one of the bosses?"

A drop of sweat is making its way down Redon's temple. It won't be visible to Evian, which is probably why she doesn't do anything about it, but to me, it's proof we're on the right track. Just for the hell of it, I trace the drop's journey down her chin. Her hand jerks up to swat at me.

This *is* fun.

Redon still has some fight left in her, though. "I certainly hope you are not insinuating my son murdered someone when he was a child, Captain. I did not realize the police were allowed to throw around empty threats and accusations without proof. I think I'll opt for having this meeting in my office, after all. And I will be filming the interview. Or should I call it what it really is? An interrogation?"

Evian shrugs, a faint smile on her lips. "I do not much care what *you* call it, Madame. I, however, qualify this as an interview. Now, if you do not wish to comment on your prior knowledge of Clothilde Humbert, that's fine. I simply hope you're aware this will look *highly* suspicious if it turns out you did have interactions with or on the subject of the young woman."

Redon clearly expects Evian to get up and leave after this speech. Her eyes are narrowed in anger, but she doesn't say anything. She knows it will only dig her grave deeper.

But Evian doesn't get out of her chair. Instead, she crosses her legs and gets comfortable. "I also wanted to talk to you about Hélori Xavier. Does *this* name ring any bells?"

TWENTY-FIVE

Hélori's name certainly got a reaction out of Madame Redon.

She was leaning forward in her chair, expecting Emeline to take her leave and now she freezes in an awkward position, her mouth opening in surprise, and her breath catching.

Emeline gets a definite feeling of da-da-da-dum, like she's in a television show with silly sound effects—which means one of the ghosts made the actual sound. It feels like something Clothilde would do.

It really is a shame Madame Redon doesn't hear the ghosts like Emeline does. Although there's a chance she wouldn't appreciate the humor.

"I take it this name is more familiar to you?"

Madame Redon eases back into her chair. "I believe I heard this name recently," she says carefully. "But only in passing and I didn't inquire." Her left cheek twitches, as if a fly was bothering her. "What does such a recent suicide have to do with your decades-old case?"

Emeline watches as Madame Redon shifts slightly to the left, then backward. She forcefully runs a hand through her hair, trying to dislodge something that isn't there. It can't be easy concentrating while being haunted by two ghosts in broad daylight.

"So you overheard enough to know it was a suicide?" Emeline opens her notebook and jots down a couple of random words. "Interesting. I'm glad you ask, though, because the link is quite obvious. Both Clothilde and Hélori's deaths were ruled suicides—wrongfully so."

Madame Redon runs a hand over her face, but all in all, she stays admirably in control and focused on the conversation. "What are you doing here, talking to me, if a murderer is on the loose?"

Emeline can't stop her eyebrow from arching. Annoyance registers on Madame Redon's face when she understands the accusation, but she's too distracted by the ghosts to do anything about it.

Madame Redon jumps out of her chair and walks to stand by the window behind her seat. A swat to her own behind shows how effective that maneuver was.

"My colleagues are investigating Hélori Xavier's murder as we speak," Emeline says. "In fact, I believe they plan to exhume the body this afternoon. I'm mostly interested in the link to Clothilde and the implications behind the timeline. Don't you find it odd that you should know both victims?"

"I told you I've never heard of the girl. And I only remembered the man's name because my nephew is also named Hélori." Madame Redon is now down to running her hands over her arms and face non-stop, trying to get rid of the ghostly intrusions.

Emeline wonders if the nephew thing is true, but it doesn't really matter. She knows the woman is lying about Clothilde and her only goal here is to try to get her to slip up, or to make her stressed out enough to do something stupid.

Which is made infinitely easier with the help of ghosts.

"What is going on?" Madame Redon finally exclaims. "Are there spiders? I can't see anything, but they're everywhere! Why do they not bother you?"

Emeline frowns, possibly too theatrically. "I don't see any spiders. Maybe it's all in your head?"

With a shriek, Madame Redon runs both hands into her hair and violently messes up her neat locks.

Emeline has a twinge of worry she has taken it too far, but it seems Clothilde and Robert have come to the same conclusion and stop their intervention.

Madame Redon stops moving, breathing heavily. "How are you doing this?"

"I'm not doing anything. I'm sitting way over here."

Seconds pass as Madame Redon calms herself down with deep breaths and murderous looks toward Emeline and the room at large.

"Tell me, Madame Redon," Emeline says when she catches the other woman's gaze. "Do you really expect to get away with dozens and dozens of murders—at the very least!—and never get caught? I realize this has been going on for awhile, but everybody makes mistakes. The fact I've managed to link you to both Clothilde's and Hélori's murder means there are lots of other clues out there, waiting for police officers to find." The woman doesn't need to know that the link to Hélori is pure extrapolation. She's not in a state to throw accusations back at Emeline right now.

If only she could find out what the deal was with the real estate in that specific area of the city. If she knew what Madame Redon and her buddies were aiming for, it would be easier to look for proof, understand their motivation, and anticipate their next move.

On a sudden burst of inspiration—so the idea probably came from Robert or Clothilde—Emeline asks, "Have you made any real estate acquisitions lately, Madame Redon?"

The other woman freezes completely and her face smooths into a perfect, inexpressive mask. Ever so slowly, she straightens, putting her back to the window and becoming mostly a silhouette against the bright light outside, and pulls on the lapels of her blouse.

"This meeting is over." Redon's voice is cold, almost robot-like. "I must request you leave, or I will call the police. The *real* police. If you try to so much as approach me in the future, you can expect to hear from my lawyers."

Looks like they really touched a nerve with that accusation. Which means she *has* made an acquisition recently. The ghosts must have seen something in her papers before she stuffed everything into a drawer.

But Emeline will have to ponder the question once she's outside. She doesn't think Madame Redon is bluffing about the police, and the truth is that Emeline isn't exactly following procedure. So if she can avoid needing to justify her actions to a colleague or—heaven forbid—Commander Diome, all the better.

Emeline gets out of her chair and smooths her hands down the front of her T-shirt. "I'll get out of your hair, Madame. But I'm certain you *are* linked to both murders in some way. Which does not necessarily mean you're the bad guy. Perhaps it's simply someone close to you. If you have any information that might help me solve this case, feel free to call."

Without waiting for a response, Emeline leaves the room, walks quickly down the hallway to the front door, and lets herself out. She has a short moment of panic when she reaches the gate and finds it closed—only to discover a switch to unlock it hidden behind a bush to the side.

Once she's out on the street, in the shade of some greenery pouring over Madame Redon's fence, she stops to take a deep breath of hot, humid air.

It's not like her to panic like that, but Madame Redon's demeanor turned downright glacial. The kind that can turn into dangerous actions and Emeline needing to look over her shoulder whenever she leaves her apartment.

Of course, there's also the feeling of being stuck, of not getting out. It's not as strong when she's outside, with the open sky above her, but her mind doesn't always latch onto such insignificant details. It registers *trapped*, and on comes the panic.

She should probably see someone about her issue. After all, she can't lecture Malik about taking care of himself if she doesn't do it herself. The significant difference being that Emeline's issues don't put herself or her partner at risk.

She just *really* doesn't like being trapped, especially in tight spaces.

Once she has her heartbeat under control, Emeline sends off a quick text to Nadine Tulle, asking if she has made any headway on her research. Then she brings up the app of Toulouse's public transport system and tries to figure out how to get to the Terre Cabade cemetery.

She has to make sure there aren't any hiccups with Hélori Xavier's exhumation.

TWENTY-SIX

EVIAN HASN'T WALKED for more than a couple hundred meters before her phone rings. Clothilde and I have left her the sidewalk, opting to stroll down the middle of the narrow street instead, ignoring the occasional car. Clothilde is much better than me at not flinching when the roaring engines run right through us.

"Nadine," Evian says. "Have you found anything?" Her pace slows down somewhat when her main focus is on the conversation with Tulle, but she keeps moving toward the closest metro station—which happens to be in front of the police station.

I can't hear what Tulle is saying on the other end and I don't bother crowding Evian to listen in. She'll tell us if our favorite researcher had something interesting to report.

"Really?" Okay, the inflection means Tulle *did* find something. "How long has this been going on? ... Wow, talk about being patient... *Three* in just the last two months? What—"

Evian stops short, her entire body going rigid.

"What's wrong?" I ask as I rush up to her, going right through a white sedan double-parked in front of a garage.

"Nadine?" Evian is close to yelling. "Who is there with you? Give me something to work with!" Her eyes wide but determined, Evian doesn't say another word, only listens to the noises coming out of her phone and moving her eyes as if she's able to watch the actions accompanying the sounds she's hearing.

"Dammit!" she yells. "They hung up her phone." With a quick glance up and down the street, she lowers her voice. "She was at the City Hall, looking through deeds and recent purchases in the area we pointed her to. There—" She shakes her head forcefully. "I'll tell you the details later. Suffice it to say she was definitely on the track of something big *and they got to her while she was on the phone with me*. I heard them telling her to put down her phone and come peacefully."

"We have to go help her!" Clothilde jogs in place, her eyes reminiscent of an Amazon warrior. "Where to?"

Evian holds up a staying hand. Closes her eyes and takes a deep breath. "Hang on. We're going to help her, but there's no point in just running down to City Hall. For one, she won't be there anymore by the time we get there, and two, I need more justification than 'I don't like it.'"

She starts pacing back and forth on the narrow sidewalk, not even noticing when her hair catches on the exploring end of a vine creeping off the garage's roof. "It sounded like they were police. A simple Capitole employee wouldn't have the power to stop a police officer doing research into publicly available documents, and Nadine would have sounded less chagrined when getting caught. God! There wasn't even anything to get *caught* for. We're definitely on the right track."

Evian stops and hangs her head. "And Nadine is the one paying for it. All right." She snaps back into action, phone in hand. "First things first: getting Nadine to safety."

While Evian makes her calls, I lean against the garage door and Clothilde jumps up to perch on the roof of the white sedan.

First comes Commander Diome. Evian explains what she asked of Nadine and the reasoning behind it. "Clothilde wanted the city to change an intersection in that area just before she died, and I've found links with several other deaths. Well, I *can't* investigate her murder without taking into account the others! Anyway, she found something. There haven't been more sales in that area than any other part of the city, but when she listed the names of all purchasers over the last thirty years, the list isn't very long."

"Wanna bet Redon is on the list?" Clothilde says in a growl.

"Madame Redon made an acquisition less than a month ago," Evian says. "Buying a building that Lise Lafargue and her non-profit organization was interested in. Yes, that's her. The sale went through a little under a month after her death. No kidding. She found a lot of other high-profile names on the list of buyers for that area. And then was stopped by what I assume was police when she was trying to tell me the other names of the list." She listens to Diome for a beat. "Thank you. Just make sure she's safe, all right?"

"He's looking into it," she says when the call ends. "Which is *not* going to be good enough, I can feel it. But at least somebody else knows." Selecting Malik's name in her list of contacts, she brings the phone to her ear again.

"Malik, Nadine's in trouble. No, I can't help with your ghost, you're going to have to get Amina's help on that one. She's the only one Constantine is likely to trust. Did you not hear me say Nadine needs our help? *Yes.* She was looking at real estate and landed on information somebody doesn't want known to the general public. Do you have the means to track Nadine through her phone? Do that, then get back to me, all right?"

Suddenly, we're just standing there, on the sidewalk, with a great sense of urgency but nothing to do.

"Do we have any idea where they might take Tulle?" I ask Clothilde. How can we be of help right now? In some cases, it's quite handy to be invisible and able to walk through objects, but right this minute I'm feeling horribly useless. So I revert to the only thing I'm good at: logical thinking.

"If it was the police, they should take her to the police station, shouldn't they?" Clothilde is sitting in her usual position on top of the car, but her legs aren't swinging. She is one hundred percent focused on our conversation and there's nothing to feel playful about.

"The people who showed up might have been police, but they weren't there on official business. Bringing her to the station would give people like Diome the power to get her free. And it would place suspicion on whoever's in charge of the operation. They flashed their badges and uniforms to *get* Tulle, but the minute they're outside City Hall, they're going far away from the station. But *where*?"

For the first time in decades, Clothilde looks her age—or rather the age she was when she died—as she worries for Tulle. "What are they going to do to her, Robert? They can't mean to just scare her into not telling anyone what she found. She's a fricking police officer. That would never work." She glances at

Evian, who is holding one hand over her eyes while the other taps a staccato rhythm on her thigh while she frantically searches for a solution to our problem.

I don't want to confirm what we're all thinking—that Tulle's life is definitely in danger—so I focus on searching for a solution. "I'm pretty sure they were the ones to cut the call with Evian. And if they're even halfway good at their jobs, they will have checked who the caller was. Which means they know somebody knows. They *could* kill her straight away—"

I reach out to place a hand on Clothilde's leg when she whimpers. "But I really don't think they will. If Tulle ends up dead, obviously murdered, yes, we will have lost the information she found, but it would also bring all kinds of attention to her case. And these guys might not have trouble with murdering people, but they have *always* tried to pass them off as suicides. They don't want attention."

"They're going to have to hide her," Evian says, proving her mind has been going down the exact same path as mine. "Until they figure out how to fake her suicide. But they can't take *too* long, because a kidnapped police officer isn't much better than a murdered one. How can they make her suicide seem believable considering the circumstances?"

"What makes a police officer feel horribly bad about herself?" I say, my chest deflating with the knowledge of the answer.

"They're going to make her guilty of something else, something horrible." Evian finally notices the vine and pulls on it, only making it longer and even more in her way. Instead of breaking it off or moving away, she stops, her gaze distant.

"There's only one thing that could make someone like Nadine feel bad enough to kill herself. Being responsible for somebody else's death."

TWENTY-SEVEN

Not knowing what to do or where to go, we wander through the narrow streets of the Minimes neighborhood, vaguely in the direction of the Terre Cabade cemetery. We still want to go there, but it feels wrong to oversee the exhumation of somebody already dead when a living person's life is in danger.

That all changes when Malik calls, though.

He managed to track down Tulle's phone—and it's in the cemetery.

"They're going after Walter, too," Evian mumbles and taps through lots of screens on her phone without bothering to share. Two minutes later, a car pulls to a stop right in front of us, so I guess she has a way of getting a driver. That's certainly handy.

"You think she's right?" Clothilde asks once we're squeezed into the back of the car with Evian. She has been kind enough to leave room for us next to her, so we don't need to get inventive. "They see Walter as a threat because he's getting the police to look into his friend's death?"

"It's possible." My eye catches on the area beneath one of the pedestrian bridges crossing the canal as we drive past. It's covered in stark, hard stones, cemented in place to prevent the homeless from setting up their tents. This isn't the first development of the sort I've seen while we've wandered the streets of Toulouse. I wonder if they expect the homeless to simply disappear.

"But why would they bring Nadine to the same place? Their headquarters can't be *in* the cemetery, can it?"

I have to smile at the idea of a group of bad guys in their sixties hanging out in some sort of underground bunker, accessed through the scariest of the old mausoleums of the city's main cemetery.

"Maybe they want to kill two birds with one stone," I muse. "Kill Walter, somehow blame Tulle for it, and then fake her suicide."

"That makes sense, dammit!" Clothilde leans forward to shout into the driver's ear. "We're in a hurry! Step on it!"

We get there in five minutes.

The car leaves us at the cemetery's main entrance. The men working at the gate barely look up from their phones as Evian rushes past. She's calling Malik as she runs, already short of breath and sweating profusely since the Terre Cabade cemetery is on the slopes of one of Toulouse's rare hills and the main entrance is at the very bottom.

"The signal is still in the same place? How precise are the data? Are we talking a meter or two, twenty, the size of the cemetery?

All right, so pretty close to the exhumation site but *probably* not right next to it? Did you call anyone else, like Diome? I don't care if they think we're imagining things, we need backup! Figure out a way to get it, then get your ass over here. Constantine will still be there tomorrow!"

Clothilde and I run ahead of Evian as she hurries through the winding paved paths of the cemetery. I don't like the number of unknowns in this situation, and something just isn't clicking.

Blaming Tulle for Walter's death could make sense, although I have no idea what they'd come up with for a motive. Maybe stage it like an accidental death? But how were they planning to do so with the number of people who would be present for Hélori's exhumation?

Speaking of Hélori, I can't hear any screaming, so I guess he has come to terms with his fate and has been let out of the casket. Once we've saved Tulle, maybe we can go have a chat with him to see what he remembers of the days before being pushed off a building.

Panting and wiping sweat off her forehead, Evian stops to look at a map on her phone—those things really have everything, what I wouldn't have given to have one when I worked as a police officer—squinting at the screen and at the street signs to figure out where we are.

"This is where Tulle's phone is emitting signals from. I'm sure Malik would have told me if they changed." She turns full circle and I do the same, looking for any sign of the short woman with the long hair, or even just a phone.

"Let's start searching," I say. "We can cover more ground than Evian."

"There's someone behind that grave!" Clothilde's yell makes me jump a foot into the air and Evian's shoulders twitch.

Clothilde is already twenty meters away, running right at the spot she pointed at. "Two guys! Both armed. Guns and one of them with a knife."

Sensitive as she is, Evian is already reaching for her gun on her hip—but it's already too late.

"Don't get any nearer that gun or I'll shoot!" The voice is coming from a half-crumbling block of a grave to my right. Which is to say the opposite direction of where Clothilde ran off to.

I run after the voice. Behind the grave, a man in his thirties with a shaved head is pointing a rifle at Evian's back. Once I get over the shock of the rifle, I realize I've met this man before.

It's the goon who got away from the kidnapping attempt on Clothilde's sister, Joséphine.

He's accompanied by another man with a shaved head. This one also has a gun but it's still in its holster.

There isn't much I can do up here—scaring the guy will only put Evian at risk of getting shot by accident—so I rush back to Evian. "Two guys, one with a gun pointed right at you," I report.

"They're on the phone with someone else," Clothilde supplies. "They're taking directions and there are clearly more people who could come in and back these guys up if needed."

Holding her hands away from her body to show she's not reaching for her gun, Evian mumbles so only we can hear, "I'm not sure if I've understood everything because of all the shouting and guns, but I'm getting the feeling I should give myself up?"

"Yes," I say forcefully before Clothilde can get her no out. "You're outmanned and a couple of ghosts aren't going to be enough to get you out in one piece. But we'll do what we can, of course."

Evian nods and turns to yell back at the man with the rifle— Thibault, I think his name was. "What do you want?"

"Throw your weapon and phone as far away as possible. No sudden movements." He's still behind the grave, only the tip of his rifle and the top of his head visible from where Evian is standing.

Evian does as she's asked. And since the guy didn't specify *where* she should throw them, she aims for a grouping of smaller, overgrown graves as far away as she can throw.

The guys yell out in anger and one of them runs over to search for the objects.

"Go after him and try to keep him from finding them, will you?" I ask Clothilde. I think getting her away from whatever will happen around Evian is a good idea. Clothilde doesn't work too well under threat, be it directly aimed at her or someone close to her. Besides, she might be able to keep the guy from searching efficiently. It's the kind of thing she excels at.

Clothilde doesn't look happy, but she goes after the guy. He's about to get haunted, big time.

"We're not laughing," Thibault yells.

"Next time, give more detailed instructions," Evian replies. "The goal is for me to be unable to use them—you've achieved your goal."

I'm on my way down to the lone guy Clothilde first spotted when he steps out from his hiding place. His gun is shoved into the back of his pants, a sheathed knife is strapped to his belt, and his hands are full of cloth and zip cuffs.

This isn't good.

Evian has her arms out, still showing goodwill. Her breathing has sped up and she's blinking a little too often, but all in all she hides her fear well. Calm and easy is what will get her out of this.

The man knows his business. He comes at Evian from the back, grabs both hands and ties them tightly behind her back. Evian clenches her fists when he does so, trying to gain some space to wiggle out of her constraints later, but the man knows this trick too, and forces her to relax her hands and wrists.

A blindfold is next, and a second cloth in her mouth to keep her from calling for help.

I can hear Clothilde yelling and doing a very believable impression of a crazy woman. I'll assume it means the phone and gun still haven't been found.

Finally, Thibault comes out from his hiding place. He seems to be the boss of this group, which means his escape from the kidnapping that ended with Madame Redon's son in jail must have given him a boost in notoriety.

"You'll walk where we lead you and not give us any trouble." His voice is low and menacing, his eyes burning with anger at Evian even though she can't see him anymore. "Any kind of trouble—and that includes the kind of stunt you pulled with your gun and phone right now—and I guarantee you'll die today. Slowly, and painfully. Follow my instructions and there will be no pain. Understood?"

I can't imagine the fear Evian must be feeling at the moment, yet she stands tall, her head held high. "Understood," she replies, her voice steady.

"I'm right here with you," I tell her. "We'll figure something out."

The guy searching for the phone and gun comes back, close to running and his eyes so wide I can see the whites all around. He's holding Evian's gun. "I found the gun, guys." He holds it out to Thibault.

"What about the phone?" Thibault doesn't take the gun, forcing the other man to keep ahold of it.

"Can't find it." He's close to whining. "There are a ton of weeds and vines and bugs and…" He shudders. "I dunno, man."

Clothilde, hair flowing around her head like it has a life of its own, skips over and hisses into the man's ear, causing him to shudder again, even harder. "This one's sensitive," she says with an evil cackle.

Thibault grumbles about incompetence but he doesn't send the man back to search more, which means they don't have a lot of time. Signing to the man who tied Evian up, he leads the group down a path no more than half a meter wide, and soon we emerge on a larger path, where a tiny van is parked. It has the name of the cemetery splayed across the side and a shovel and two brushes stuck into holders next to the driver's door.

Thibault walks over and opens the doors to the cargo area. "Get her in here," he says to his men. When Evian stumbles past him as she searches for footholds climbing in, he leans in and speaks, much in the same way Clothilde and I do when we want to freak someone out, "We're going to have a little chat."

TWENTY-EIGHT

EMELINE EXPECTS ONE of the men to get into the driver's seat and the engine to start. Depending on how long it takes before someone—Malik, he's the only one who knew where she was going—figures out she's missing, they could be halfway to Spain before a search begins.

But that isn't what happens. After the main goon shoves Emeline inside the small space, all three of them pile in after her, then shut the doors.

Within seconds, the air gets suffocatingly hot. Emeline can smell the sweat off one of the men, and an excessive dose of deodorant on another. Because of the blindfold, Emeline can't see a thing, she can only determine it's darker than when they were out in the sun. Some grumbling from the men seems to indicate at least one of them is using his phone to get some light in the space.

"All right, Captain," the leader says. Emeline seems to remember his name being Thibault. He was the one who got away at Joséphine's house. "We all have bottles of water to keep us going, as well as the possibility of stepping outside. You do not. The sooner you answer our questions, the sooner you can hydrate."

A quip is at the tip of Emeline's tongue, but she refrains. Unfortunately, the man has a point. She's already thirsty from her rushed trip from Madame Redon's neighborhood and this tiny van is going to turn into a furnace in no time with the midday sun bearing down on them full force.

"How many people know about your little forage into local real estate?" Thibault asks, followed by the sound of him guzzling water.

"You'll have to be more precise," Emeline says. "I have no intention of buying a place in Toulouse, if that's what you're asking. Once I've finished my current case, I'll be moving back to Paris." Yes, Emeline has no doubt Thibault has the upper hand and has a very good chance at success, but that's no reason to give up immediately.

She needs to buy time. For Malik to find Tulle, and for him to realize something has also happened to Emeline. With her phone still lost among the graves and all of them just sitting here, cooking in the cemetery heat, there's still hope of discovery.

But only if she doesn't provoke them too much. She has no doubt where this game will end up if the men get their way.

"Cute." Thibault doesn't sound like he's amused. "You had your friend Nadine Tulle look into the records of real estate purchases in one specific neighborhood over the last three decades. Why?"

Emeline's heart sinks. If he knows that much, it means they definitely have Nadine and that they've managed to make her talk.

"Is Nadine all right?" Emeline keeps her voice as hard and impersonal as her captor's.

"I'm the one asking the questions, Captain."

"And I won't answer a single one until you can prove to me Nadine Tulle is alive and well." It's a bit of a gamble, but the heat is already getting to Emeline and she's increasingly convinced they have no intention of letting her out of here alive. She needs to obtain as much information as she can as quickly as possible.

There's a grunt and a grumble. "Fine. Not like it's going to cost us anything. Marc, get her on the phone, will you? Marc! You gotta keep drinking the water, dude."

More sounds of the men shifting in the small space and the entire van rocking, making Emeline fall with her back against the inside of the van. It's scorching hot.

"Get him out of here," the leader says and a breath of "fresh" air swoops through the van when they open the door. "Nobody's poking you in the gut, idiot. Learn to follow orders and maybe you won't start hallucinating."

So the ghosts are messing with her captors. Good.

Emeline hears the sound of a phone call being connected. After the second ring, a gruff voice says, "What?"

"We need proof of life for your little prisoner," Thibault says.

The huff seems to imply whoever is on the other end doesn't think it should be necessary for the job at hand, but he complies anyway.

Some sounds of mumbling in the background. A female grunt. A highly threatening, "*Now*, lady, or I'll be giving them proof of death instead."

"I'm all right." Definitely Nadine's voice. Clear and strong, but also decidedly scared. The young woman may be a trained police officer, but she never wanted to be out in the field getting in trouble. She's at her best alone in front of her computer.

"Less than thirty minutes in a car to—" She's interrupted by a loud slap, making Emeline jump in her seat in surprise.

"You got your proof," the man on the other end growls. And hangs up.

"She's alive and well," Thibault says. "Now explain why you asked her to look into those records and who else you've put in harm's way for your thirty-year-old cold case."

Emeline got her proof of life, but at what cost? Nadine attempting to give information on where she is being held might have put her in *more* danger than before the phone call. And unfortunately, thirty minutes in a car from the City Hall makes for quite the large area.

Including this cemetery.

"You don't seem too stupid," Emeline says, squirming as sweat pours down her front between her breasts and down her back. Her hair must be clinging to her scalp by now. "You knew when to run away when the police arrested your two accomplices at the Humbert residence the first time we met. Now you've successfully lured a police captain here and captured me. You know perfectly well what Nadine was looking for, and you know she found it. Having me spell it out for you isn't going to change what happens here today in any way."

More gurgling as the two remaining men drink water, making Emeline's eyes twitch in want and envy. Luckily, with the blindfold, the men can't see it.

The man who isn't Thibault, who is sitting on Emeline's left, keeps shifting around on his seat. It *could* be the heat. But in case it isn't…

"Somebody poking at *your* belly now? Or maybe some other spot? A poke in the eye must feel really uncomfortable, don't you think?"

Robert and Clothilde follow along to perfection. The man yelps and jumps across the van—at least that's what it feels like to Emeline—and opens the door.

Another blessed rush of fresh air.

"Hey! What do you think you're doing? It's not *that* warm in here! A couple of idiots letting your imagination get away with you. You make sure we're not bothered while I finish up here, all right? Think you can manage that? That means *not* brandishing your weapons in a cemetery, Marc!" With a couple of expletives, he pulls the door shut and it feels like all the air of the small van lands on Emeline's shoulders immediately.

She's so thirsty and hot, she's starting to feel incoherent. She's trying to remember what she can say to the man without jeopardizing anyone or the case, and what she must keep secret. But it's so difficult when her captor keeps drinking water and making sure she hears it.

Just *one* mouthful of cold water would be enough to—

"So we agree your colleague was looking for the group buying up that part of the city. She doesn't seem to know exactly why, but she did recognize most of the names on the list. She's been living here for awhile, after all."

It feels like he gave something away in what he just said, but it's so hard to concentrate. Remembering the two ghosts are still with her—and there's no reason they would be affected by the heat—she lets them remember and analyze. Emeline is going to have to focus on her own survival. And that of Nadine.

"But she couldn't give any other names than yours. She seemed to think her friend Malik Doubira was *not* in on it for some reason.

Now, if I can get rid of just two police officers instead of three, that would suit me just fine. You lot are a load of trouble to get out of the way in a manner that doesn't draw attention."

"You have enough experience with it," Emeline says without thinking. "You got rid of Robert Villemur when Clothilde died."

There's a sniff that might have been a laugh, followed by torturous guzzling. He seems perfectly calm, which means that either Clothilde and Robert have decided not to bother him, or he's completely impervious to ghostly interventions.

"That would have been way before my time, Captain. Tell me why your partner isn't part of this investigation and he'll be spared. Make it convincing. I'm of the kind to err on the side of caution but am not interested in killing for the pleasure of killing."

At least it's clear he's not planning on letting Emeline go. In a way, it's freeing. If she isn't able to foil his plan, she will die. Which means she can take more risks in trying to get free.

If she could only get some water.

Focus on Malik, Emeline. It might come from the ghosts, it might be her own mind pushing through the fog in her brain. In either case, it's true. She has a chance to make sure Malik isn't pulled into this unnecessarily, and she's going to take it.

"Malik hasn't worked with me since the day of your foiled kidnapping attempt on Joséphine Pradel. Some old history came back to haunt him, and he's been on paid leave for almost a month while working through it. He's only been back on the job for a few days, and he's not working with me on this case. He's on a completely different ghost."

More gurgling but no reply from her captor.

"A completely different *case*," Emeline corrects, trying to clear her throat only to feel even more thirsty. "Could I have some water, please?"

"Who could corroborate what you say?"

"My boss, Commander Diome."

A true laugh this time. "Yeah, sorry, I'm not going to call the commander."

Emeline shifts in her seat, rolling her shoulders in an attempt to loosen some of her muscles straining from having her hands tied behind her back. She's sweating so hard now, even her pants are completely soaked.

"You could call the morgue." The idea must have come from one of the ghosts. Emeline is beyond thinking. Which might make her even more receptive than normal to repeat what her friends are saying to her from the other side of the veil. "Malik has been working on the case of a dead body discovered in an old apartment and has spent a lot of time with the person responsible for the autopsy at the morgue. He wouldn't be there if he was working with me on my case."

The last words are little more than a croak. Emeline is seeing lights move across her eyes and they're not from an outside source. She's minutes from collapsing. Her focus is only on Malik, on doing her best to protect him.

"All right." Thibault gurgles even more water, then crumples the empty bottle, eliciting a small moan from Emeline. "I'll check out your story. Not because I owe you anything, but because having a third body in the mix would mess with my carefully laid plans."

The door opens, the van shifts as Thibault steps outside, and a little bit of cool air reaches Emeline's face.

Then the door closes again, and she's alone in the dark. Thirsty, scared, tied up.

And trapped.

TWENTY-NINE

Evian crumbles to the van's floor less than thirty seconds after Thibault leaves. I'd have loved to go after him, but I'm stuck where Evian is, inside this van.

It's almost completely dark in here now. The only light comes from a narrow crack between the van's back doors, but it's enough for us to see an outline of Evian's form, and to confirm her chest is heaving softly with each breath. She's soaked through with sweat and I'm very, very worried about her.

I hope Thibault's plan is something close to what we've guessed—meaning he wants to set Tulle up for the murder of the police captain—because it means he needs her to stay alive for a bit longer.

Survive the next fifteen minutes to have another chance at thwarting the attempted murder.

Clothilde has settled down on the floor by Evian's head and is singing the same lullaby as when Evian had her panic attack during Hélori's funeral. She's stroking Evian's hair and keeping an eye on our friend's breath.

There isn't much we can do except wait.

Fortunately, Thibault doesn't take long. When he whips the back doors open less than ten minutes later, it's like I can feel the coolness of the air pouring in, allowing me to breathe a little easier. Except I don't need to breathe, of course.

"Oh good, I won't have to knock you out," Thibault says without inflection. "You'll be happy to know your story checked out and I'll be leaving your partner alone. At least for now." Pulling Evian unceremoniously toward the door by the foot, letting the side of her face drag against the van's floor, he removes Evian's handcuffs before getting help from one of his colleagues to hold Evian's sagging body between them.

Clothilde and I leave them be for the moment, not wanting them to drop her to the ground by accident. And in any case, Thibault is practically immune to our interventions.

While Clothilde stays close to Evian to keep her company, I try to move as far away as possible, searching for help. It still gets *very* uncomfortable when I'm about fifty meters away from the bracelet on Evian's wrist, but I push outward as far as I can take, hoping to encounter someone who can help.

I can't find a soul.

I don't know if it's because it's mid-afternoon on a weekday and the sun is murderously hot, or if Thibault and his men have somehow found a way to clear out the entire cemetery, but the only movement I see is from ghosts. And not the helpful kind.

I'd have loved to run into Hélori, but he'll be busy overseeing his own exhumation—if he has been let out of the casket by now, that is. I don't hear his screams, so I assume he's free.

Thibault and one of his men carry Evian between them along one of the narrower paths going uphill while the third one trails a few meters behind with his gun in his hand. The tall tombs, mausoleums, and trees hide them from view in most directions.

Once they reach the northern corner of the cemetery, they choose a path parallel to the crest of the hill, passing in front of an enormous tomb with roman columns the size of a small house and the statue of a grieving angel. I'm curious enough to go over and have a look—the guy apparently invented something to do with hydroelectric plants—then I continue my forage left and right, looking for help.

I even find it. Sort of.

While Thibault is keeping to the smaller paths, I can move to the larger avenues, and this allows me to see about one hundred meters ahead of me.

Coming through one of the small gates in the east wall, Doubira strides across the main path, his nose in his phone, and quickly disappears out of sight. Wasn't he supposed to be looking for Tulle? Does he think it will help his career to drop in on the officers in charge of exhuming Hélori?

I try yelling after him and push as close to him as I can get, but it doesn't work. Doubira isn't sensitive enough to hear me from this far off, and I simply cannot move more than sixty meters away from the bracelet. It doesn't hurt, exactly, but I'm fairly certain I'd disintegrate if I push any farther. It feels like my very soul is cracking.

Thibault stops in front of a large family tomb with the name George inscribed across the top. While the guy with the gun continues on down the path, the two others pull Evian inside the tomb. It's set up like a tiny chapel, with plaques on the walls listing the names of everyone buried there, two tiny windows with iron bars allowing some light to enter, and two stone benches running along each wall. They drop Evian on the right-hand bench, then sit down to wait on the left-hand one, their eyes on their phones.

"What do you think they're waiting for?" Clothilde asks. She has squeezed into the corner so she can continue patting Evian's head. I'm not sure it's only for Evian's benefit at this point.

"Someone to leave or someone to arrive," I guess. "I'll keep a lookout."

Since the tomb doesn't have a door, we're not stuck in here with Evian. I wander outside and find the guy crouching behind a smallish grave a short way down the path. He has shoved his gun into the back of his pants and is stretching his neck to look at something going on downhill from where we're standing.

I suddenly recognize the location. And sure enough, we're looking at Hélori's casket being loaded into a hearse under the supervision of Walter and no fewer than three police officers, neither of which I recognize. The grave is an open maw—a view that brings back many memories from my time in our old cemetery. It usually meant we'd have a new arrival shortly.

I don't see Doubira, so he either didn't find them or he had other business here. Maybe he was looking for Constantine's husband's grave and didn't know there are two large cemeteries on this hill?

I can't spend much time mulling over Doubira because all those people leaving was what my guy was waiting for. When the last officer disappears from view on foot and the hearse has left the premises, he takes off running to give the information to Thibault.

Five minutes later, we're all standing at the foot of Hélori's open grave, Evian's head dangling as she is held up between Thibault and his goon. Clothilde is staying close, but I can tell she's getting agitated. Her hair is moving as if there's a wind—even if there were one, it wouldn't affect us ghosts.

"Why are we here, Robert? I don't like this."

"Neither do I." I try to sound as calming and as confident as possible. Having a stressed-out Clothilde isn't going to help Evian get out of this situation.

"He sent off a text to someone named Kevin before we left the tomb back there. It just said, 'Go.'"

I'm about to tell her we're waiting for this Kevin person when I hear the putting of an engine behind me. Turning, I see another of the cemetery vans coming up the path. I'd love to know how they've managed to steal at least two of the vehicles without getting caught. Adding in the fact that there's nobody else around, I think they must have at least one of the cemetery employees on their side. As part of the team or simply bought off to turn a blind eye.

It pulls to a stop in front of Evian. Thibault nods in greeting to the man at the wheel before making his way to the back. The man I'm going to assume is called Kevin follows and opens the doors.

"Why is there a casket in there?" Clothilde asks, her voice shaking with fear.

We both know why there's a casket, but I'm not going to say it out loud.

When I spot the unmoving body lying in the corner, I stop pretending to breathe. Nadine Tulle. I rush in to check if she's alive.

She's breathing. If the lump on her temple is anything to go by, she was knocked unconscious, but I don't see any other wounds.

The casket is as basic as they come, probably close to the one I was buried in. No fancy paint or decorations, only a brown wooden box in the right shape and size and with handles on the side for it to be carried.

Honestly, I'm not sure why they bother with the box at all. Why not just throw her in the gaping hole and be done with it?

I'm not going to complain, though. Anything buying Evian time and the opportunity to survive is okay with me.

And my question is partially answered when Thibault grabs Tulle's hand and uses it to place her fingerprints at strategic locations on the casket. I notice all four men have put on plastic gloves.

They're going to frame Tulle for Evian's death.

Clothilde lets go of all pretense of control. She starts screaming at the men manhandling Evian so she'll fit into the casket, going from one to the other like an otherworldly whirlwind, screaming, hitting, spinning…anything she can think of.

While Thibault stays immune to her interventions, the others can feel Clothilde. They change positions to move away from her, keep throwing worried glances over their shoulders, and fumble Evian's body, making her fall to the ground with a sickening thump.

I wince at the lump Evian is going to have on her forehead in addition to the scrapes from earlier, but it's a small price to pay if it can save her life.

I alternate between helping Clothilde and running as far away as possible, searching for someone—anyone—who can help, yelling at the top of my lungs for Doubira.

There's nobody but us.

Finally, they get Evian inside the casket. It's a little big for her, there's at least a foot of space over her head. I see her chest heaving slowly and her eyes moving beneath her eyelids but no amount of yelling or pleading wakes her up.

When they bring the lid, Clothilde loses all semblance of human shape. She focuses all her efforts on the one named Kevin because he seems to be the most sensitive. He ends up stepping away, holding his head—but that doesn't stop the others from dropping the lid in place and bringing out nails and hammers.

Clothilde disappears.

What—?

Her screaming resumes. From inside the casket.

She was pulled in when Evian—with the bracelets—was locked in the closed space. Wherever the finger bone is, the ghost is.

So why am I still on the outside?

THIRTY

I don't know if the zip cuffs weakened the homemade bracelet or if it got torn when they were manhandling Evian's body into the casket, but it's no longer on her wrist. It's lying between two cobblestones by the cemetery van's back tire, only one end of the blue string easily visible for passersby.

Worry about what this means for me simmers at the back of my mind, but I can't focus on it right now. They're going to bury Evian alive in Hélori's grave, and Clothilde is stuck in there with her. Tulle doesn't have long before it's her turn either.

I'm not even sure which of the two in the casket I'm the most worried about. Evian is still alive, and I *really* need her to stay that way, but at least, if she becomes a ghost, she'll be let out of the casket eventually.

Clothilde is stuck wherever that bracelet is.

Will she be let out of the casket to roam the cemetery once Evian dies?

I can't let myself think down those lines. If we do end up on that scenario, I'll figure out how to deal with it when it happens. My priority has to be *avoiding* the scenario.

First, I try stopping them from lowering the casket into the ground. I keep screaming at the top of my lungs, hoping it will bother Thibault and his men, or draw the attention of ghost-sensitive visitors, but my only result is a middle-aged ghost woman settling in on a grave three plots down, dispassionately watching the show.

When they get the casket to the open grave and use ropes to lower it to the bottom, I try to communicate with Clothilde but she's past listening. Her screams are worse than anything I heard in thirty years of funerals. The men grab a shovel each and drop enough of the dug-up dirt lying next to the grave to cover up the casket so casual passersby won't see it.

All the equipment goes back into the van with the still-unconscious Tulle and I'm flitting back and forth between the men and my friends in the grave, not managing to stop the former or calm the latter. Kevin takes the wheel and Thibault gets into the passenger seat while tapping away at this phone, while the two others take off on foot, I assume toward the van we abandoned earlier.

And I'm all alone.

In a cemetery I'm not familiar with, limited to a fifty-or-so-meter radius around the bracelet wedged between two cobblestones, one friend dying in a casket nobody knows about, a second buried and stuck in a casket for the second time in her life, and a third unconscious and in the hands of men meaning her great harm.

I have no idea what to do.

When I've stood there for several minutes, not moving and my heart breaking anew each time Clothilde screams, the woman ghost from earlier comes strolling toward me, moving straight through the tombs.

"They buried a ghost," she says with her head cocked as she glances curiously into the half-filled grave.

"That's my friend." My voice breaks and I'm irrationally furious that my body doesn't reflect my stress. No furiously beating heart, no tears forming, no shaking hands. Is this really all I can do for my friends? "I need to get her out of there. Her and the woman they buried alive."

Elegant eyebrows shoot up. "Alive. Well. That's new." Her clothing seems to indicate she might have died around the same time as me, maybe a little later. Her hair is in a neat bob around her head, and I think she's wearing makeup.

"I need to find someone to help them," I plead with her. "I'm stuck here, much like my friend. Can you see if you can find someone alive in the cemetery and try to get them to come here?"

Her non-blinking dark-eyed stare is unnerving. This woman hasn't tried to appear alive in a while. "The dead cannot touch the living."

I don't have the time to get into metaphysical discussions with this woman, so I get straight to the point. "If you speak to them, their subconscious can hear it. If you touch them, some will feel it, like a fly touching down on their skin. If you've been here a while, I'm sure you know this. Will you help me, please? Can you make a quick circuit through the cemetery and see if anyone other than the men who were just here can be convinced to come?"

"They've closed the main entrance," she says without inflection. "Claiming there's an incident with a water pipe."

That would explain why I haven't seen a single visitor since we came here. Except…

"A man came in through one of the back gates not long ago. Tall, brown-skinned, dark hair, wearing a police uniform." I'm speaking faster and faster, clinging to this new sliver of hope. "Can you please see if you can find him? He might still be here. Mention the name Emeline Evian. It's the woman in the casket and a close friend of his."

The woman studies me silently while I ramble on, her head cocked to the side. She lets the following silence stretch for unbearable seconds until she finally gives a slight nod.

"I admire your dedication to your friends. I will see if I can find this man and try to get him here."

"Thank you." Relief lifts some of the weight bearing down on my chest and my feet actually lift off the ground. I'm losing all control and I don't even care.

While the woman is gone, I return to the grave. In some spots I can see the wood of the casket through the dirt. Evian and Clothilde aren't buried deep.

I've never been more frustrated at not having a body.

Clothilde's screams are calming down somewhat. I hope it means she'll be able to hear me.

"Clothilde?" I try shoving my head through the casket's lid, but it's impossible. We tried this a couple of times in our old cemetery and never managed, but it was worth a try. Whatever keeps a soul inside the casket until it's ready to come out also keeps others out. So I settle for being as close as possible and hope the sound travels both ways.

"I'm doing my best to find help," I tell my friend. "I've got another ghost looking for Doubira and I'll be on the lookout for visitors coming close enough for me to talk to them. Can you hear me, Clothilde?"

A scream is her first response. Then followed by a sullen, "Yes. I hear you. Why aren't you in here too?"

"My bracelet fell off out here. How is Evian?"

A sigh. "Alive. But her breathing's really shallow. Do you think air can get into this thing? At least I think it's cooler than out there in the sun."

I try to remember what the casket looked like before it was covered in dirt. "It seemed like it had been put together quickly and not by a pro. They just needed a box to hold her for a day or two. So there's a good chance *some* air can come through cracks and stuff."

"Then why can't I come *out* through any cracks." It's not a question and Clothilde's fear and frustration are clear. "I want *out*!"

"And I'm going to get you out, Clothilde. But I need you to focus on Evian right now, okay? You have to help her stay calm in there. If she panics, she'll use more oxygen and we'll have less time to find help."

"She doesn't like small spaces," Clothilde says.

"I know." I run a hand down my face. I don't envy Clothilde's job when or if Evian wakes up. "It might be better if she stays unconscious."

"Nothing we can do about that." Clothilde seems to have put her own fears aside to focus on Evian. She should have her physical form under control if her no-nonsense tone is anything to go by. "I'll do my best to keep her calm. You work from out there."

"Will do," I promise her.

Climbing out of that grave is one of the most difficult things I've ever done.

Fortunately, I spot movement almost immediately.

It's Doubira.

The ghost woman is flitting around him, speaking into one ear then the other, shoving him in the direction she wants him to go. Her expression is as neutral as earlier, but her tone seems encouraging.

"That's it," I hear her say when they come close to my fifty-meter limit. "Your friend Emeline is that way. She needs your help."

Doubira, poor guy, looks like he's had the fright of his life. His eyes are wide and darting left and right, his skin is almost gray, and his steps are those of a drunken man—one straight, the next staggering to the left, the next two correcting toward the right.

"That's right, Malik," I tell him. "You're on the right track. We desperately need your help. Emeline is in danger."

We continue speaking to him and pushing at him until he stands in front of the open grave.

The ghost woman steps away, settling in to watch from the neighboring tomb. She has done what she promised and now she'll go back to being a spectator. I give her a nod of thanks.

Once the barrage of otherworldly influences has stopped, Doubira takes a deep breath. Closes his eyes. "What the hell just happened?"

I do believe he's getting more sensitive to ghosts, which is all kinds of interesting.

"Look in the grave," I tell him. "It's not as empty as it seems."

But Doubira still isn't *as* sensitive as Evian. He opens his eyes but doesn't look into the hole in the ground. His gaze is caught by something else—the bracelet.

"Hey, that's Emeline's." He bends down to pick it up and

my little finger tingles as he rolls it between his fingers. "Does this mean one of you was the one to pull me over here? Emeline dropped you and you need me to get you back to her?"

"I'm thrilled you found the bracelet," I say. "But you need to look into the open grave over there. Emeline is buried alive! You can see—"

"That's cute and all," Doubira growls. "But I was in the middle of something important when you tricked me to come over here." He shoves the bracelet into the front pocket of his pants. "Nadine is in trouble and I've traced her phone to somewhere in this cemetery. No offense or anything, but you guys are already dead. I need to prioritize the living."

I'm torn. I *am* prioritizing the living—Evian. But Tulle is also definitely in danger. Thibault said he'd kill both women. It seems probable he's going to frame her for Evian's demise. If her phone is still in the cemetery…

"Go find Tulle," I tell him. "Let's save her first, then we'll come back for Evian and Clothilde."

Doubira is already moving. I rush into the grave before he hits those fifty meters. "Clothilde," I croak out. "I'm going with Doubira to find Tulle. Then we're coming back. I promise!"

I don't have the time to hear Clothilde's response. I'm pulled after Doubira.

THIRTY-ONE

N̲o̲t̲ ̲a̲g̲a̲i̲n̲.

Emeline keeps her eyes closed when she comes to, wishing that if she cannot confirm where she is, it isn't really happening. Denial isn't usually her thing, but desperate times call for desperate measures.

The situation is definitely desperate. She can feel the rough wood under her with her hands. The walls on each side. The smell of earth and sweat. The echo of her labored breathing.

Such a small space.

No air.

As memories assail her, Emeline's throat spasms as she fights for air. Her hands curl into fists and start pounding on the wood above her.

So dark. Can't breathe.

Fingers bloody from scratching at the wood.

The cold. The fear.

Except it's warm. Very warm, in fact. She remembers the heat of the van and the sound of her captor gurgling water.

Forces herself to stop pounding. Realizes she's been screaming herself hoarse. Stops.

She fights the panic. If she wants to survive, she can't let the rising emotions win. So she focuses on the things that are different from the last time she fought death from inside a box.

It's warm, not cold. Her hand on the coarse wood above her face confirms it. There's still air, at least for the time being. Her fingers haven't been scratching at the wood—yet.

She measures out her breaths, counting under her breath. When she forces herself to count slower, she realizes the thought didn't come from her.

The ghosts.

"You guys in here with me?" she whispers. Somehow, that makes her feel a little better. Even if she is to die today, she won't be alone.

She touches her wrist—and finds only one bracelet. "Where's the other one?"

A calming presence. No point in worrying about the other bracelet. She needs to focus on her own well-being.

"Guess it's just you and me then, Clothilde. I'm sorry you're stuck in here with me." A focus on someone other than herself helps.

She needs to take tally of the situation. She survived once before. She can do it again. But only if she stays calm.

She opens her eyes.

Darkness. Her entire body tenses again, remembering how hard she fought the last time, and how little it helped.

The darkness isn't absolute. There's a sense of light on her left, just above her left eyebrow. Once she starts focusing on it, she can make out a hair-thin crack between two planks, and what she hopes is sunlight behind it.

Right. She was in a cemetery. She's in a box that is definitely shaped like a casket. And the smell of dirt gets stronger the more she focuses on it. It mixes with the smell of her own sweat and terror.

She's been buried alive. Again.

Her throat constricts. When she tries to curl in on herself, her head hits the top of the casket with an empty *thunk*.

There's room for her to pull her legs up to her chest, though. Focus on that.

"Thank you, Clothilde."

Why didn't she deal with her claustrophobia? Keeping away from elevators and small spaces wasn't dealing with the issue, it was putting her head in the sand. How could she judge Malik for not being over all his issues when hers were still so decidedly fresh and active? Stupid of her to think Malik's issues were more of a problem because they involved guns.

Clearly, suffocating to death in a box is just as common a cause of death for police officers as being shot.

Still, how can this be happening *again*?

A calming song permeates her mind, and she feels a slight pressure against her scalp, like the memory of someone brushing through her hair.

Clothilde.

She lets the lullaby soothe her for awhile, using the calm rhythm to slow her breath and focus on her heartbeat. Still beating. Still alive. Sunlight above her somewhere. Just a couple of planks and some dirt between her and freedom. She places the palm of one hand on the spot closest to the light, using it to give herself hope.

When this happened eighteen months ago, she was saved at the last minute by her partner. This time, she has no partner. In fact, nobody even knows she's missing. Her phone is lost—but in the same cemetery, so that might be a point in the plus column.

She's starting to make out the notes of Clothilde's lullaby. It starts each stanza quite low, only to go high and pure toward the end. She can even make out a few words. A thousand stars to guide you.

The outline of a hand passes in front of her eyes.

Another ghostly caress through her hair.

Two beats, the song continues. And the hand comes back. Attached to an arm.

"Clothilde," Evian whispers. "I can see your hand."

This cannot be a good sign. Is she becoming a ghost herself? Was she deluding herself into thinking she could survive this? Was it all a fevered dream and her body is finally letting go?

Afraid of what she'll find but unable not to do it, Emeline turns her head to follow the line of the blouse-covered transparent arm with her gaze.

She looks into Clothilde's wide eyes.

"This can't be good." Emeline blinks several times, hoping the apparition of the young woman will disappear. She has seen plenty of pictures of Clothilde Humbert. This *could* be a hallucination.

But the ghost stays put, meeting her eyes and giving a tentative smile. Only the top of her torso is visible, the rest seems to disappear into the ground.

"Where is the rest of you?" Emeline asks. "Can you leave the casket?" Was she staying here only to keep Emeline company?

Clothilde shakes her head. "Don't have a body," she seems to say—it's a world easier to interpret the thoughts intruding on her subconscious when she can see the young woman's lips move—"Stuck here with you."

"I'm sorry."

Clothilde shrugs and Emeline marvels at the fact she can see the ghost. She doesn't need light to be visible. With the rest of the world around her being perfectly black, Clothilde is like an apparition in the darkness, a beacon of hope.

Clothilde points upward. "How about we get out of here?"

"Sounds like a great plan," Emeline mumbles. "But I'm afraid I didn't bring any of my tools. A jigsaw, for example, would have been nice."

Clothilde grins.

It seems being close to death makes it easier to communicate with ghosts. It might explain why Emeline is so much more sensitive than for example Amina. Emeline has been close to death herself, whereas her lovely neighbor has lived a blessedly normal life.

This doesn't bode well for her current situation, of course. But somehow, it calms her nerves. She's as good as dead anyway—what does she have to lose? She has wonderful company and a guide to the other side should she need it.

The weird thing here, though, is that Emeline has done some research on how to escape being buried alive. Going to see a therapist wasn't necessary but Googling how to get yourself out of a grave seemed like a perfectly normal pastime.

She needs to use her legs because they're the strongest. And when the dirt comes down, she needs to move it down underneath her body, thereby digging herself upward little by little.

BENEATH THE SURFACE

Then there's always the detail of breathing under a mound of dirt, but she's going to keep that problem for when she comes to it—meaning after she breaks through the wood.

Emeline pulls her legs up against her chest and places her feet as best she can on the underside of the casket lid.

And she starts kicking.

THIRTY-TWO

Doubira is using a map on his phone to guide him through the cemetery. There's a red blinking dot that I assume represents Tulle's location. It's jumping a bit back and forth, as if the signal isn't perfectly clear on where it should be sending us, but it's also moving slowly downslope, toward the north-western corner. If my memory serves, it's the general area we were in when Thibault questioned Evian in the cemetery van.

I run ahead as far and as often as I can, trying to function as a lookout for Doubira. Since it's far from certain he'll hear or heed me if I try to tell him anything, it's probably futile but I can't just tag along and wring my hands while my friends are fighting for their lives. If I can give Doubira one extra second or hint of what to expect, maybe I can help him save Tulle. The sooner we save Tulle, the sooner we can go back to Evian and Clothilde.

And I need for Doubira to stay free and safe too. He's the only one not currently in mortal danger and he needs to stay that way.

I've noticed he's wearing his gun, shoved into the back of his pants as usual. And no Tazer in sight. I hope this means his therapy is working and that he's ready to use the gun if needed.

Hidden behind a large cedar tree in a bend of the path, I spot a cemetery van. There's no way to tell if it's the one that held Evian, the one with Tulle, or a third one. They all look the same. Still, there can't be that many of them—this cemetery is huge but no bigger than a large parking lot.

I rush back to Doubira to tell him where to go, but as I reach him, his phone pings with a message.

"It's from Nadine." Doubira stops and taps on the message, a large frown appearing on his forehead. "What the—"

I lean in to read over his shoulder.

Malik, I'm so sorry for what I did to Captain Evian. It was an accident, I swear. I hope you can forgive me some day. I can't forgive myself, though, and I don't know what I would become without my job. So this is my goodbye. Take care of yourself and move on. Don't put yourself in danger like the captain did. Nadine.

"What did she do to Evian?" Doubira's eyes are wide and he's clutching his phone so hard I'm worried he'll break it. "What the *hell* did she do?"

"She didn't do anything!" I yell straight into his ear. Partly in the hope he'll hear me better and partly because I'm scared shitless of what he'll do if he believes that message is really from Tulle.

"Evian sent you to look for Tulle, remember? It's because she's in danger, not because she's one of the bad guys."

"Oh my God, she's one of the bad guys."

Lesson learned: negations don't come through very well with non-sensitive people.

"Tulle is in danger," I insist, holding the despair at bay. "They're setting her up to take the fall for Evian's death—but *she isn't dead yet*!"

Doubira isn't listening anymore. At all. His cheeks are flushed with anger and he's grinding his teeth together so hard I can hear it from where I'm standing—which is, admittedly, pretty close since he can't see me and worry about me being in his personal space.

"What did Emeline ever do to her?" Doubira fumes to himself as he taps on his phone to come back to the map with the blinking red dot. "She asked her for help and didn't even take credit for it like so many officers would do in a similar situation. What did you *do*, Nadine?"

Stalking off toward the blinking dot, he tries to call Tulle. Nobody answers, of course.

Since he's still looking for Tulle, I decide not to try any more interventions at the moment. It doesn't really matter if he believes Tulle is on his side or not, as long as he keeps searching for her. Since the van is out of reach for me, I fan out, like earlier, hoping against hope I'll find something useful. Something that might help Doubira prepare for whatever is waiting for him in that van.

Miraculously, I do find something.

While running between two crumbling tombs that are mostly hidden from view because they're a lot more modest than the larger ones in the prime spots along the paths, I hear a strange buzzing. It comes in bursts, like someone pressing an intercom rather angrily, leaving only second-long pauses between each ring.

Intercoms being rather rare in cemeteries, I stop and try

to locate where the sound is coming from. It stops for twenty seconds, then starts up again.

It's coming from the overgrown narrow space between the two tombs. Reminding myself my body isn't corporeal, I shove my head through the brush, and partially through stone, to find, wedged between a rock and an empty beer bottle, a phone.

Evian's phone.

No wonder the goon from earlier couldn't find it.

According to the screen, Doubira is trying to call Evian. I try swiping my finger across the screen like I've seen Evian do so many times. Sometimes ghosts can influence the world of the living in tiny ways. I once managed to write in a layer of dust, and Clothilde moved the lock of a door a millimeter or two not so long ago. Touching a screen should be within my reach.

But it isn't. For one, I'm not as good at this as Clothilde, and two, I think moving things is easier than influencing something that needs touch.

When the phone stops ringing, I give up and rush back to find Doubira.

According to the map on his phone, he's standing on top of the blinking dot representing Tulle's position. I guess it means the phone is in the van hidden behind the next bend, with whoever sent that message in Tulle's name.

Even though Tulle certainly wasn't the one to send the message, I hope she's in the van too. Saving her phone won't get us anywhere.

Doubira seems frustrated. He's in the spot indicated by the tracker, but he doesn't see anything of note.

"I can help you a little," I tell him. "But you have to be open to actually listening to me. I can guide you toward what I think is Tulle's location, or I can give you proof your friend Evian is also in trouble." Saying it like that doesn't make the second option sound very appealing, but it would help Doubira get a better picture of what is going on, meaning he'd be more on his guard, and it would bring me a step closer to saving Evian and Clothilde. Evian's time is running out and Doubira doesn't even know it.

Doubira tries calling Evian again. "Why isn't she answering? I know she isn't very high-tech, but she usually has the phone with her. I spoke to her an hour ago!"

"Her phone was dropped behind two tombs back there when she was attacked earlier. I can show you, if you want?"

The ringtone continues while Doubira paces in place. He pulls my bracelet out of his pocket, making my finger tingle. He rubs it between his fingers, his breath speeding up.

"I guess you're still here if I have the bracelet," he grumbles. "And now I'm talking to ghosts. Not sure if it's better than a fear of guns."

"Can't really argue with you there," I say. "But being in a position to know ghosts are real, I'm rather partial to the first option. Evian's phone is at two o'clock, between two decrepit tombs. If you keep calling her, you should be able to hear the vibrations when you get close enough."

Staring at the bracelet, Doubira grinds his teeth together. "How do I know I'm not feeling a tug because I want to feel it? How do I explain to Commander Diome that I started wandering aimlessly through the cemetery when I was supposed to be looking for Nadine?"

"Did Diome really send you here? The way you explained it, I was under the impression you were here because you care, not because your boss ordered you to."

"Come to think of it," Doubira says with a slight frown, "Diome doesn't know I'm here. So I won't need to explain every little detour. Why am I taking a detour?" The question is addressed to me.

"Evian is in trouble and that's where her phone is," I say. "Come, follow my voice. Don't think, just go wherever your feet want to take you."

I stay ahead of him and keep talking, encouraging him to follow. Surprisingly, he does. He might not have been in the best state of mind lately, because of his reaction to accidentally killing an old man in the line of duty, but he still has a healthy respect for Evian. He didn't really question her when she told him about communicating with ghosts. Didn't quite believe her either but was at least open to the possibility.

Step after step, he moves toward the phone. I walk in a straight line, right through tombs and mausoleums, so that the direction he's drawn in is always the same. He makes his way around or over the obstacles, frequently looking around, checking if anyone sees him.

Nobody does, of course. The bad guys have managed to empty the cemetery.

"Try calling her phone again," I say when I'm standing right above the location of Evian's phone. "You'll hear the vibrations."

Standing at the foot of one of the two tombs, Doubira frowns, a faraway look on his face. "No more pull." He holds up his phone. "I should try calling her again. That thought didn't come from me, did it?" With a sigh, he places a call to Evian's number.

"Don't hold your phone to your ear," I tell him. "You won't be able to hear the vibrations of Evian's phone over the sounds coming from yours."

Doubira lowers the phone and holds it by his thigh.

The vibrations start up again between the tombs.

"It's hidden beneath the weeds," I say.

Doubira hears it. Doesn't take him long to identify the source, and only a minute or two to extract the phone without cutting up his own arm.

"Why is Emeline's phone lying here?" Doubira's gaze whips from left to right, searching for something. I'm not sure if he's looking for me, Evian, or the bad guys.

"She was attacked and is in trouble." I talk loudly and enunciate as best I can. "She needs your help, and you need to call this in to the station."

"I should call this in to the station." Doubira brings up Diome's number on his phone and places the call.

THIRTY-THREE

WE'RE BACK AT the spot where Doubira's map indicates Tulle's phone to be.

"I can guide you to the van where her phone is," I tell him. "But you need to be careful because there are at least three guys there, and Tulle is most likely unconscious, so she won't be able to help." I move along the path to the spot where I saw the van earlier. It's still there. "Come this way, you'll be able to—"

The van starts up and drives in the opposite direction of where Doubira is standing.

"They're moving! We have to follow them!" I rush to Doubira's side and force my voice down. I don't want to spook him. "Can you hear the engine, Doubira? You need to follow it."

He cocks his head—he does hear it.

"You have to follow the van," I plead with him. "That's where the bad guys are."

Frowning, Doubira glances down at his phone. The red dot is moving.

He takes off running.

I stay ahead of him, as far as I can go without losing touch with myself, guiding him toward the moving van. From time to time, I catch a glimpse of it, sometimes I can hear it. At one point I think it must have hit a tree root, the squeaking of worn shock absorbers followed by the scraping of something metallic against stone breaking the heavy silence of the cemetery.

Doubira follows. No hesitation, always choosing the right path to keep up. He's guided by his phone, by me, by the sounds. He's as focused as I've ever seen him, and it gives me hope that we might have a not completely catastrophic outcome today.

Suddenly, I know where they're going. This cemetery is huge, sure, but there's still a limited number of spots that could be of interest to this gang. If they were going to hide a body, the number of potential locations would be limitless, but they're looking to hide two murders as something else, linking the two.

"They're going to Hélori Xavier's grave," I say to Doubira as he jumps over a modest grave during a shortcut between two paths. "You can aim a little more to your right. The van has to go around on the main paths, but you can take shortcuts."

Miraculously, Doubira listens.

I don't think he's even conscious of what he's doing anymore. He's focused on running, and on not tripping over headstones or crosses. He follows my instructions perfectly.

Until we find ourselves by the large cypress tree that Evian used for cover during Hélori's funeral. Doubira grinds to a halt, eyes wide with confusion since he doesn't realize he stopped on my instruction. The man's in good shape but he still needs to catch his breath and rests his hands on his knees as he looks around.

It doesn't take long for the van to come into view. It's actually coming from the opposite direction, proving they had to stay on the main paths to navigate the cemetery. They had to move in a half circle where Doubira could go straight.

This is where I'm supposed to give some instruction to Doubira, but I actually don't know what to tell him. Well, except, "They outnumber you, and have your friends. You should stay hidden until you get a better overview of the situation."

The instruction wasn't necessary. Doubira is already kneeling between two roots and his phone is pointed at the scene below, filming everything.

"Good idea," I tell him.

Thibault and one of his goons exit the front of the van. A third jumps out of the back.

Doubira swears under his breath. Checks the map on his phone. The red dot has moved with the van, meaning Tulle's phone is with one of the men.

We can't see into the van from where we're hiding—I've opted to stay with Doubira for the moment, in case I need to talk to him—but all three men gather at the back, and two minutes later, they emerge with Tulle draped over Thibault's shoulders. Her body is limp, her long braid dangling down to below her captor's ass.

"She didn't send that message." I'm pretty sure Doubira can come to this conclusion by himself, but I'm not taking any chances. We're one and a fraction against three—we're going to need all the advantages we can get. "She's being set up to take the blame for Evian's death."

"Why here?" Doubira whispers. "Is that a random open grave and they're planning on throwing her in, or does it have some significance?" He chews on his lip as his sharp gaze follows the men as they line up at the foot of Hélori's grave. "Nadine mentioned she'd helped Emeline on some open case, a guy they thought was linked to de Villenouvelle's victims. Is this his grave? Did they exhume him?"

"Yes, that's exactly right." From Doubira's slight nod, I think he has figured out how to open up to listening to me.

"Emeline's phone was in this cemetery, but I haven't seen her. That wasn't a spot where you accidentally drop your phone. Nadine sent a message apologizing for harming Emeline, except from what I'm seeing down there, she wasn't the one to compose the message. She's being set up. So *where is Emeline?*"

"She was buried alive in that grave down there. Remember where you found the bracelet?"

Doubira swears. And sends off a message to Diome, telling him both Tulle and Evian are in immediate danger. He also seems to set it up so the video feed from his phone is available to his superior in real time.

I hope the commander still has enough power to come through on the call for help. I'm convinced he's on our side, but equally certain many other elements in the chain of command are bought by Redon and her group. They're not going to want that video to be widely seen.

Thibault has lain Tulle down on the ground by the open grave. One of the goons has brought a hammer—the one they used to nail Evian's casket shut, if I'm not mistaken—and they put it into Tulle's hand. Making sure her handprints are on it. Then they do the same for a shovel.

Setting her up all right. And it can only work if Tulle isn't alive to contradict the story.

Of course, if Doubira shows himself, this will also ruin their plans. There will be no point in setting up an elaborate scheme if someone can prove it's all a lie. But if he steps out and shows himself, will that save Tulle, or will it simply mean they kill her more quickly?

Doubira seems to come to the same conclusion as me and stays hidden.

"Emeline is in that grave, isn't she?" he whispers after a while, as he watches the men leave Tulle's fingerprints on anything they can around the grave. I'm almost surprised they don't jump into the pit to put her hands all over the casket. "They killed her and now Nadine is going to take the blame for it." He glances at his phone. "Except she isn't."

I tell Doubira that Evian isn't dead yet—at least I'm praying she isn't, I haven't been down there to check on my two friends because right now I prefer the doubt—but I'm not sure he hears me. In any case, it doesn't change much. What we need is to take out the bad guys. The rest will follow.

It's when Thibault pulls out a gun that we spring into action.

The two goons are holding Tulle up between them, at the edge of the open grave. As I rush down the short incline, I notice he's wearing gloves so as not to leave any prints, and he folds Tulle's hand around the gun.

He's going to have her "kill herself," with her own service weapon if I recognize the gun correctly and drop her into the grave on top of Evian's casket.

We have one minute, tops, before he has all he needs and pulls the trigger.

I'm about to yell out to Clothilde, to check on her, when her head pops up from the pit.

"You got out?" I ask stupidly.

"Emeline managed to make a hole big enough for me to get out." Clothilde takes in the situation as she jumps up to stand behind Tulle. "Where do you need me?"

Pushing all thoughts of Evian to the side, I focus on saving Tulle. "Doubira is on the way." I glance behind me and see him rushing down the path toward us, gun drawn. The men will notice him in a second or two. "We need to distract the men."

Clothilde's hair is already lifting, her eyes pitch black. "On it," she says in her midnight voice.

And she jumps *into* the man on Tulle's left.

Remembering Thibault has no sensitivity to ghosts, I follow Clothilde's lead. I step into the second goon's form and focus on trying to touch him. Reaching out, imagining ripping through his insides, squeezing his heart, shaking his stomach. I roar at the top of my lungs, right into his head.

Clothilde is much better at this than me, of course, so her goon lets go of Tulle first. But mine isn't long behind.

Tulle's body tumbles into the pit.

As long as the fall didn't kill her, at least she's out of harm's way for the moment.

"Don't move!" Doubira yells from behind me. "Police!"

A shot rings out.

THIRTY-FOUR

If Emeline ever gets out of this box of horrors, she is never getting into a closed space ever again. She will leave her window open at home year-round, even in the heat of summer and cold of winter. She will never take an elevator, no metros. No meeting rooms without windows.

No. More. Caskets.

How is it possible to be locked into a casket to be buried alive *twice* in a lifetime? Surely once was more than enough?

To be fair, the people shoving her into said caskets probably never expected her to wake up. Today, she was unconscious when her captors had put her inside, and the last time…

She had been hot on the tails of a guy killing prostitutes.

He was one of those jerks who thought women who sold their bodies were worthless, to their families, to society, to him. So he picked them up along the Canal Saint-Martin, brought them to a secluded spot in his van, and killed them. Rape, mutilation, murder, this guy did it all.

And the solution to finding him was in the mutilations. Emeline spent hours and days with the coroners at the morgue, looking at the bodies, studying the reports, searching for patterns. She *knew* there was a pattern, she just couldn't make it out.

She fell asleep there one night, while poring over a report for the tenth time.

When she woke up, she was in a casket.

She wouldn't be alive today if it hadn't been for her partner. Solène stayed awake for over twenty-four hours as she searched for Emeline, never giving up. As it turned out, the killer gave away the key to the pattern by taking Emeline at the morgue. It limited the number of potential candidates considerably.

Solène figured out the only way to have gotten Emeline out of the morgue without being caught on camera would have been inside a casket. So she ordered the exhumation of all five bodies that had left the morgue since Emeline's disappearance.

Emeline was in the third one and was just about to run out of air.

Together, they put the last pieces of the puzzle together and arrested the killer.

And Emeline has been scared of small spaces ever since.

Now, here she is again, six feet under and fighting for her life. Only difference: this time she's accompanied by Clothilde's ghost. Although it makes no sense, she is reassured by the young woman's presence. Sure, the fact that she sees her can't be a good sign, but at least she's not alone.

She has tried screaming for help since she woke up in here. At times, she has been so panicked, she couldn't do anything *but* scream for help. If someone comes by, they should be able to hear her and come to her aid—or run away screaming in fear. But nobody came. This cemetery seems suspiciously empty.

When Emeline's voice cracks from the strain, she squeezes her eyes shut and tries to take calming breaths. She can't die in here today, not like this. Her chest seems locked in place, unable to take in any air.

Is she already running out of oxygen? Are the cracks between the casket and the lid not enough? Is she farther into the ground than she first thought?

A song resonates through her body. Soothing, sweet.

And inaudible.

Emeline opens her eyes and comes face to face with Clothilde. Who is singing and running her ghostly fingers through Emeline's hair.

She can see the lips moving. Feel the song in her veins. But she can't hear a thing other than her own labored breath.

It helps, though. Clothilde's kind eyes and soothing movements, the intent behind the lullaby. It all adds up to Emeline being able to draw a decent breath, filling up her lungs.

She lets it out, and images of dragonflies on the moon and a million shining stars appear in her mind.

"Thank you, Clothilde," she whispers when the song is finished.

She receives an encouraging smile in reply.

If Emeline dies in here, what will become of Clothilde? Will anyone find the bracelet and wear it? Or will she end up in the trash and spend eternity haunting some landfill? Or the bottom of a drawer in her mother's house?

She isn't only fighting for herself. She also needs to consider Clothilde. At this thought, she realizes she still has some strength left. She won't let fear be what kills her.

If she dies, it will be without the fear.

To save her strength, she only tries calling out every now and then, just in case, but without much conviction. She focuses her every effort on kicking off the casket's lid. Just because she couldn't get it open on her first attempt doesn't mean it's impossible.

It should be feasible. The lid is basically a wooden plank which is nailed to the casket in six spots, three on each side. Emeline manages to move it sufficiently for her to identify the nails, to see light seeping in through the crack. But she can't get her legs in the right position to push in the direction she needs to finish the job.

Clothilde encourages Emeline at every kick, every pounding fist, and even tries to have at the lid herself. It doesn't seem like her efforts are yielding any tangible results, but the intangible ones, to Emeline's psyche, are enormous.

At one point, Clothilde waves her hand to catch Emeline's attention. She points to the lid above Emeline's feet and mimes kicking at it.

Isn't that what she has been doing all along?

No, Clothilde wants her to kick the middle of the lid, not at the sides where the nails are.

There's no reason for that to be more effective than what she's been doing so far, but since she isn't having any luck, Emeline tries it anyway.

And on the second kick, she feels the wood start to give way.

She cracked it!

With renewed energy, she keeps kicking at the same spot. The wood groans, pebbles trickle across the lid above her, and

Clothilde is behaving like a demented cheerleader. The ghost throws in a few kicks of her own, screaming some war cry while she does it.

Emeline gives a shout of her own when the lid finally cracks. She still can't get out, but the tip of her foot went through, which means she *will* be able to break through eventually.

She's about to give the next kick when she hears the engine.

Her first reaction is pure joy. Somebody's here! She's saved!

Then Clothilde's frown registers, and reality hits. She's in the middle of a huge cemetery. No vehicles are allowed in here, except for the cemetery vans and hearses. A hearse would mean mourners, which she should have already heard. And the vans… were in the hands of the people who put her here.

The claps of two doors opening and closing sound out. Male voices.

Clothilde holds a finger to her lips, signing for Emeline to stay quiet. Then she points to the hole in the casket.

She wants to leave?

It makes sense she can, once the opening is big enough. At first, Emeline panics. She's going to find herself alone in here, and she'll die alone.

Clothilde reaches over and touches the bracelet still on Emeline's wrist. She's still tied to it—she won't go far.

And she zips out of the casket.

Emeline hears voices out there, but she can't make out any words. She distinguishes at least two different voices, and some grunting and scuffling. What are they doing?

She's fairly certain they are the guys who put her in this casket, so if possible, it would be best if they don't discover the fact she is awake and has almost broken the lid.

However, she cannot stop trying to get out. Instead of

sending out kicks, she wedges her foot into the hole and applies constant pressure. Upward, and toward the far end of the casket, since it's the most natural movement from her position.

Slowly but surely, the lid continues cracking down the middle. Along the grain, from her feet all the way up to her head. Some dirt falls into her eyes, but not before she sees actual sunlight hitting her thigh.

Emeline is so happy she feels like screaming in joy.

Instead, she suddenly feels a great urgency and a panic, as if someone was screaming at the top of their lungs. Without actual sound: a ghost is screaming.

Clothilde needs her help.

Not caring anymore if she makes noise, Emeline wipes the dirt from her eyes and pushes at the lid with both arms and legs, using all her remaining strength.

The lid cracks in two and sunlight floods in, accompanied by even more dirt.

Coughing and with her head swimming, Emeline sits up, *needing* to get out and help her friend.

She gets her eyes open just in time to see the body tumbling down to fall on top of her.

Real screams have joined the inaudible ones. One of them seems to yell, "Police!"

Then a shot sounds out.

THIRTY-FIVE

Since I'm mostly inside one of the men when the shot is fired, I don't see who shot at who. I see flashes of cemetery, flashes of darkness, and catch a glimpse of the whirlwind that is Clothilde in and around the other man.

I stretch my neck to get a clear view—but keep trying to pull on the guy's insides. Any confusion on the bad guys' side is a win in my book.

I can't see Doubira. Did Thibault shoot him?

A grunt behind me.

Thibault on his knees on the ground. He still holds Tulle's gun, but it's pointed down at the ground and loose in the man's grip. His head is bent, his breathing labored. I realize his free hand is on his right shoulder. Covering the wound where a bullet just went through, with blood seeping into the material of his T-shirt.

"Doubira's the one who made the shot?" Only when I say the words do I realize I assumed it wasn't him. With his fear of guns, I didn't think he'd be able to be the one to shoot first. Second maybe, but not first.

I'm impressed. And proud.

I get no answer because Clothilde has given herself up completely to haunting her designated goon. And it's working. The guy is bent in half with a hand to his stomach and the other on his head, whimpering like he's a second away from calling for mommy.

I hope Clothilde will be able to find herself again when this is over. I can't even make out a human shape. She's just anger and mist.

"Police!" The yell comes from my left somewhere, so I rush toward Doubira's voice. "Drop your weapons!"

He's behind a fancy-looking mausoleum with two roman columns and a severe-looking angel on the top. He's glancing out from his hiding spot, his gun in hand, and only a slight tremor to his hand.

"You're doing great," I tell him. "The guy with the gun is down and one of the goons is having…technical issues."

I suddenly realize that in the heat of the action, I've taken up a spot behind Doubira, hiding from the bad guys, like I still have a body that can be hurt. I run back out into the line of fire, so to speak, to work as lookout for Doubira.

Unfortunately, I don't like what I see.

Although Clothilde's target is definitely out of the equation, the two others have rallied. My guy seems as good as new now

I'm not there to pull at him and he has pulled a gun out from somewhere, pointing it in Doubira's general direction. Thibault has rallied and has switched the gun to his good hand, leaving the bleeding shoulder to fend for itself while he deals with the more immediate threat.

Doubira is still two against one, dammit.

I try calling out to Clothilde, asking her to change targets, but she's too far gone. She's keeping the third guy out of the fight and that's all I'm going to get from her right now.

Thibault stays in place while the other guy moves away. Making sure Doubira can't keep his gun pointed at both of them and moving to a position where Doubira is going to be exposed.

I go back to pulling at the man's insides. I feel like it's the only thing I can do that might be helpful. I'm not as good as Clothilde, but it could mean a shot missing Doubira instead of hitting its mark.

"One more step and I'll have to shoot you!" Doubira's voice is strong, but unfortunately it cracks on the last two words. He has already fired one shot and the risk of him accidentally killing someone will only increase if he has to take them all out.

Thibault is holding his healthy arm out straight, gun pointed at the spot where Doubira is hiding behind the grave. Doesn't look like he's worried about using his left.

Despite my best efforts, the second guy keeps moving. He winces from time to time when I manage to catch onto something, but it's not enough to stop him. Neither are Doubira's words.

He takes the last step that will put him in Doubira's line of sight, and I follow.

I can see the whites of his eyes from over here. He's scared to death.

But as the goon grins and starts to pull the trigger, Doubira fires a second shot.

This one rips through the man's midsection.

A lot more effective than when a ghost pulls at it, that's for sure. Two down, one to go.

But Doubira has reached his limit. I'm guessing he didn't intend to aim for the soft bits, and comes rushing toward the man he just shot, his gun dropped to the ground where he had been hiding.

With Thibault still there, armed and aiming for Doubira.

I rush forward. I'm not sure what I'm trying to do. Take the bullet for Doubira. Scream loud enough to finally distract Thibault. Run in *to help*. Somehow.

Just as I see Thibault's finger tighten to fire his shot, something barrels into him from behind.

From the open grave.

It's Evian.

Somehow, she has managed to fly out of the grave and land on Thibault, making his shot go wide and the man tumble to the ground.

I think she's alive. Her legs are moving. And her head lifts up to check the gun has fallen out of reach, then to inspect the man she is sprawled across. She shoves her dirty, matted hair out of her eyes and clears her throat.

When she speaks, her voice is so hoarse I don't even recognize it. "You're under arrest, Monsieur."

Then she passes out.

THIRTY-SIX

Tulle was the rocket launcher. She's in the open grave, sitting on the remains of Evian's bust-open casket, one hand on each side of the pit as if trying to hold herself in place. She has a large lump on the side of her head and some dried blood in a streak going into her shirt. Her long braid is coming apart, and large strands of blonde hair are hanging in front of her face as she squeezes her eyes shut, trying to regain her senses.

I don't know how she managed to find the energy to boost Evian out of the hole like that, but I don't see a trampoline so it's the only explanation. This woman is a lot stronger than she looks.

Right now, I don't think she'll be of much help, though. It seems like she's holding on by a thread just to stay conscious and upright, and in any case, climbing out of a grave all on your own is no easy feat.

Clothilde is still a whirlwind and her victim a sobbing mess on the ground. I try to talk to her, yell at her, but I'm not having any luck. The only positive side is that the guy is in no shape to harm any of my friends.

I just hope I'll be able to get my *best* friend back from whatever pit of anger she has fallen into.

Doubira is trying to save the man he shot in the belly. He seems to have someone on the phone, yelling, "Two minutes isn't good enough!" as he applies pressure to the wound, pleading with the guy not to die.

He has both his own and the other guy's guns shoved into the back of his pants, so at least he has made sure the man can't suddenly wake up and shoot at will.

But I'm not going to be able to get him away to help Evian.

They look rather odd, the two of them, lying there at the edge of an open grave in the heat of the glaring sun, like a couple who decided this was the perfect place for an afternoon nap. Thibault is spread-eagled, his gun no more than ten centimeters from his left hand, the blood stain on his right shoulder expanding every moment. Evian is lying on top of him, her head in the crook of his neck. Almost idyllic if it weren't for the matted and dirty hair and clothes, torn hands and fingers, and streaks of tears having run through the dirt on her face, then dried.

Which of them will wake up first?

"Evian, you have to wake up." I speak loudly but avoid yelling for fear of scaring her. "You have to secure the man you're arresting, or he could harm you or Doubira or Tulle."

Thibault wakes first, of course. I hear sirens approaching but that isn't going to be enough to save Evian if this guy reaches the gun first. He pulls in a sharp breath and his body jerks as his consciousness returns.

Which—thank God!—is enough to rouse Evian.

"You have to subdue him!" I yell. "Knock him out again! Kick him in the balls. Head-butt him. Anything!" I realize I'm panicking but I absolutely *hate* this. Being the only one consciously present but the only one not to have the slightest influence on the world of the living. There's nothing I can do. Except keep yelling at Evian.

She hears me. Or her reflexes are on point, as always.

As her eyes flicker open, she takes in the man starting to move beneath her—and head-butts him right in the nose.

Thibault collapses back into unconsciousness.

"Excellent work, Evian," I tell her. "You have to secure him. This scene is far from safe."

Evian looks right at me. "Thank you, Robert," she says. And pulls a zip cuff out of Thibault's jeans pocket before pushing him over on his side to secure his arms behind his back.

I vaguely notice she keeps him off his injured shoulder, but I'm too shaken to focus on such details.

"You can see me?" I sit down on the ground, feeling light-headed despite there being no reason for it, since blood hasn't run through my veins in decades.

Evian glances up from her work, a frown on her face. "I can see you, but the sound, or lack thereof, is still the same. I can sort of hear you without hearing you. Where is Clothilde?"

Talk about a reversal of roles. I'm supposed to be the one to help her, being out of physical danger and all, yet I've completely lost my footing.

I point to the guy whimpering on the ground, and the whirlwind that is Clothilde. "She got too angry, I think. I've never seen her like this. I don't know how to bring her back."

The sirens are getting closer. I think they're inside the cemetery now. Doubira is yelling instructions to his phone, still applying pressure to the goon's wound, threatening him with bodily harm if he doesn't survive.

We've all lost it, I think.

Except Evian, of course. She quickly assesses Doubira's situation and concludes there's no point in intervening. Doubira isn't in danger and he's doing everything he can to keep the other guy from dying. Tulle is still in the grave.

"You all right in there, Nadine?" Evian yells down. "Help seems to be on the way, but I can try to pull you out if you need it."

Tulle shakes her head but keeps her eyes closed. "Secure the scene, Captain."

"Right." Evian crawls over to the third guy and what's left of Clothilde. She finds another zip cuff, pulls on the man's arms until she can secure them behind his back, all the while trying to avoid touching the whirling mass of Clothilde.

"I've secured him now, Clothilde," she says loudly. "You don't need to do this anymore. We're all safe."

Doubira's head whips around to stare at his colleague, incredulous. "I could need some help over here, Emeline," he all but growls.

A police car appears around the bend of the main path, followed by an ambulance. Which distracts Doubira so Evian won't have to explain why she prefers talking to thin air over staunching the gunshot wound of a bad guy.

"Clothilde," she pleads. "See all the people coming? We're safe now, and I can't continue talking to you like this once they get closer. Please come back to us." She reaches out a hand to touch the whirlwind, but it doesn't have an effect.

I join in the conversation and add my voice to hers, trying to convince my friend to come back. But it's no use. Clothilde keeps spinning and the man keeps moaning. Evian even tries to surreptitiously move the man, so he'll be outside of her reach, but the swirling mass follows.

After worrying for so long about my live friends, will I end up losing the dead one? The one I care about the most?

I can't give up on her, and I won't. But a feeling of dread settles over me. Was it all worth it? Will catching Thibault and his goons get us any closer to catching the people who killed us? Would Clothilde consider this sufficient to settle her unfinished business?

I know she wouldn't. We have to get her back to normal so she can settle her business like everybody else.

As the EMTs approach Doubira to take care of the wounded man, three police officers approach Evian, their guns drawn, searching for additional dangers.

"They're all taken care of," Evian says. "Your first priority should be getting that man to the ambulance." She points to Thibault. "He has been shot in the shoulder. Then you need to get Lieutenant Tulle out of the grave."

While she's giving her instructions, I continue talking to Clothilde, pleading with her to come back, to calm down. To remember who she is.

When the officers execute Evian's orders, she turns back to Clothilde. She sits back on her heels and sighs. Neither of us knows what to do.

Then she starts humming. Her eyes are glazed over, and her breathing is very slow. It's like she's in a meditative state.

I think I recognize the tune. It's the lullaby Clothilde sang for

Evian when she was overwhelmed with the screams from Hélori's ghost, and when she was trapped in the cemetery van.

Clothilde's whirling mass slows down a fraction. She's still spinning, but not as fast, and not as smoothly. Evian keeps humming, I keep up the talking, reminding Clothilde we're here and that we need her.

I think I see an arm. Floating hair. It's starting to look like a person caught in a whirlwind instead of a person being a whirlwind. I give Evian the thumbs-up, although I'm not sure she's really seeing anything right now.

Doubira comes stalking toward us, his hands covered in the blood of the man currently on his way into the ambulance, his gaze furious.

I can't have him messing with Evian's concentration now that she's getting through to Clothilde. I don't want his anger to somehow fuel Clothilde's. So I rush toward him. "Please leave her be," I plead. "She has been through a lot and needs to calm down. She's just decompressing by humming a tune. Please leave her be."

Maybe he hears me, maybe he comes to the same conclusion by himself. For someone who doesn't see or feel the Clothilde whirlwind, it looks like Evian is gathering her wits after a great trial, and Doubira still has enough hero worship for his partner to give her the benefit of the doubt.

He changes direction and moves to help the officers with getting Tulle out of the grave instead. When the short woman is safely out, Doubira envelops her in a hug, burying his nose in her hair. Tulle doesn't look like she expected this—I'm guessing it's the first hug she's ever gotten from her friend—but she definitely needed it.

In the meantime, Evian keeps humming. The same melody,

over and over, and even I'm getting sleepy.

Clothilde is recognizable now. Still in a whirlwind, but a slower-moving one, and her entire body discernible, with her arms out and her head back, like she's dancing.

When the officers come for the poor guy who's still whimpering on the ground, Clothilde forgets to follow. She's not focused on hurting the man anymore. I'm hopeful we'll get her back.

I'm in the middle of a sentence, reminding Clothilde of who she is, when I'm suddenly pulled away. That awful feeling of being in one place, then suddenly another, like my body disintegrates only to reform.

Doubira still has the bracelet with my finger bone in it. And he's seated at the back of a second cruiser that pulled up a moment ago, cradling Tulle in his arms as a female officer carefully maneuvers the car toward the exit.

I'm cut off from my friends again.

Evian will have to save Clothilde on her own.

THIRTY-SEVEN

Emeline isn't entirely certain she's still conscious. She has entered a trance-like state, where she hums a melody she has never actually heard before but knows by heart, while watching Clothilde's otherworldly dance performance. She's vaguely aware of her body hurting, her throat begging for water, fresh tears coursing down her cheeks, but all that doesn't seem to matter in the face of Clothilde.

The young woman is beautiful, and a whirlwind of emotions. The anger is ebbing away now, giving place to the joy of the dance and the music, but there's always something. Never apathy or indifference from Clothilde.

A young officer, a woman with short, black hair and light

brown eyes, come over to kneel next to Emeline. "Captain, are you all right? We have an ambulance waiting for you."

Emeline doesn't want to stop singing for Clothilde, but reality rears its ugly head. Nobody else can see the beautiful ghost and the longer she stays here humming to herself, the longer it will be until they let her go back to work. The break they're going to force on her after such a trial is already going to grate.

When she stops humming, Clothilde slows to a stop.

"It's been a long day," Emeline says to the officer. "I zoned out there for a moment. Would you mind helping me—"

Robert isn't there anymore. Where did he go? Where is the bracelet?

Clothilde says something, the whirlwind she was spinning in earlier completely gone, leaving place for the young woman from the photos Emeline has spent hours perusing. Except without any color, and slightly transparent.

"Malik took it?"

Clothilde nods. And the officer, who is holding out a hand to help Emeline stand, frowns.

"I need to see Malik Doubira immediately," she tells the woman, using her sternest tone. It probably isn't very convincing, given her general state. "We have to act on what we learned here today as soon as possible."

"We'll contact Lieutenant Doubira," the woman says. "He's on his way to the hospital too. But even finishing up your case can't come before your own health. You need hydration and some rest."

As long as she is being taken to the same place as Malik, Emeline can let that statement stand. A glass or three of water wouldn't hurt. "Has anyone seen my phone?" she asks. "I need to call Commander Diome."

They've reached the ambulance and to Emeline's surprise, the officer climbs in with her. An EMT straps Emeline onto a stretcher and starts taking vitals and giving her fluids. She's apparently not even allowed to drink the water by herself.

"Here," the officer says and hands Emeline a phone. "I don't know where your phone is, but I'm dialing the commander for you."

Emeline smiles in gratitude and feels her lower lip crack. "Thank you."

The woman nods and holds the phone to Emeline's ear when she discovers her arms are otherwise occupied with tubes attached all over the place. The EMT isn't wasting any time.

When Diome's deep voice answers, Emeline feels another tear break free. It seems she has been bottling up emotions at least as well as Clothilde—who is currently perching on one of the cabinets at the back of the ambulance, worried eyes fixed on Emeline.

"Commander," Emeline says, "It's Emeline Evian. I need you to arrest Delphine Redon."

"Is that so," the commander replies calmly. "I hear you've had a bit of an adventure in one of our cemeteries?"

Emeline snorts, then coughs, earning a stern glance from the EMT. "Got buried alive for the second time in my life. Great fun."

The officer's eyebrows shoot up and the EMT looks up from his work in surprise.

"Glad you made it out alive, Captain," Diome says.

"Me too. I really need you to go pick up Redon. I went to see her earlier today."—*Was that really mere hours ago?*—"And I'm certain that's what triggered their attack here today. That, and Lieutenant Tulle's search in the real estate records at the City Hall. Look through Redon's phone history and find the link with one of the men arrested at the cemetery today. His name is

Thibault, and he was shot in the shoulder. Clearly the leader and the one who would have gotten the instructions from Redon. And get your hands on the information Tulle found at the City Hall before they destroy all of it."

"I cannot simply arrest a member of the Regional Council because one of my officers thinks there is a link between two independent events. I will look at your evidence—"

"You have to act now, before she can get rid of any evidence!" Emeline is beyond caring about internal politics, or even rules. She *knows* Redon was behind the attack. And therefore, more. "I will not let your fear of your superiors stop me from doing my job. I will not let yet another murderer go free while I'm waiting on a system that doesn't work. If you act quickly, before she knows her men failed, you *will* find the evidence you need."

Wide eyes all around, except for Clothilde, who is clapping. She seems a little more faded than earlier.

Diome stays silent for several moments. The ambulance rocks as they drive over a speed bump and the driver activates the sirens to get through a red light.

"I will see what I can do, Captain Evian," Diome finally says. "I will not break any rules or laws, but I can push a little harder where there is resistance. I will expect you at my desk the moment the doctors clear you at the hospital."

"Yes, sir," Emeline replies and nods to the officer to indicate the conversation is finished.

Five minutes later, her stretcher is pushed through the doors of the Purpan Hospital emergency room. After some yelling, she's allowed to be treated in the same room as Nadine and Malik. They apparently asked if the two officers were okay with this situation before clearing it, which annoys Emeline to no end.

She may be getting grumpy.

Emeline sees Robert before she sees Malik. The ghost is leaning against the wall by the window, giving the two patients some space. When Emeline's stretcher rolls through the door, his brows draw together in worry—then his face breaks into a huge smile when Clothilde follows.

The two ghosts embrace in a hug. They seem a little more transparent than earlier. Is it because Emeline is more tired and therefore can't see them as well? Or is it because she's not at death's door anymore?

That last explanation makes a certain amount of sense.

But right now, Emeline has to focus on securing evidence against Redon. That woman is *not* getting away again. First though…

"Malik, I think you found one of my bracelets?" she says by way of greeting. Her partner is the only one not in a horizontal position. It seems they cleaned off all the blood only to discover none of it was his. He's in the room's only visitors' chair, a hand on Nadine's as she sleeps.

Malik grunts in reply and rolls his eyes. "Don't know how you deal with that crap on a regular basis. Messes with your head." He shoves his free hand into a pocket and throws the bracelet over to Emeline's bed.

He misses, of course, but the nurse who is getting Emeline settled is kind enough to pick it up. She seems surprised someone would find something so tattered and dirty important enough to come *before* asking after your colleagues' health but keeps her thoughts to herself.

Emeline's hand closes over the bracelet and she lets out a relieved sigh.

"Oh, and I also found your phone." Malik makes the effort to get up from his seat to place it in Evian's hand. "The screen's cracked, but I think it still works." He returns to holding Nadine's hand.

"Thank you, Malik." Emeline nods toward Nadine. "Did she say anything about what she found before she passed out?"

He shakes his head while keeping his eyes on his friend's face. "She was pretty out of it. Doctors gave her some medicines that knocked her out cold." His dark gaze lifts to Emeline. "You sent her on a dangerous field mission all on her own?"

Emeline sighs. "There was no reason to believe it was dangerous. And I asked for information without knowing she would need to go physically to the City Hall to find it." French bureaucracy and their love for paperwork.

Although he's still angry, Malik lets it slide. "Do you at least know what she found before they kidnapped and almost killed her?"

"Most likely a complete list of the people we've been looking for for months. They've been buying up real estate in one specific area for decades and killing whoever stood in their way."

"The supposed suicides?"

"Yes. Starting with Gisèle Grand and Clothilde Humbert, and all the way up to Hélori Xavier less than a month ago."

Malik whistles softly. Then his brows draw together in a frown. "Any chance of them being able to get rid of the evidence? That's public records, right?"

"Should be." Emeline closes her eyes. Now that all the excitement is over and her body knows it's safe, she wants nothing more than to sleep. "Would you mind making sure the evidence is secured, though, Malik? Diome said he's taking care of it but having someone offer to do that part of the job might help. Make sure you bring a partner or two along for the ride."

Emeline forces one eye open and sees Malik studying Nadine

Tulle's small form on the bed. He squeezes her hand and stands up. "I'll do what I can. It has Diome's support, you say?"

"As much of it as he can give, yes. I still don't know what his restrictions are."

"Fine." He walks over to the door, and with a hand on the knob, turns to point a finger at Emeline. "But once this is done, you're going to help me get rid of the ghost haunting the morgue. One of the coroners' assistants almost quit yesterday."

"Deal." And with a smile on her face, Emeline falls asleep.

THIRTY-EIGHT

THE RELIEF AT seeing Clothilde again, safe and sound and perching on things, leaves me without words. We share the longest hug we've ever had, while being frustrated at the lack of physical touch. I can pretend to hold her, but if I don't pay attention, I'll go right through. There's nothing like touch to make sure someone is really okay. In our case, a visual inspection will have to do.

The bracelet with my bone is back in Evian's keeping and she's getting the treatment and rest she needs. All in all, things are going well.

While the two policewomen sleep, I catch up with Clothilde, listening to her adventure in the closed casket and telling her about getting through to a reluctant Doubira.

At first, it's peaceful, nice to catch our breaths after an action-filled day. But as the hours trickle by and the sun approaches the horizon, I get impatient to get back to the case. We're so close to having a breakthrough, I can feel it. But while Diome and Doubira are out there working our case, we're waiting, completely useless, in a hospital room.

Evian's phone pings with several messages, but since it's placed face-down on her chest, I can't see what they say or who they're from. On the third ping, I growl in frustration—and Evian wakes up.

I should feel guilty about waking her up when she needs more rest, but I really want to know who's messaging her.

I point to the phone. "You have several messages."

Evian squints, seems to look through me. Looks toward the door. "I can only see you in my peripheral vision now," she says hoarsely. "Not when I look directly at you. Guess I won't be dying today after all."

I exchange a confused look with Clothilde. Why would she think she was dying? Okay, except the obvious reasons. Why would she think there's a link between her almost dying and seeing us?

Huh. Actually, that sort of makes sense.

Evian picks up her phone. She grimaces at the cracked screen but gets straight to business when she sees Diome's name on the screen.

Will interrogate the leader when he's out of surgery, the first one says. The second: **Will drop by after interrogation, you are apparently in the same hospital**. Then, **What is your room number?**

Evian doesn't need to get out of bed to find the room number; Diome finds her first. His large body fills the doorway perfectly, his salt-and-pepper hair newly cropped close to his head, and his uniform crisp as always.

"Captain Evian," he says in his deep voice. "I hope I am not interrupting."

"I almost died, but now I'm doing much better, thank you." Evian waves him into the room. "Did he give you anything to work with?"

Diome rumbles a laugh, closes the door behind him, and comes to stand at the foot of Evian's bed. "Being shot and realizing his colleagues would do nothing to help him out of his current predicament loosened his tongue considerably."

Evian narrows her eyes at him.

"Being offered a lighter sentence in return for turning in his superiors also helped. You know how this works, Captain."

I'm thinking having a giant like Diome interrogate him while he's still weakened in a hospital bed influenced the man slightly, too.

"As long as he doesn't get out of prison until I'm back in Paris, I don't care." Evian looks around, searching for a way to sit up in her bed. She finds a remote, and after only one false start, gets into a seated position. "Did he give you Redon?"

Diome doesn't smile but the tightening around his mouth says he wants to. "He did. Said she was the one paying him and his colleagues, showed us the logs on his phone from today, when he was told first to take out Lieutenant Tulle, then you. We do not have the actual conversation, but the logs plus his testimonial should do the trick."

"So she's under arrest?"

Diome gives a slight nod. "Being brought to the station as we speak."

Clothilde lets out a whoop of joy from her perch. Evian glances in her direction and she visibly retains a smile.

"And the information Nadine was looking for at the City Hall?"

Diome glances over at the young woman sleeping in the second hospital bed. Her hair is spread across her pillow. Being so used to seeing it contained into a tight braid, I almost feel like I'm trespassing.

"Lieutenant Doubira is collecting and analyzing the data." I think Diome is trying to keep his voice down but with a deep register like his, the entire room is resonating with his words. "Anything that was bought in that area over the last thirty years will be under scrutiny. Any repeating names are being brought in directly for questioning. They all called their lawyers before we could even get them out of the house."

"Let me guess," Evian says. "They're all represented by Laurent Lambert."

Diome grunts. "Good guess, Captain. All except two, so far."

"The two are most likely innocent, then." Evian waves a dismissive hand. "Lucky not to have been killed by the rest of them when they bought the land."

Sobering thought, but she's probably right.

She meets her boss's gaze. "The lawyer is one of the bad guys. You realize that, right?"

"He was not one of the names on the list from City Hall," Diome says after a beat. "As long as we have no proof against him, I cannot arrest him. Nor bring him in for questioning."

Evian shrugs. "We'll get him eventually. I'm not going back to Paris until that man is behind bars. He might even be the brains behind the entire operation. Maybe having him on hand like that won't be a bad thing. We can observe him."

Clothilde has come down from her perch. She walks up to Evian's bed, across from where I'm standing, and places a hand on Evian's shoulder. "Thank you," she says. "Lambert is the guy I need to see pay for his sins before I'll be able to let go. We *have* to get him."

"We'll get him." No more than a whisper, but we hear the words.

Diome and Evian have a monster case ahead of them. Today's events were enough to take a large number of people into custody. My guess is that any sale they can link to a "suicide" or an accidental death will result in an arrest. If the sale went through without hiccups…they'll walk free. For now.

We won't let them get away with it, though. This first wave of arrests should help us figure out *why* they are targeting that specific part of the city. Once we know the why, we can move on to the how and who.

And once we do, justice will be within our reach.

THIRTY-NINE

We hear Constantine the minute we step into the building. The wails and screams are distant but most definitely audible. From the wince on Evian's face, I'd say she hears—or rather, feels—them too. She squares her shoulders and takes off down the dimly lit hallway on our right, toward the crazy ghost.

"You can hear her, can't you?" Doubira asks. "How did you know which direction to choose?"

Amina, walking between the two officers, looks excitedly from one to the other, practically skipping along, beautiful eyes gleaming with anticipation. I think a great part of it is from finally being able to help her resident ghost, but part of it is also excitement at watching Evian communicate with ghosts. This is something she is *very* interested in.

"That is one loud ghost you got there," Evian says with a sigh. "No wonder the people working in the room with her have tried to quit."

"You think you can calm her down?"

Evian glances across at her partner—again *officially* her partner since Diome redid the assignments following Doubira's success with extracting the information they needed from City Hall—the beginnings of a smile playing on her lips. "*I* won't be the one to convince her."

"Right." Doubira gulps and sends a nervous glance over his shoulder.

Clothilde grins and waves at him—not that he sees her, of course.

"How do you feel about our chances of success here today?" I ask as I mirror Evian's poise, with my hands clasped behind my back.

"For calming her down while still in the morgue?" Clothilde snorts. "Ten percent chance, max. That woman isn't going to believe a word we say until we get her out of here. She wasn't very stable to begin with and then we went ahead and betrayed her."

I hum my agreement. I think Evian and Doubira know this too. Our goal isn't to calm Constantine down so she'll play nice. It is to let the coroners and their colleagues get a breather so we can get the woman out of here and to her husband.

And then we'll pray the two crazies will cancel each other out.

Doubira opens a door on our left, and the volume of the screams increases tenfold, at the very least. I can see Evian gritting her teeth before walking through, and even Amina's smile loses some of its intensity.

Nobody can be insensitive to this level of anger and despair.

At least she has somewhat maintained her own shape. As she

turns on herself in the air above a body bag I assume contains her remains, Constantine's hair rises around her head like she's drifting downward in water, but it's still recognizably hair. Her face is blocked in a rictus as she screams mindlessly at us, but the features are still human. The poor wedding dress is in tatters, even worse than when she haunted Amina's guest room. It looks like she's been wearing it while crawling to hell and back.

"Hi, Constantine." Clothilde approaches the other ghost, walking on air so she's on the same level. "We've come to take you to your husband. Jacques?" she adds when Constantine shows no signs of relenting.

I want to hold my hands over my ears to shut out the noise, but I know from experience that nothing can dampen the volume of a ghost screaming. Evian does cover her ears but drops them just as quickly.

"We'll keep working on her," I say into Evian's ear. "Try to calm her down a little. You should focus on getting us to the cemetery."

Doubira managed to get in touch with Constantine and Jacques' next of kin. Béatrice Larcher confirmed that her cousin never recovered from being left behind by his wife. For a long time, he refused to believe she would do such a thing, but after a while, he came to accept the version everybody else kept pushing at him.

Doing so broke him.

When Doubira told Jacques' cousin that Constantine's body had been found, she broke down in tears. And lost no time in authorizing the burial of the wife in the husband's grave.

The grave was dug up yesterday and Constantine's casket is ready in the corner.

Clothilde keeps talking to Constantine in soothing tones, explaining what we're about to do and that her husband is also a ghost and waiting for her.

It doesn't stop the screaming and we don't get any response from Constantine, but we keep at it anyway.

The only positive thing about her non-responsiveness is that she doesn't seem to realize what is happening to her dead body. Doubira, Evian, and Amina lift the body bag into the casket and nail shut the lid. I half-expect Constantine to disappear into the casket—which will *not* help with her panic—but it appears that having accepted she's a ghost long ago means she isn't stuck inside the box.

When they push the casket on its trolley out the door, Constantine is still spinning in place in the middle of the room. As the door slides shut, she is pulled forcibly out—just like Clothilde and I who choose to stay with her instead of following Evian and waiting for our friend to appear—and the screams cut off.

Evian lets out a relieved sigh and the two others glance around, frowning. Wondering what just changed, why they feel a little lighter.

This is a temporary reprieve, though.

"What are you doing?" Constantine yells at the top of her lungs. "Where are you taking me? Take me back to my room! Amina!" When she spots her longtime host, she swoops down on her, seemingly trying for a hug. Or an attack. Right now, I'm not sure Constantine knows the difference.

Amina shudders but keeps walking alongside the casket.

Evian stops. Stares really hard at the Amina/Constantine combo. Shifts her gaze to the right—to bring what she's interested in into her peripheral vision.

"Constantine!" she roars, making both the two living people and all three ghosts jump in surprise. "Get away from Amina. She's helping to get you reunited with your husband and going inside her like that is *not* the right way to show your gratitude."

Doubira looks up and down the hallway, worried someone might have heard the outburst. Amira stares slack-jawed at Evian—she's either impressed or scared. Let's hope for Evian's sake it's the former.

And Constantine stops.

Head cocked and hair falling limp for the first time since we got here, she takes one step away from Amina and studies Evian. "You can see me?"

Evian growls. "I can't see you if I look directly at you, but I perceive your general form when you're out on the side like this. We're here to help. Which we won't want to do any longer if you start haunting us."

Constantine seems to finally notice Clothilde and I. "Help?"

"They're taking you to Jacques," I say. "You'll be buried alongside your husband."

"But what's the point if he isn't—"

"He's there." Clothilde signs for Evian to get the procession moving again, and our trusted medium gets the message and returns to pushing the trolley with the casket. "We went to Jacques' grave and met your husband's ghost. He's waiting for you."

That might be an extrapolation but I'm not about to correct her.

Clothilde ushers a shocked Constantine toward the door, so we won't be sucked out again when Evian and the casket go outside.

I thought we'd be done with cemeteries for a while now that we're out in the world with Evian. At least this time, there's some hope of ghosts finding peace as a result.

Or they'll go into a tailspin together. We shall see.

FORTY

This thing with seeing ghosts when she isn't looking directly at them is going to take some getting used to. In her small rental car, with Malik behind the wheel, Emeline keeps catching glimpses of the two ghosts sitting next to Amina in the back seat when she turns her head, making her turn to face them directly—and thereby not seeing them anymore, but always meeting Amina's smiling and inquiring eyes.

She's pretty sure she saw a gleeful grin on Robert's face just now. So glad he's finding this funny. Emeline's face must be turning permanently red.

When they arrive at the Salonique cemetery, the hearse is already at the grave site and the two reluctant drivers look immensely relieved to see them arrive. No wonder: Constantine is rushing from one to the other in a flurry, screaming her head off again.

Is there a way to turn *off* this capacity for hearing ghosts?

This is one of the most beautiful cemeteries Emeline has ever seen, with mostly well-maintained graves, large old trees giving shade from the harsh summer sun, and benches along the paved paths so visitors can sit and relax and profit from the calm haven in the middle of the large, busy city. But right now, it's impossible to relax even an iota because of the inaudible screams.

While Robert and Clothilde attempt to calm Constantine—again—Emeline and Malik thank the drivers and send them on their way as soon as the casket is on the lift that will lower it into the ground. They'll be back in an hour to fill the grave and get everything cleaned up.

Amina places a hand on the casket, saying a last goodbye.

Now, where is the husband?

Emeline sees him coming out of the corner of her eye. He's yelling, he's running, he's malicious.

Emeline doesn't think, she only reacts. And throws herself on Amina to protect her. The two land in a heap, at the edge of the pit, Emeline's body covering Amina's from head to foot.

"What is going on?" Amina's eyes are wide, her breath short.

Emeline frowns. This may have been a bit of an overreaction. After all, the ghost can't actually harm them. "Sorry," she says, wondering why she isn't moving away. "Constantine's husband was coming, and I acted out of reflex."

There's that brilliant smile again. "Don't be sorry for protecting me. I quite like it."

Yep, time to scramble away.

And step right into Jacques' ghost. Emeline catches glances

of a man in his thirties, marked by grief and anger. From what they learned from his cousin, he's mostly angry at himself, but there's nothing better than finding a different target to take the pressure off from time to time.

Why is he attacking Emeline and not Malik or Amina? Does he remember her from her last visit? Does he realize she's the one in charge? Or that she's the one his antics will have the most effect on?

Robert rushes to her aid while Clothilde keeps gesticulating and trying to get through to Constantine.

"We're here to help!" Emeline says as forcefully as she can. She resists the urge to swat at the ghost like he's a mosquito. "We brought your wife. That's Constantine's casket in your grave."

Jacques stops. Apparently right in front of Emeline because she cannot see him, but she feels the relief of not being under otherworldly attack.

"Your wife has been waiting for you for all these years," Emeline says, hoping she's looking approximately at the man's face. "She's not in the best of shape, as you can see. Perhaps you can get through to her?"

Emeline gets the feeling of a conversation going on just out of earshot. Robert taking over. Confirming it is, indeed, Constantine. Explaining what happened.

They move toward Constantine and Clothilde, and Emeline finds herself staring into Amina's comically wide eyes.

"That was amazing," she whispers.

Emeline doesn't know what to say to that, so she only shakes her head and works on calming her heart. What happens if the husband and wife don't recognize each other? Have they just created a haunted ground in the cemetery, where nobody will ever willingly set foot because of the ghosts?

At least nobody would know it was Emeline's fault—except her partner and her lovely neighbor, that is.

"What's going on now?" Amina asks.

"The husband is trying to get through to her," Emeline replies, keeping her eyes on Amina while her real focus is on the debacle going on between ghosts on her left. Constantine *seems* to be slowing down.

Malik is working the lift to get the casket into the ground, intensely focused on his task so he has an excuse not to observe Emeline's weird behavior. Or maybe feel the ghosts himself—if Robert was able to guide him while Emeline was underground, he must have developed some sensitivity to them.

Amina's hand lands on Emeline's forearm. "Thank you so much for doing this."

"Uh." With Amina suddenly so close, Emeline loses track of what the ghosts are doing. There's no way she can focus on what's going on in her peripheral vision when her crush is right there, no more than an arm's length away. "I don't think I did much, really."

"Oh, but you did!" She steps *closer*, and Emeline's heart takes off at top speed again, but for an entirely different reason this time. "I wouldn't have known where to start or what to do without your help. And Constantine would have been stuck in that room forever. Now she's reunited with her love." A sigh. "I'm so happy for her."

Emeline feels a surge of emotions. Surprise, happiness. Love. They consume her, making her lose all train of thought—or sense of propriety.

Before her conscious brain catches up, Emeline lifts her hands to cradle Amina's face, and leans in to kiss her.

The emotions disappear as quickly as they arrived—oh God, she was projecting the ghosts' emotions—and she's left with a surprised-looking Amina in her arms and a stunned Malik across the open grave.

And some emotions, of course. It wasn't *all* the ghosts' doing.

She lets go of Amina and takes a step back.

Hoping she hasn't ruined her relationship with her neighbor for good.

FORTY-ONE

In a way, I'm happy to be back in a cemetery. After all, I spent almost as much time in my old cemetery as I did in the outside world before dying. The gray granite and the worn paved paths are like old friends. The mourning angels a reminder of the innumerous expressions of love and loss we witnessed over the years. And the reuniting lovers a callback to our main occupation while waiting our turn: helping other ghosts find peace.

There's no doubt in my mind that Constantine and Jacques will find peace now they're together. They may both have somewhat gone off at the deep end, but only because they were missing each other.

The moment Evian gets through to Jacques, and he realizes his wife is here, he takes over the operation.

"Constantine, *chérie*," he almost sings at her as he joins her in her furious dance around the casket. She's not as lost as in the morgue; she still maintains her normal shape and the dress is recognizably a wedding dress, but she also hasn't been hearing a word Clothilde is saying.

Luckily, Jacques has more success. His clothes transform into a three-piece suit—I'd bet anything it's what he wore at their wedding—and he hums a waltz as he catches his wife in his arms to pull her into a dance.

At first, Constantine resists. But when he doesn't give up, she finally looks at him—really looks at him—and her dress becomes so white it's almost blinding.

"Jacques!" she exclaims. "They weren't lying, you're really here?"

"Of course I'm here, my love. I've been waiting for you."

Their dance continues, turning in a slow circle around their grave, ignoring people and other tombs alike. Jacques keeps humming and Constantine's entire being is transformed by her giant smile. Just as they pass through Evian and Amina, who are standing surprisingly close, Jacques leans down to kiss his bride.

They explode into a ball of light, brighter even than the sun.

When it disappears, they're gone.

And Evian is kissing Amina.

Clothilde gives out a whoop. "Finally! Good for you, Emeline." She jumps over to slap Doubira on the shoulder. "You're gonna catch flies, Malik. I'm sorry to say you never stood a chance there, anyway. Now your friend Nadine…"

Evian takes a step back, horror and embarrassment on her face, and my heart drops. Was she caught up in the moment? Will this make everything awkward?

Then Amina blinks. Frowns at Evian stepping away. And firmly steps right after her to grab another kiss.

I let out a relieved sigh and sign for Clothilde to leave the two alone for a bit. We can't leave entirely, but I'd like to give our friend and benefactor as much privacy as we can.

After, all, we're not done working together yet. We have schemers and murderers to catch, evidence to collect and trials to prepare for, and who knows, perhaps other ghosts to assist. At the end of the line, our own nirvana may be waiting, but I'm not in a rush to get there.

I plan to enjoy the journey and make sure that when I reach my destination, I'll be found worthy.

AUTHOR'S NOTE

THANK YOU FOR reading *Beneath the Surface*. I hope you enjoyed it! I certainly had a blast writing it.

This story isn't over yet. We keep getting closer, but we're not yet in the clear. This series will continue. If you want to make sure you're informed of any future updates, you can sign up for my newletter on my website.

If you haven't tried out the *Ghost Detective* short stories yet, the first one (the one that started it all!) is available for free for my newsletter subscribers.

R.W. Wallace
www.rwwallace.com

Also by R.W. Wallace

Mystery

Ghost Detective Novels
Beyond the Grave
Unveiling the Past
Beneath the Surface

Ghost Detective Shorts
Just Desserts
Lost Friends
Family Bonds
Common Ground
Till Death
Family History
Heritage
Eternal Bond
New Beginnings
Severed Ties

The Tolosa Mystery Series
The Red Brick Haze
The Red Brick Cellars
The Red Brick Basilica

Short Story Collections
Deep Dark Secrets
A Thief in the Night

Short Stories
Cold Blue Eternity
Hidden Horrors

Critters
Gertrude and the Trojan Horse
First Impressions
Let Them Eat Cake
Out of Sight
Sitting Duck
Two's Company
Like Mother Like Daughter

Romance

French Office Romance Series
Flirting in Plain Sight
Hiding in Plain Sight
Loving in Plain Sight

Fantasy (short stories)

Unexpected Consequences
Morbier Impossible
A Second Chance

Science Fiction (short stories)

The Vanguard

Lollapalooza Shorts
Quarantine
Common Enemies
Coiled Danger
Mars Meeting

Adventure (short stories)

Size Matters

ABOUT THE AUTHOR

R.W. WALLACE WRITES in most genres, though she tends to end up in mystery more often than not. Dead bodies keep popping up all over the place whenever she sits down in front of her keyboard.

The stories mostly take place in Norway or France; the country she was born in and the one that has been her home for two decades. Don't ask her why she writes in English—she won't have a sensible answer for you.

Her Ghost Detective short story series appears in *Pulphouse Magazine*, starting in issue #9.

You can find all her books, long and short, all genres, on rwwallace.com.